misfit · fatherless · oddball · loser · outcast · eccentric · lowlife · scumbag · zero · bastard

©2025 Matt Starr
Cover ©2025 Robyn Leigh Lear (inspired by the art of Mary Leigh Lear)

-First Edition

Publisher's Cataloguing-in-Publication Data

Starr, Matt
    American bastard / written by Matt Starr
ISBN: 978-1-953932-40-2

1. Fiction - Short Stories (single author) 2. Fiction - Southern
3. Fiction - Small Town & Rural I. Title II. Author

Library of Congress Control Number: 2025945885

contents

For my mama and my Winnie. We sure do miss y'all.

"I've been brought down to zero, pulled out and put back there."
–John Prine

where bright angel feet have trod

In May of 1983, a Boeing 707 lost hydraulics on its way from Tampa Bay to Charlotte and crashed into a river baptism at the fringe of my hometown, killing all 130 people on board and fifty-four more on the banks.

We made the national news. There was an investigation. Men in suits placed big takeout orders from Libby's Deli.

Thirty-eight years later, and that's still all anyone talks about. Every day around lunchtime, things get real still. A phantom hand unzips the sky. Then you hear this sound like you're driving through a tunnel at full speed with all the windows down. You don't see anything, but there's the godawfulest exploding noise. A mosaic of screams.

Some folks stop what they're doing and remove their hats. Most people simply shake their heads. Children cover their ears, and their mothers tell them it will be okay. Some people—not as many as there used to be, granted—go to where it happened and join hands.

Mr. Overcash flings open his storm door, puts his hands on the back of his head, and howls no. Then he runs circles around his front yard, singing: "Yes, we'll gather at the river. The beautiful, the beautiful river. Gather with the saints at the river. That flows by the throne of God." He's 102 years old. This happens every day.

I'll probably die in this town, and I've made my peace with that. That's what people do here: They are born here, and then they die. Z has different plans, though. We work at the One Buck on the corner together, but for how much longer, I'm not sure. She's heading off to college in a few days.

She's facing the product in aisle 3, and I'm staring at her when a customer approaches the register. The man tosses a dog toy onto the counter and reaches for his wallet.

"That'll be a dollar six," I say.

He cuts a look at me. "I thought everything in here was one buck."

I can see Z rolling her eyes behind him.

"Well, yessir," I reply. "But there's tax."

He sighs, gives me exact change.

"Have a nice day," I say as he heads for the door.

He turns back. "Don't you fucking tell me what to do."

I drop my head like someone's giving the blessing before supper, but it's just me up there. Feeling like an asshole. I put up with a lot of shit, I really do. Still, every day I'm optimistic. I wake up, I look at myself in the mirror, and I tell myself that I'm going to make the best of it—that I'm going to make another go at it and be a more positive person. Then my first customer comes in and looks at me like they've smelled a fart, and I give up all over again. There are those people out there. The ones who say they think everyone should be required to work retail at some point in their lives. To give them an appreciation of what we go through. But I wouldn't wish this on anyone.

"Fuck that guy," Z says, her smile real wide under her septum ring. Is there something different about her today? I swear her hair gets shorter every time I see her. "I wouldn't put too much stock into anything someone like that tells me."

We've known each other for two years, but I still overthink what to say. "Good thing I'm too broke to buy any," I respond. Then I do that thing where I cringe inside. Die a little.

Z laughs and squats to straighten the bottom row of disposable cooking pans, and I find myself looking at the sweep of bare skin between the bottom of her shirt and the top of her pants. But I remember what my mama told me about objectifying women. *A sunset's purdy, too, but if you look at it long enough, the Good Lord'll blind you.* I turn away. Feel my cheeks blush.

Overhead, I hear a deafening commotion. Z described it one time as a band-aid being peeled from the hairy arm of God Almighty, and I thought that was as good a way to put it as any. There's the fracture of impact, dirt and water rising from the earth and coming back down someplace else. There's the chorus of cries. Could you ever dream up a more bizarre sensation than barreling toward oblivion with a bunch of people you don't know?

"Well," Z says, standing to her feet. "Guess it's time for lunch."

She disappears for a moment, then comes back to the register with a bag of rolled tortilla chips. I key in her two dollars and separate the change in my hand. When I go to give it to her, her fingertips trace the love line in my palm. We share a look, a moment. But I doubt it's the same one.

It's not like people haven't tried to make it out of here.

Biff Goodnight was a first-team All-American and got a full-ride scholarship to play college football in Georgia. But after one season of pro ball, he returned. Rumor has it he refused to fly with the team. You can find him these days walking his geriatric cattle dog mix in a stroller. The two of them shipping up and down the sidewalk, easy as you please.

Then there was Rhonda Lord, who was as gifted a singer as anyone around here ever heard. She packed service after service at the local church and recorded one song that made it to the radio. She played The Opry twice, but up and came home one day with one show still left on the schedule. Said her place was by the river. When she's not there, she's sharing one-dish recipes and rightwing conspiracy theories on Facebook.

Mr. Overcash even went away twice for war, got shot on both tours, but admitted it was just obvious that he wasn't going to die outside of this place. Couldn't if he tried.

Most people don't make it that far. They get to the welcome sign and think better of it. Every time someone leaves, it's not goodbye. It's see you later.

We're hanging tags for the upcoming sales week when Z's boyfriend walks in. He's tall and bearded and tattooed, and he's the assistant manager at the record store. He looks like a walking energy drink, smells like a body spray that would be the sponsor of a motocross show. His vape pen glows as he takes a hit from it and glares at me. He knows. Sometimes, I wish I would have met Z before she started dating him, but we only went to high school together for one year before I graduated.

Z's boyfriend heads to the stationary aisle where she's putting orange doorbuster signs on end-of-schoolyear clearance. He pinches her arm, and she playfully slaps him. I pretend it doesn't bother me, but it does.

When I return to the register, Mr. Overcash is standing there in clothes fit for a dead man. He's staring straight ahead, eyes like fogged glass.

"What can I do for you, Mr. Overcash?" I ask.

He places a soda bottle and a can of potted meat on the counter, hands me two rolls of pennies and six loose cents.

"Say, y'all sell cigarettes?" he asks—like he does every time.

"No, sir."

"Oh," he says. Then he leaves to wait for tomorrow's mayday.

I peek around an endcap, and it appears that Z and her boyfriend are still talking. But something tells me it's not light conversation. Her expressions are very animated. That's how she gets when she's pissed off. I see him grab her arm. She tells him to let go and pulls away. They notice me standing there, and now they're quiet.

After an awkward pause, he scratches the back of his neck. "I'll catch you later," he says to her.

"Yeah," she says.

He passes by me without saying a word. I'd like to take his head and shut it in the freezer door.

"You okay?" I ask her.

"Yeah," she replies. She won't look up from the pricing gun in her hand.

"Did he hurt you?"

She smirks. "Not today."

I wish I knew how to respond. I dig in my pockets, hoping I'll scare up the answer there, but there's only a boxcutter and a tin of mints.

"We've been fighting about whether or not we'll still date when I leave for school tomorrow."

"Will you?" I ask.

"I'm not sure."

"Well, you're going to a really good school," I say. "I'm sure there'll be plenty of smart and funny guys who'll treat you nice there. Or girls."

She smiles for a moment, then mashes at the pricing gun's keypad. It beeps uncooperatively. "Shittinass thing," she says, smacking it.

I laugh.

She does, too.

"Anybody there?" a customer calls from the register.

I start to head that way.

"C," Z says.

I look back.

"There's supposed to be a supermoon tonight. Wanna watch it with me after work?"

I was nine years old when I was baptized in the river. I didn't understand what it meant to be saved, but I didn't want to disappoint anybody, and I didn't want to go to Hell. That was the biggest thing. We stood hand in hand on the banks, the mud cold under our bare feet. Preacher said the first man rose from it. He said he'd wager most of the town was baptized by him. Said he was doubtful that everyone on the plane was saved, but that those who were baptized seconds before the crash were lucky.

That made me think about all the people on board and all the people in this town. All the men, women, and children. How many were saved, how many were lost, how we were all left behind. How this was a cursed place.

Rhonda Lord sang with her eyes closed as we lined up. When these things happen in the movies, they show people wearing white robes, but I was in a striped t-shirt and bluejeans. I waded waist-deep in the water, and I felt like I'd forgotten how to swim. Maybe I had. Preacher held my nose with one hand and dunked me under with the other. And at that moment, the rushing water in my ears became indivisible from the tearing of the wind, ripped open forever by that plane. Preacher pulled me through the surface of the water, and some people cheered. But I heard hollering, too.

Once the last person had gone, Preacher said: "The like figure whereunto even baptism doth also now save us, not putting away of the filth of the flesh, but the answer of a good conscience toward God, by the resurrection of Jesus Christ."

I wondered if God could resurrect the plane. Dig it from the riverbed and cast it back into the air in a holding pattern until it was safe to land.

We're sitting on the tailgate of my truck in the One Buck parking lot, sharing a single beer from a brown paper bag. The moon is massive and slightly red in the sky above us, and if I didn't know any better, I'd say it's only a matter of time before we collide with it.

I take a drink, look at Z. "What time do you have to be home?" I ask.

"Who cares?" she says, grinning. "I'm outta here tomorrow." She checks her phone, and there's at least a dozen missed calls.

"Can I ask you something?" I say.

"Go for it."

"Why do you date that guy?"

She motions for the beer, and I give it to her. "Familiarity," she says. "I guess. I mean, why do people go to the high school football games ten, fifteen years after they've graduated? Why does everybody eat at Libby's even though it's gross?" She drinks. "It's just easier."

She's got a point. I can tell that she doesn't want to talk about it, though, so I try to change the subject. "You ever decide what you're gonna major in?"

"I wish you'd just stick to questions about why I gravitate toward assholes," she says.

I laugh.

"Kidding," she says. "I don't know, I'm torn. I wanna do something with lit, or maybe design, because art's important. But so is science. And girls aren't encouraged to be scientists."

"Sounds like woke bullshit," I joke, and she rolls her eyes. "Seriously. I think you'll be great at whatever you do," I say.

She smiles, but I can tell she's distracted.

"What is it?"

She breathes in real deep and looks up. "You ever think about the crash?" she asks.

"Does anybody around here ever *not* think about the crash?"

"I'm serious," she says, raking a hand through her hair. "184 people here one minute, gone the next." She snaps her fingers. "Or maybe they're still here. Who the fuck knows? It's all so wild to think about. I've heard the impact force created such a loss of space in the cabin that only a few of the bodies weren't completely mangled. They had to identify them by fingerprints and dental records and tattoos."

I say, "Damn." That's all I can say.

"I don't wanna be like that, C," Z says. "I don't wanna be lost. I don't wanna be inseparable from the droves of lifeless, faceless bodies in this town."

"You won't be," I say. "Look at it this way: At least you won't have to hang any more ad tags."

If she laughs, I can't tell. If she laughs, it's lost in the here and there traffic scraping the road in front of the One Buck. It's lost in these streets and these alleys that have been stuck in purgatory for thirty-eight years. It's lost in the blackbox of a Boeing 707, the last wish of a damned crew. If she laughs, it's lost in Mr. Overcash's dark house as he sings: "Yes, we'll gather at the river. The beautiful, the beautiful river. Gather with the saints at the river. That flows by the throne of God."

I grab Z's hand. She looks at it, then at me. She scoots toward me a little. I'm close enough to hear her breathing, feel her breathing, feel her hip on my hip.

"I hope you get out, too," she says.

"Y'all wouldn't happen to sell cigarettes, would you?" Mr. Overcash asks. Today, he's wearing a plain white buttondown, all of his medals pinned over the right breast pocket.

"No, Mr. Overcash," I say. "Afraid not."

"Oh," he says. He picks up his soda and heads for the door. He turns. "Did I ever tell you they shot me?" He points to the left side of his chest, then his right thigh. "Here and here. Seen me a man cut in two at the waist with an MG 42."

"Yessir," I say. "Thank you for your service."

He leaves.

The new employee, who to this point hasn't stopped talking about her extensive retail management experience, looks at him like he's crazy. She looks at me next, and I know she wants me to say something—to make a lighthearted watercooler joke.

But I don't have it in me. All I can think about is Z. I think about us breaking down totes in the stockroom. Doing voice impressions together on the PA system. Playing rock-paper-scissors to decide who has to clean the bathrooms. I dream of drawing pictures below her navel with the tip of my finger. Masterpieces that only we can see.

Five minutes later, the door slides open. It's her, standing there in a sweatshirt even though it's warm outside, the sleeves so long they're covering half of her hands. Her normally sleepy eyes look wet and alive. Like the ground Preacher said the first man rose from.

She walks around the register, and she kisses me. Once. Then she hurries through the door, and she doesn't look back.

I imagine her leaving. I imagine her going to someplace where people are born, but maybe they leave, too. If they want. I hope she makes it through. So many haven't. I think about following her, ripping off my nametag, my vest. Jumping over the counter and sprinting past Biff Goodnight and his white-muzzled stroller dog toward the county line.

But I know what will happen once I get there. I will stop as if dumbstruck. There will be a loss of gravity, a breath of fuel and smoke, a burst of life happening in reverse. My eyes will glaze over, I'll walk backward, and I'll be like everyone else. And then we'll gather at the river. The beautiful, the beautiful river.

out of the ground the lord god caused

Paw Paw said the tree in his backyard must have matured half a century before he was born. That would have been 1863 or so. It was a towering American Beech with a thick trunk and deformed yet brawny arms that threw crisscrossed shapes onto the earth below when the sun set. Veins of fading light in the dirt. I can see it nestled in the valley, a young drummer boy lying beneath it, stoic, bleeding out of a hole in his head.

The tree had a hole in it, too. It was a cavity that ran longer than wide, about five feet up the north side. Paw Paw said that ghosts lived in there. That you could talk to them if you wanted. Said if you waited long enough, they might just talk back.

Genesis was the first book in the Bible. Paw Paw knew that, but he couldn't have found France on a map before he stormed its beaches. Paw Paw was a carpenter in his spare time, like Jesus. He built the house when he came back home. Everybody told him he was off his rocker. Said, "You're craziern a shithouse rat for buying land downwind a hog lagoon." But all he cared about was the quiet, and he was too damn stubborn to quit once he'd made up his mind about something. He started laying the foundation during an Indian summer, his hammer percussing the psalm of the camel crickets surrounding him, unseen in their vast battalions. As the house came together, the tree's misshapen branches gave way to dark green leaves with tiny teeth. He'd heard tell that certain bands of the Tuscarora had sworn by their healing power. Some gobbledygook about the veins being blessed. Or was it the bark?

For the first few years, Paw Paw lived with a bluetick coonhound who'd wandered up one day and wouldn't leave. He named her Misty. Every night she'd bark at things that shouldn't have been there—cannon blasts and carbine smoke and screams whispering from the horizon. One summer day, she had a bad run-in with a cottonmouth down by the crick, and Paw Paw had to give her back to the Good Lord. He buried her under the shade of the tree. From time to time, she came back to visit him.

Paw Paw met Maw Maw in the weave room on first shift. It was her hazel eyes that drew him in. It would be her talent for telling him what was on her mind that kept him around. How he was the most bullheaded man she had ever known, how he looked foolish with a plug of tobacco in his cheek, how there was no use in trying to comb over his bald spot. What she lacked in height, she made up for in spunk. Their first date was a picnic beneath the tree. She looked up at its silver-streaked brown skin, a spine of moss crawling toward its crown, sun splitting through its twisted points.

"It's purdy in its own way," she said. "But I prefer magnolia trees."

A hiss fell from the tree hollow like a shallow breath.

"Don't mind them," Paw Paw said, biting a corner off his tomato sandwich.

She tried not to.

The first night Maw Maw stayed over, a thunderboomer lumbered through the valley on drunken, leaden feet, and the tree moaned a sad lullaby. Then Maw Maw heard a deep woof.

"What in the sam hill was that?" she asked.

"Don't worry," Paw Paw said. "That's just Misty."

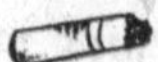

A bloody skirmish happened here. The boys had marched from Mudcat Holler in the thick of a monthlong, blue blazes heatwave and were dropping left and right, falling out of rank like a bunch of drunks. An hour before dusk, the enemy opened fire from the cover of the bramble near Sugar Knoll. Cut down scores of disoriented soldiers with the first volley. Addled by exhaustion, the commanding officer dismounted his horse, drew his saber, and ordered an ill-advised bayonet charge into the shrubbery. Witnessing even more of his company fall at this rash decision, not to mention the strength of the force before him, he beat a hasty retreat southward on foot. As he fled, he heard a symphony of horror behind him. Wails, childlike in their pitch. The unnatural squelch of metal entering flesh. Voices crying out for the women who gave them life. Music akin to the War in Heaven. The noise never disappeared altogether, but it did grow quieter. More distant. Blended with cicada song.

On he ran, only stopping once he reached the tree. He took refuge on a carpet of beechnuts. There, in the cool of the tree's shadow, he realized two things: one, he'd been shot in the right shoulder, no exit wound; and two, he hadn't given the order to pull back. He was alone. The bullet ached in his shoulder, a white-hot agony. A hellacious thirst seized hold of his mouth, and for reasons only known to him, his first reaction was to reach for a beechnut. He peeled the burr and chewed on the bitter fruit within until a providence came upon him, not unlike the one promised in the Good Book. He sat, listening, waiting on the battle to find him. Waiting on the moon.

"Now," he said, something like a smile on his bearded face. "Who among you will join me?"

The tree had grown crooked out of the ground, but it became even more slanted as the years went by. Paw Paw said that's just the way it was, and some things you couldn't change. When my mama came along, he hung a tire swing from the sturdiest branch. She played there every afternoon, told Misty about what she'd learned at school that day.

When she was in the fifth grade, the branch snapped and sent her plunging toward the ground. She rolled over to find her knee scuffed, speckles of dirt in the blood where flesh was just a moment ago. She scooted up to the base of the tree, crying a little, and sat there for a spell. Slowly, the skin grew back as the tree shivered in the breeze.

Later, Paw Paw went out there with a bucket and tossed fertilizer onto the ground.

"I wish you'd just cut that damn thing down," Maw Maw said, pinching her nose at the smell of the work. "I wouldn't trust it as far as I could throw it."

"I love you," Paw Paw said.

The ice storm came the night the president was assassinated. Freezing rain weighed heavy on the tree's limbs and sent many crashing to the frosted grass, narrowly missing the back deck of the house. Something weighed heavy on Paw Paw's chest, too: It felt like a backhoe, sitting there and digging. Misty bayed, and the tree hollow sighed as Maw Maw helped Paw Paw into the car, still in her slippers, and, sitting on a phone book so she could see over the steering wheel, drove him to the hospital. They had to resurrect him five times with the paddles. A hail of machine gun fire found him behind a Czech hedgehog, between worlds. Sand in his boots. Then he was back.

I used to ask Mama how someone could be revived like that. The only thing she would say was, "Well, look at Jesus."

On the way home from the hospital several days later, Maw Maw said, "When my time comes around, don't you lay me under that tree." Then she held Paw Paw's rough hand to her cheek.

When he felt up to it after a few days of bedrest, he went out to the tree. It was jagged and bare and didn't feel much like talking, which was okay because he didn't, either. There were burn marks in random places that would take time to heal—if they ever did.

"Me too," Paw Paw said. "Me too."

The tree was at a forty-five-degree angle when Maw Maw started chemo. As her hair came out in clumps, the tree's scaly bark started to peel. Once she was relegated to a wheelchair, its roots began to protrude—spreading out like the rotten tentacles of some deep-sea beast. It shed leaves when it wasn't supposed to and creaked like an old rocking chair at all hours of the night. Misty pitched a fit at first, but she eventually got used to it.

Paw Paw told Maw Maw: "I cain't live without you."

She smiled and said, "I know."

The air surrounding the tree began to smell like gunpowder. Paw Paw noticed it one day while he was out mowing the grass. He also noticed that some of the tree's sapwood was exposed. So he took his pocketknife and removed segments of his own skin. Used them to patch up the damage.

He showed up to Maw Maw's funeral wrapped in bloody bandages. He laid a magnolia blossom on her casket.

Mama came back just before the hurricane made landfall on the coast. She found Paw Paw on a ladder with a pruning blade in his palsied hands, sawing away at the tree's dead appendages. He was hunched over and frailer than he let on, his once-brown hair a dirty white horseshoe, his natural teeth, the ones he had left, like pieces of bark.

"You don't need to be out here doing this, Deddy," she said.

"It's all I got left," he replied.

It was true. Maw Maw had done everything for him. She'd cooked and cleaned and managed the checkbook. After his heart attack, she'd patted his steaks and liver mush with paper towels to remove the excess grease. All he knew how to do was look after the damn tree.

"Look at that thing," Mama said, pointing to it. "It's liable to fall on your house and kill you dead. You could at least come stay with me til the storm passes. They're saying this one's different."

"It ain't gonna come this far inland," Paw Paw said. But he knew, deep down, it would.

<hr>

Paw Paw lay in his bed with the covers up to his chin as the wind howled by his windows. Power was out; it was full dark. It had rained hard as hell for four days, and floodwaters had driven waste from the hog lagoons into the valley. The stench was unimaginable. Somewhere a bugle sounded, and the rum pum pum pum of tree limbs breaking joined this dolorous chorus.

The storm door opened and closed. From the middle distance came the thump of an LCVP, its momentum halted by an invisible embankment. Then there was a crack, sharp and quick. The tree sliced through the ceiling of Paw Paw's bedroom, the branches it had left impaling and fracturing his eighty-year-old body. The night got quiet and still all of a sudden, and he could see the stars through the gash in his roof. He reckoned it was the eye of the storm.

A sibilant voice came. It spoke once. It said, "O, Mother."

He rose, something panting at his side. It was going to happen. It was time. He didn't want it to be, but he had to leave. The drummer boy with the hole in his head told him so. She did, too. He knew. He was bone tired. Jesus was a carpenter. Genesis was the first book in the Bible. He didn't live there anymore. He understood. Had all the while. He knew. Charge.

phoenix

During games of hide and seek, her demons always find her in the most obvious of places. They don't manifest themselves physically, but rather as auras and shadows and whispers. She isn't a psychic, and she has never pretended to be. She doesn't have premonitions, and she never will. Billie is a medium. She talks to the dead. But the spirits that burden her aren't like the ones that burden the other clairvoyants. She can't communicate with departed mothers or reunite distraught parents with their prematurely deceased children. But if someone is yearning for a long-lost connection with their beloved household pet, then Billie is their best chance.

The media has been after her for years about a human interest story. "Animal telepath brings closure to owners left behind," the tribune pitches. "Local woman reads stories from beyond the pet cemetery," News 5 proposes. They've heard that Billie can bring voices back from the grave, and whether they find that to be true, they hope, Billie reckons, that supernatural features can do the same for their freefalling ratings. Billie doesn't pay attention to the news.

Sitting in the dimmed living room of a millhouse she shares with her sister, Nadine, and a random assortment of anemic plants, Billie watches some afternoon rerun cop drama through eyes like smoke. Everything moves languid, reeks like cigarettes. Just as the smolder of a handsome detective fades into a commercial break, the phone rings, breaking the otherwise quiet of the day-to-day routine. Nadine cuts her eyes and picks up the phone. "Hello," she says. Her voice is vinegary.

Billie looks across the room to her sister, a top-heavy woman whose hair has been dyed so many times that she can't remember what her natural color really is. She sits in her recliner as if it is part of her, her back molded into its cushions and her leg propped on its armrest.

"I ain't interested," Nadine says.

Unintelligible mumblings seep from the earpiece of the phone.

"Well, I ain't *got* ten dollars," Nadine says, her tone growing sassier by the syllable.

The voice on the other end becomes louder, faster.

Billie shakes her head.

"Look, Mack, I'm on The Disability. Every time y'all call, my blood pressure goes out the roof. Take my name off whatever list you got and don't call back no more." Nadine slams the phone.

"Who was it?" Billie asks.

Nadine swallows. The conversation has left her breathless. "Them sorry bastards at the Family Video. Always wanting to put their grubby hands in someone's pockets."

Billie nods in agreement as the show resumes. She looks on, but something doesn't feel right. A vague light wraps itself around the television like a thin veil. Billie blinks, hoping it's just one of those aggravating eye floaters she gets, but she knows better. She tries to ignore it and devote her attention solely to the Pavlovian cadence barking from the surround sound speakers, but she can't. Billie looks in Nadine's direction, and her face furrows into a grimace.

Still calming down, Nadine locks eyes with her sister and sighs. "Billie. Again?"

"Yep," she says listlessly.

Nadine raises her hands and drops them, slapping her knees. "Damn. I just had this house cleansed."

"You know it don't matter. They just follow me."

Billie hobbles down the uneven brick of Main Street on her way to work in a wilted posture, the whistling wind at her back echoing deep in her bones. Winter's morning breath chews on her exposed face as she pulls her scarf over her mouth and wonders what motivates the local fitness nuts and power-walkers as they pass by. They all follow the same pattern: They offer her a fleeting glance before returning their eyes to the pavement. She does the same. She knows all their names, and they know hers.

Billie grew up here in Planerville. A town where places are like people, with stories and memories, sorrows and dreams. She passes the orange-and white-checkered water tower that she and her girlfriends used to climb to smoke cigarettes they had stolen from their parents. She passes the mausoleum along the spaded black fence of the cemetery. She ignores her reflection as it dances through storefront windows and rounds the corner at the First Baptist Church where she was baptized as a little girl. She nearly reaches the awning of the old mill offices when she stops. She has never been able to put the feeling into words, but it begins to happen around the same time almost every morning. The onsets vary from something as subtle as a mood change to something as profound as a shift in the brilliance of hues in her visual plane. Oftentimes, she can hear them. They reach for her with faint whimpers and nonhuman language. And she understands them.

Today's onset finds Billie as an unavoidable awareness of a presence that wasn't there before, and in the strangest and most inexplicable of ways, a numinous sensation comes over her in a soft storm: She feels as though she has just stirred from a dream, the fragments of which she can piece together as each second becomes the next. Her maw maw, who noticed it in Billie from an early age, called it "rising."

Billie searches her surroundings and looks at an elderly couple ahead, their bundled bodies nestled on a bench in Town Square. She contemplates trekking on in the opposite direction, her body right woozy now, but her conscience doesn't let her. She approaches the man and woman as the steam from their coffee cups drapes about them like swaying curtains. She stands in front of them momentarily, and they smile at her before looking at each other as though they hope she'll take the hint and continue on her way.

"She wants to say thank you," Billie says.

"I'm sorry?" the man replies.

"Your rescue, Boo. She wants to thank you for the ball of yarn. And the little wicker chair y'all sat out at the screen door so she could watch the road." Billie turns to the woman. "And movie nights in your lap. Even though y'all rarely made it through a whole one without falling asleep."

The couple watches her with awe-frozen faces.

"And for being her angels," Billie says. "Holding her at the end. She was half deaf, but she heard every word you sang in that cold, cold room with the teaberry walls."

She closes her eyes and begins to croon in a raspy baritone, a memory that isn't hers crawling through the cinders. The Patsy Cline version of "Anytime."

The man grips the woman's hand as they continue to stare, now misty-eyed. Billie opens her eyes and adjusts the strap of the threadbare bag on her shoulder. She lingers for another moment, uncomfortable and fatigued, before she departs in the other direction, the gray of the morning softening behind her.

"Put that shit back, Randy," Billie says, her Southern voice dragging like heavy feet. A gaunt man with more fingers on his hands than teeth in his head reaches into the pocket of his coat and returns a bottle of shampoo to the shelf in front of him, a defeated scowl stretching across his leathery face. At least he isn't harassing her for pseudoephedrine today. Billie has been a medium for as long as she can remember. Maybe forty years. But rather than charge for services rendered, she earns her living at a daytime job as a technician in the Planerville drugstore. She counts pills in between cigarette breaks, and when she's not foiling petty thieves or clocking fake scripts for opioids, she's disregarding looks and whispers from regulars.

Standing bent in her baggy teal scrubs, Billie pecks away at an old keyboard and watches as Randy exits the front door. In the corner of the store, two women stand wide-eyed, exchanging gossips. Two small children squirm uneasily next to the gumball machine as they try to see for themselves whether the rumors their classmates have spread in the schoolyard are true or not. An older man pretends to read the active ingredients of an anti-diarrheal, just so he can get a closer look at the woman the preacher condemned on Sunday.

Billie zones out as if it will make her invisible. She has tried to keep certain parts of her life as private as possible, but there are no secrets in a town where people talk like they breathe. She was once supple-cheeked, with hair like nightshade, but decades of casted stones and a crowded mind have salted her gray. Aside from her inclination to tell it like she sees it, she isn't as feisty as she once was. She still fans flames, but only dwindling embers remain from a once-hungry fire.

Despite being sought after by failing rags and TV stations, Billie isn't a local celebrity like Mute Maddie. Mute Maddie is the town's other resident clairvoyant, and her talents are more traditional: She can communicate with actual people who have crossed over. Stepping into buildings and offices and homes with her composition notepad, she'll scribble her reads with her arthritic fingers. Nobody really knows how old she is; they just know that her wrinkles are saturated with far too much makeup and that her wiry hair has been bleached white since the 70s. And since then, she has never been one to back down from her cosmic calling.

Billie, on the other hand, has avoided mediumship whenever possible. Once, as she lay in bed when she was very young, a dark figure approached her, panting. A damp, moldy smell pervaded the air. Billie closed her eyes and prayed to God for it to go away. It was Dirk. An Australian Shepherd. He was the first one who ever sought her help. He wanted his owners to know that he had died of old age and not from years of ingesting paint chips from the backyard shed, as they had long suspected. He had traveled from the other side of town to tell her this information. Although Billie considers her abilities a curse, she still has positive thoughts of Dirk, nonetheless. He was a good boy.

She surfaces from her memories and turns her attention back toward the line forming in front of her. A mustached man from Billie's high school class casts a crumpled prescription onto the counter in front of her. She smiles at him warily, only to be stared at like she showed up to church naked in return. This isn't anything new. As her generation grows older, she knows their children and grandchildren will be taught to judge her, too. Maybe even fear her.

Billie purses her lips and nods as the gentleman goes on his way without a word. Before she can enter the prescription into the computer, a doughy, middle-aged creature waddles to the counter, bristly eyebrows arched on his mango-shaped head. The type of harmless, albeit nervous-stomached man you might see in a commercial about dating services for fortysomethings.

Billie looks up and sighs. "Picking up for your mama, Dewey?"

He clears his throat. "Not today."

"Then what can I do for you?"

Dewey places his palms on the countertop and leans forward. His eyes dance back and forth between Billie's forehead and the bins along the pharmacy wall. Tears begin to brim atop his red cheeks. He tries to blink them away, but it's no use.

Billie rolls her eyes. "What's wrong, Dewey?"

He sniffles and glances at the people in line behind him before he settles on Billie. "Do you think you could do another reading for me?"

"Dewey."

"It's the last time I'll ask you," he says. "Cross my heart and hope to die. I just need to know, you know?"

Billie shakes her head. "I've tried three times, Dewey. He ain't in there."

Softly, Dewey begins to weep, and every eye in the building falls on his wet face. Billie's mouth curls as she hands him a tissue. She can be coarse, but she has always had a weakness for people who need help. It's the only time she chooses to access her abilities. "All right. But if I cain't get him this time, don't come in here bothering me no more."

Dewey smiles beneath glassy eyes and nods. He mouths, "Thank you," before blowing his nose into the tissue as he walks off toward the front door.

The next customer in line approaches cautiously, her face drawing with disgust. She stops, hugging her handbag close to her chest. "You know, I think I'll just come back tomorrow."

Billie smiles a muted smile. "Who's next, please?"

The two women climbed the front steps of the cozy, vinyl-sided house that sat across the street from Plant 4 on the corner of what the locals called "Mill Row." Mute Maddie poked at the doorbell as Billie stood under the eaves of the porch, finishing her cigarette and wondering why the hell she had been duped into tagging along. A well-liked machine fixer had died unexpectedly in this house the week before, leaving behind a wife and eight-year-old daughter. When the wife had called on Mute Maddie for a reading, the old mystic had done everything short of pulling Billie's ear to get her into something she wanted no part of.

Standing there with her black- and white-dappled notepad tucked under the arm of her polka-dotted housedress, Mute Maddie prodded at the doorbell once more. A petite, pallid woman answered the door with dried tears streaked into her round cheeks. "Missus Maddie," she said with an almost mellifluous drawl.

Mute Maddie tipped her head toward the widow.

"I'll be accompanying Missus Maddie if that's all right," Billie said, stepping forward with an extended hand. "I'm Billie."

The widow took it and answered with a reluctant smile. "By all means," she said. "Y'all come on in."

Mute Maddie and Billie followed the widow into the living room of the house, a quaint den lit by candles and the tuliplike bulbs of an antique ceiling fan overhead. A child in a cream-colored dress lay on the floor in front of the television watching her favorite show, "Mindy McStubbins, the Crime-Fightin' Corgi." She looked over her shoulder, skeptical of her mother's guests.

"Would y'all like a glass of sweet tea?" the widow asked.

Mute Maddie shook her head no.

"No, thank you, honey," Billie said.

"Of course," the widow replied, unsure of how to proceed.

Mute Maddie put her pen to work against the wide-ruled lines of her notepad paper. She faced it toward the widow. In broken letters, it read: What can I help you with?

The widow smoothed out the creases of her dress and clasped her hands together. Her daughter joined her, standing at her side with a stuffed replica of the tri-colored Mindy McStubbins burrowed into her tiny arms.

"Since my husband passed, strange things has been happening in the house. Sometimes in the dead of night, we hear funny noises. Or sometimes this odd feeling like a cold draft'll come through just up and out of nowhere and then leave."

Mute Maddie nodded her head up and down. She gestured down the shotgun hall, seeking permission.

"Please," the young widow said.

Billie followed Mute Maddie down the hall as the widow, daughter at her side, led them through the house. They stopped in the child's room first, a stuffed animal shrine with meringue walls.

"This is a purdy room, darlin," Billie said to the little girl, hoping to warm her out of her shyness.

The little girl drew closer to her mother, and Billie smiled in understanding. Mute Maddie pushed on to the master bedroom. The widow flipped on the light switch just inside the doorway, revealing a beige-colored room with a large burgundy tapestry occluding light from the outside world. A vintage cherrywood vanity sat at the foot of the queen-sized bed, and a golden-handled dresser stood kitty-corner at the far end of the room. The widow wore a hopeful gaze as Mute Maddie hovered next to the waterbed and lingered for much longer than she had in the other room. Aside from sadness for the child, Billie felt nothing.

After a moment, Mute Maddie's mouth puckered and she carried on into the kitchen, her slippers sliding on the linoleum floor beneath her. She combed the room up and down with eyes suited for the deepest of meditations. Billie reckoned the old woman had a mind for spirits the way a portable metal detector had a knack for picking up iron, copper, brass, and so on and so forth.

The widow pointed to the fixture just above the sink. "That light flickers on and off from time to time since it happened."

Mute Maddie pointed to the same light with her pen. She turned and questioned the widow with lifted eyebrows.

"Yes," the widow said. "It was the light we left on so he could find his way through the house when he come home from the graveyard shift." She laughed a longing laugh and dipped her head toward her daughter. "So he wouldn't break his neck on this one's toys."

Mute Maddie stood at the kitchen sink for so long that Billie became restless. She began to tap her notepad with her pen, and after at least a minute of doing so, she let out a sharp grunt like the wince of a hurt animal. She approached the widow and frowned. She scribbled on her notepad and handed it to the young woman. It read: I'm not getting anything, I'm sorry.

Tucking her chin, the widow teared up. She gasped and began to cry.

Billie remained in the corner next to the refrigerator, feeling helpless as Mute Maddie wrapped her arm around the widow.

The little girl pouted and stepped away from her mother with hurt in her eyes. "He lied," she said.

The three women looked at her, taken aback by the power behind her words.

Mute Maddie stepped toward her. What do you mean? she scrawled in her signature chicken scratch.

The girl gripped her stuffed dog. "He said he'd never leave us. He said he'd always be here," she said. "He lied to us."

Mute Maddie squinted at the child and knelt down in front of her. She wrote in the most precise lettering her shaky hands would allow: He is with you, youngin, and he will be forever.

The little girl started to cry as her mother looked on, and Mute Maddie took the child into her bony arms, grasping her as if she would fulfill the promise herself. Billie fidgeted in the corner, trying to choke back tears of her own because she did not like them. Did not like to feel things in general. Mute Maddie patted the little girl on her back and rose to her feet. She took the widow by the wrists and offered more reassurance with a look than Billie imagined most people could with words.

The widow led the pair of mediums back down the hall and escorted them out of the house. "Thank you," she said, embracing both of them and sniffling.

As the door shut behind them, Billie buried her eyes into the flowerbed beneath the edge of the porch, all the petals within beginning to strip off their color and wither. She placed a cigarette between her lips but didn't light it. She felt a tap on her shoulder and turned to find Mute Maddie standing in front of her, the notepad in her hands chest-high and outward. Black ink read: You have the gift, you can do this too.

Fifteen minutes after quitting time, Billie arrives at the little pea-green house, strands of multi-colored holiday lights flashing around its gutters. Dewey is already waiting at the screen door, and when he opens it, Billie can see the grooves of its wire mesh imprinted into his forehead. "I cain't thank you enough for this, Miss Billie," he says, clutching Billie's hand with his clammy mitts. "Maybe you can get him this time."

The "him" Dewey refers to is his dearly departed parakeet, Herbert. Billie nods warmly and enters the house behind him, finding herself in a sparsely lit den that smells stale and old and vaguely of mothballs despite the presence of numerous candles. Herbert, who got sick in late summer, died perched atop the stoop inside his iron cage, where Dewey found him board stiff. This is Billie's fourth time attempting to make contact with him. She isn't optimistic, given that she has felt next to nothing during the previous three visits.

"Dewey," a hoarse voice questions from the next room. "Who's that?"

Dewey rolls his eyes and becomes flustered. "It's Miss Billie, Mama."

"Oh, Hell's bells, Dewey, I wish you'd give that nonsense a rest!"

"Don't you start!" Dewey yells, his voice cracking at the end.

Billie stands there quietly, resisting the urge to shake her head.

A diminutive, owllike woman emerges from the doorway at the left of the room, the ridges of a scowl permanently embedded into her browline. She's hunched over and purple with crabbiness—dressed for a night on the town, her box-dyed beehive hairdo done up, but she's not going anywhere. She never does. "Don't you holler at me!" she scorns.

"Evening, Missus Lilly," Billie says.

Dewey's mother turns toward Billie, the frown in the skin of her neck matching the one on her face. "Don't you 'evening' me. I know what you're up to, hussy."

"Mama!"

"In cahoots with the Devil, Dewey. You need to get right for even talking to her."

Dewey shakes his head and exhales.

"Have fun. I ain't sticking around for it," his mother says, storming back toward the other room. "Y'all need Jesus!"

"Evening, Missus Lilly," Billie says again.

Dewey wipes his chapped lips and grumbles. "I'm so sorry, Miss Billie. Please carry on." He stands there in awkward and impatient stillness. He's trying to be polite, but he's anxious for answers. It's a quality with which Billie is all too familiar. She wants to help him, but her rising can't be forced. She doesn't throw out feelers or manufacture cold reads like primetime mediums of the small screen. The spirit world is a murky place; it's never cut and dry. This hard truth doesn't bode well for someone who wants to know whether their iguana has unfinished business or someone who craves assurance that their hedgehog is okay on the other side—but it is what it is. Billie doesn't make the rules.

She stands in front of the silver Christmas tree, her head tilted and her arms to the side as if she has just asked a question that no one else heard. Enveloped in an almost palpable silence, Dewey remains where he is, staring in wonderment. Billie scans the room, hoping that the familiar energy will find her again. She looks at the walls, dressed top to bottom with framed photos of Dewey and Herbert. She searches for answers, but all she finds is the same dumb picture dozens of times over—the only difference is the background. Dewey and Herbert in the backyard. Dewey and Herbert in the park. Dewey and Herbert at the Lutheran Church Nativity Scene. Herbert sticking his little head through a photo stand-in of The *Mona Lisa*.

Dewey begins to fidget as his excited smile wanes. "He ain't talking, is he?" he asks.

Billie doesn't respond.

Dewey sighs. "I knew it was too good to be true."

"He was a little bastard anyway," Dewey's mother calls from the next room.

"Stay out of it, Mama!"

Billie stands there just the same, her body language reminiscent of a performer stricken with stage fright. She stands there like she hasn't done this hundreds of times, but she has. She stands there like she doesn't remember standing the same way four decades ago in her own backyard.

"What're you doing over there, Wilhelmina?" her daddy would ask.

"Don't you pay that child no mind," her maw maw would say, over the back-and-forth rhythm of the porch rocking chair. Liverspotted hands folded in her lap. "She's justa rising. That's all."

Billie now digs deep into the corners of her mind, reaching out for anyone or anything that might be hiding. She turns to Dewey as if fresh out of a trance. "He's in a better place, Dewey."

Dewey's eyes glimmer with hope as he looks on.

"And he don't have cancer no more."

Dewey opens his mouth to speak like he might die otherwise.

Billie holds up her hand. "And his wings," she begins before pausing and nodding in thought. "And his wings work real good."

"He said that?" Dewey questions.

"He said that. He ain't here. He's already moved on. But I can hear him. And I can see him. And there's plenty of food in his feed. And the cage door is always open."

Dewey erupts into tears. He lunges forward, and Billie embraces him reluctantly. His cheek feels like snakeskin against her neck as he holds her far past the point of comfort. "Thank you, thank you, thank you, Miss Billie," Dewey says, backing away from her at last. He wipes his nose and sniffles. "Let me go get my checkbook."

Billie shakes her head. "No, Dewey. You know that ain't necessary." She offers her hand one last time, and he accepts it, interlacing his fingers with hers, squeezing. She turns and makes her way toward the door.

"Miss Billie," Dewey says.

She turns. "Yes?"

"Thank you."

Billie gently takes a bow and heads out the door, her stomach in knots over telling Dewey what he wanted to hear rather than what she felt to be true in her heart.

Billie slouches on a bench in Town Square. Her mind wanders. A cloudless sulphur, capering from bush to bush. She thinks about Dewey. She has an idea of why she lied to him about making contact with Herbert, but she doesn't know completely. She doesn't know a lot of things. She doesn't know what it is about her that draws the animals who seek her. She has never owned any pets herself, and she isn't particularly fond of them. At the same time, she doesn't know if they would be lost without her, or if it's she who would be lost without them.

She hears a clamorous twang of voices ringing in the distance and turns to her right. Mute Maddie shuffles toward the town hall ahead. A drove of people trails her as she gesticulates and jots jagged-footed words and sketches onto her notepad. Her neon-flowered muumuu pierces the dimming daylight as her fingers bridge the gap between life and death for those who follow behind her. To them, Mute Maddie is fascinating, mysterious, and charismatic. A star. Billie, on the other hand, is no better than a fraud behind a superimposed 1-800 number on a television screen, peddling magic tricks.

Billie's focus on the mob is broken by the patter of feet drawing near on the pavement ahead. She turns to see a young boy with chubby jowls hanging beneath his fuzzy knit cap. Little Andy Timmons had written a personal letter to Billie when his bunny rabbit died. When she had done a reading for him with no success, he was inconsolable. He now studies her up and down, eyes beaming as mucus gleams from his upper lip. Billie studies him in return and offers a slight smile, a half-assed wave. The boy leans backward for a moment, reaching into his overall pockets. His hand emerges with a small rock. He stares for another moment before stepping forward and hurling it with such force that it lifts him from his feet.

Billie flinches as the rock glances off her left shoulder and the boy darts off clumsily in the other direction. She remains seated with downcast eyes as a warm pain radiates from the flesh beneath her coat. After a few minutes, she stands to her feet and saunters down Main Street, the sweetgum trees along the road bare and dead in her wake. She crosses the street in front of the train station. The windows behind the white antebellum-style columns glare at her, watching and knowing and judging.

She makes it to her house—the same one that belonged to her mama and daddy—as the night's first stars begin to glow behind the clouds above. She enters through the storm door and proceeds to the living room sofa without any intentions of turning the lights on. She wraps herself in the patchwork of the quilt her maw maw had made and passed down to her. Leans her head against the cushion behind her and closes her eyes. And at the end of the day, the meows and the barks fall heavily, quietly, like snow in the windless night. But in the morning, they rise like new monsters.

Waiting in line at the grocery store checkout, Billie tries to ignore the man in the next lane, who is poorly masking the fact that he's staring at her. It feels like being awake but not realizing it yet. Foggy. She checks her watch before gazing out at the parking lot beyond the storefront window as the man's mindless, empty eyes swallow her whole. She imagines Dewey's parakeet, fat and green, bouncing from one cottony platform to the next somewhere in the firmament. A garden of clouds where nothing has a name.

She places her bag of apples onto the belt and sighs. Turns and finally acknowledges the man with a weary expression.

"Is it true?" he asks, stuttering at first.

"Is what true?"

"Do all dogs really go to Heaven?"

don't look up!

When I was twelve years old, the apocalypse reared its ugly head at our small town of Perch, North Carolina. The first total solar eclipse in almost two decades was set to blanket the country with darkness from sea to shining sea on a late-August afternoon, and this time, there was more to it than there had been with previous events. But I'll get to that directly. Three Sundays before the big day, I was in the bathroom brushing my hair for church.

"You almost ready, Junie?" my mama asked as she entered the doorway, her finest pearls gathering around her neck.

"Yessum," I said. "Just need help with my tie."

She bent her knees to get eye-level with my collar and knotted my wrinkly blue tie into a half-Windsor—just like she had with my deddy. It wasn't perfect, but it worked. That was true of a lot of things. Mama had done the best she could after Deddy got thrown fifteen feet from a powerline he was working on and died the week before I entered kindergarten. She worked two jobs between Monday and Saturday—one at the hospital and one at the general store around the corner—and even though I didn't always have new clothes to start every school year, I didn't want for nothing, neither.

"Grab your Bible," she said. "We're gonna be late."

We took my deddy's old five-speed pickup through the town's main intersection. Mr. Errol was there like he always was, chugging away on his big red bicycle, two six-foot-tall American flags flapping off either side on the back of the seat. Sweat sheened his brown arms and soaked through his muscle shirt as he stared straight ahead and followed the same loop he had day-in and day-out since I could remember. Mama had said one time that the Lord worked like that, too—always pedaling and pulling on the gears of your heart. Most people had told me that Mr. Errol wasn't right, but I hadn't made up my mind one way or the other.

We drove through the backroads toward the county line, where the cotton rose and fell in sweeping green ranks, aching to bloom under the sun's fury, though harvest time was still months away. If you looked real hard, you could see the wild horses in the spaces between the fields, the last of their kind in this part of the state, running and bucking and rearing with grace and strength that didn't seem possible. Singing, no shame in their voices. Answering to no one save for each other.

The Baptist church was the only building in sight for miles, the one exception being a fish house up the road that got the majority of its business from our congregation. The church was a converted barn situated a quarter mile as the crow flies behind the Perch Confederate Cemetery. It was the only structure that had been spared in Sherman's pursuit of Johnston over 130 years before. According to the old timers.

The choir was already singing "In the Highways" when we entered the double doors at the front of the building. Preacher Mills, a squat man who kindly put you in mind of a bullfrog, was there to greet us. He leered at my mama. "Well, howdy, Sister Coralee," he said to her, ogling her up and down. "Ain't you just purdy as a peach this morning?"

Mama nodded uncomfortably, and we found a seat at the back of the sanctuary. The good news was that we wouldn't be in sight of the preacher when the sermon started. The bad news was that we were on the same pew as Mr. Tuttle, and one time during an Easter prayer, Mr. Tuttle had farted and tried to blame it on everyone besides himself, me included. We were also on the same pew as Wade Furr, a bully at my middle school who was in all my classes. He smiled at me wolfishly as I took my seat.

Preacher Mills entered the pulpit and silenced the choir. "Y'all been getting out in the highways and the hedges?" he asked.

The congregation replied with amens.

"Y'all been somewhere working for your Lord?" he asked.

More amens.

"I hope so. Let's pray."

I bowed my head and closed my eyes as he rambled. I never paid much attention to what he said. I just sat there uncomfortable and blue and unsure of why I felt that way. Most of the time, Mama told me to use it as an opportunity to pray for my uncle, her brother. That wasn't the worst idea: I figured he could use all the praying he could get.

Once the opening prayer had concluded, Preacher Mills looked up and smirked. "Boy, it's a good morning. Don't y'all agree?"

Most did.

"It's a good morning, all right." He bounced up and down, hands in his pockets. "If'n you have that peace which passeth all understanding, that is."

"Right," someone called.

"Because I gotta tell you, friends: God is working out here, and I think he's about to wrap this thing up."

Something pricked at the side of my neck. I turned to find Wade Furr sneering across the pew, a straw in his hand. He'd blown a spitball at me. I scowled at him and rubbed my skin.

Preacher Mills continued, a fresh layer of sweat now beading across his red face. "The signs is all around us, folks. We got babykillers and sissies speaking for us in Warshington. They're taking God out of our schoolhouses and replacing him with fornicators. Natural disasters is happening all across our wicked world. Shootfire, just last week, a cloud in the shape of a fist streaked through the sky in Brazil. And this black sun we're fixing to have might just be the proverbial nail in the coffin."

"Preach it, brother," a deacon cried from the first row.

And Preacher Mills would have, too—of that I have no doubt—but at that moment, a mangy, reedlike man burst through the church's side entrance and stumbled toward the front row. Uncle Dipper wore an old hand-me-down corduroy jacket, tattered bluejeans, and tennis shoes with holes at the toes. He had the kind of beard that would never get full no matter how long he grew it out, and he smelled like roadkill and booze, even from the back of the sanctuary. He plopped down at the end of a pew.

People were whispering, and when I looked at Mama, I saw that she'd closed her eyes and dropped her head. She was mouthing something, maybe a prayer. This hadn't happened for months.

Preacher Mills looked Uncle Dipper up and down with disgust in his eyes. "I told you before," he said. "You ain't welcome here, Dipper."

"Ain't welcome?" Uncle Dipper slurred. "What happened to hate the sin, love the sinner?"

"You ain't a sinner. You're an abomination."

Uncle Dipper withdrew a flask from the pocket of his jacket and took a swig. "'And be ye kind to one another, tenderhearted, forgiving one another, even as God for Christ's sake hath forgiven you,'" he recited.

"I know the scripture," the preacher replied, offended. "Christ only forgives them that ask for it."

Uncle Dipper sighed. "I didn't come here to argue with you, Rick," he said, returning his flask to its home. "I come here to see my family." He looked over his shoulder wildly but couldn't seem to track us down. "Why don't you carry on with that nonsense you was spewing before?"

"Nonsense? You're the one needs to hear it most."

Uncle Dipper made an "O" with his right hand and motioned it suggestively.

"Good heavens," someone gasped.

"You know what I think?" Preacher Mills said.

"Naw."

"I think you're scared, friend."

"You mean like you was when you pissed your britches in the Scouts that one time we was telling ghost stories around the fire?"

Some members shrieked. A lady in the second row smiled toothlessly and nudged her spouse with her elbow. Wade Furr pointed at me, laughed, and stomped his feet. Mr. Tuttle coughed in an attempt to mask a fart, but each were heard separately. Preacher Mills was as ripe as a Cherokee Purple tomato.

Two deacons rose to their feet, rolled up their sleeves, and closed in on my uncle. Mama grabbed me by the arm and pulled me toward the parking lot.

❦

"I told you to get lost for a while, Pete," Mama hollered through the screen door of our house. That was Uncle Dipper's Christian name, though I'd never heard anybody call him that aside from her. He got his nickname from being a decent baseball pitcher once upon a time. We've got a newspaper clipping somewhere around here from the time he threw a perfect game in high school. When he'd wind up on the mound, back then, he'd dip his hand past his hip like he was submerging an egg in Easter dye. Then he'd toss a fastball that most people around here couldn't touch. Now, he pretty much only moved his arms to deliver a bottle to his lips.

"Where's Junie?" he asked, holding himself up by the doorjamb.

"In here with me, and he ain't coming out," she said. "You can keep carrying on til the cows come home for all I care. He needs a better role model in his life than a drunk heathen."

"I ain't drunk."

"Yeah, and water ain't wet." My mama was a slight woman, but she was scrappy and quick to the draw.

"Come on, Coralee," Uncle Dipper pleaded. "I come all this way on foot."

"Can I just go sit with him for a minute, Mama?" I asked.

She squinted at me.

"Don't let the sun go down," I said. This was a phrase she always used on me when I was fixing to go to bed mad at someone or some*thing*.

"All right," she said, crossing her arms. "Remember what I told you."

"Yessum."

"Say it."

"'Don't drink nothing he gives you or you'll be laughing at things that ain't funny and Jesus'll be crying.'"

49

"Good boy," she said, patting me on the back. "Go on."

The screen door creaked as I stepped out on the porch and fell into my favorite rocking chair. Even in the shade, the afternoon was hotter than Hades, and the katydids around us sounded like paper maracas shaking a million miles an hour. Uncle Dipper had popped a squat on the stairs and was smoking him a handrolled cigarette. A brown bag sat next to him. "Howboutya, little man?" he asked, his eyes on the road in front of our house.

"Hey, Uncle Dipper."

He puffed. "You doing okay?"

"Fair to middling," I responded, even though I wasn't entirely sure what that meant. I had heard adults use that phrase before.

"How's your mama?"

"She's getting by." I always tried to talk to Uncle Dipper with a deeper inflection. He wasn't around but once every few weeks, if that, but I still had this unavoidable desire to impress him.

"Can I ask you something?" he said.

"Yessir."

"Is that Preacher Mills courting her?"

I looked back to see if Mama was standing in the doorway, but she wasn't. "No, sir. Why do you ask?"

"I heard it through the grapevine," he said. "I hope it ain't true. I'd rather run through Hell with gasoline britches on than for her to date that imbecile."

I slowed my rocking down to a gentle sway. "Mama says you ought not talk about a man of God like that. Says it ain't where you wanna be when Jesus comes back."

"Well, a man of God ought not talk like he *is* God," he coughed. "He seems to have everything figured out, but your Bible says don't nobody know the hour. Know what I mean?"

For a moment, there was only the rattle of the katydids. Then I could hear the television through the open window. Some man with a chalky voice was talking about how eclipse fever had a stranglehold on the nation.

He talked about how totality would stretch over the entire contiguous United States at some point or another. Said the last time that'd happened was 1979. Then the program went to commercial.

"Uncle Dipper, are you saved?" I asked after a wordless minute or two.

He took a drink from his brown bag. "Are you?"

"I don't know."

"Well, if you're looking for someone who's gonna come and save you, it ain't me."

I didn't have nothing to say to that. One Sunday when I was real little, I'd answered the altar call at the end of the sermon. Deacon Chip knelt down next to me and said that if I confessed my sins and came to Jesus, He'd remove them as far as the east is from the west. I told him I didn't have any sins, except for maybe not finishing my peas at supper. He told me that we all had sin. I asked him if he meant like when he was running around town with a married woman. He grimaced and didn't really answer one way or the other. So I prayed and prayed with him, and he told me I was born again—that I had a new heart. I didn't feel any different, but Mama was real proud. Preacher Mills said that most people carried a false profession of faith, though, and I was worried because I didn't have any way of knowing if I was one of them.

"How's school?" Uncle Dipper asked, changing the subject. "You doing good in your classes?"

"We just started back, but my grades are good so far," I said. "I don't fit in too much, though." That was a euphemism. I caught hell in class every day. Mama said the other kids made fun of me because they thought my name was girly, but I knew the truth. They say in a small town, people know you as good as or better than you know yourself. There are no secrets. That was the case for me in Perch, at least, after Wade Furr got ahold of my personal journal and told the whole school I liked boys as more than friends.

"Anyone giving you a hard time?"

"There's this boy, Wade Furr. He hounds me pretty good."

"Aw, I wouldn't worry too much about him," Uncle Dipper said. "I hear he's thicker than cold grits, just like his deddy. That ole boy'd try to hotwire a truck that was sitting on blocks."

"He ain't too bright," I agreed.

"Well, I'd like to tell you it gets a lot better from here. I really would. But it don't. You gotta make do with what you got. Sometimes you'll get a little help. Probably when you least expect it." He paused. "You're a good boy, Junie."

I thought about that for a spell.

"Uncle Dipper."

"Yeah?"

"Is it true you was there?"

"Was where?"

"When Deddy got thrown off that powerline?"

He dropped his head. "Yeah," he said.

After a time, Uncle Dipper stubbed out his cigarette and wobbled to his feet. "I better git. I got your mama madder than a wet hen. Just thought I'd check on y'all." He picked up his brown bag and staggered off.

"What do you think about the eclipse?" I called to him. "You really think it's the end of the world like they're saying?"

He turned. "The world's gonna end, all right," he said. "But it ain't gonna be then. Who knows? This might just be a good thing, yet."

The bell rang in science class right as Wade Furr hit me on the cheek with a rubber band from two rows back. Most everybody but me had a good laugh about that while the teacher scrambled to her desk and unloaded her bag. Miss Spears was a pretty, full-figured lady of her late twenties whose facial expressions suggested she'd already become disenchanted with her profession. Some said it's because Preacher Mills had tried to get her kicked out for teaching evolution—and had almost succeeded. Mama said it's because her deddy was black and her mama was white, and people around here gave her a hard time for that. I didn't really know the reason; I just knew that she'd always been sweet to me.

"Morning," Miss Spears said.

Wade Furr shouted, "Penis," and buried his head into his arms.

The room erupted in laughter.

"Who said that?" Miss Spears asked. "Wade Furr, was that you?"

Nobody fessed up, least of all Wade.

"We're not gonna start that nonsense today," she said, brown eyes wide and luminous. "Turn to page twenty-one in your textbooks."

Half of the class did.

"We're talking about the Solar System today," she started, "and I'd like to stay focused on the planets. If you have any questions about the eclipse, see me after class or wait til we cover it next week." She read a brief introduction from the teacher's copy. Then she walked over to the chalkboard. She had no more than finished writing the names of all nine planets when the first arm shot up. "Yes, Caleb?"

"Is the eclipse gonna send one of them planets crashing into the earth?" a skin-and-bones boy in the first row asked.

She sighed. "No."

"Sometimes I like to create my own planets and doodle them in my notebook," a girl with a bow in her hair called from the other side of the room. She kicked her legs. "I give 'em names and surface temperatures and whatnot."

"That's nice, Ellen Anne," Miss Spears said. "Now—"

"How come we read out of this here book and not the Bible?" Caleb chimed in again.

"Let's not get off topic," Miss Spears said. She turned off the lights in the classroom, flipped on the overhead projector, and threw on a semi-transparent sheet that showed the sun and each planet attached to its own line.

Wade Furr was in the back, giggling about Uranus. I remember looking at Pluto and thinking about how small and far away it felt. It was a little fish in a big sea, and I reckon I could empathize with that. The other planets were shiny, and some had rings, but Pluto was just there and didn't seem like it really knew if it wanted to be or not. I scribbled my notes as Miss Spears talked about masses, distances, radiuses, and orbital periods. The only time she hit another snag was when she talked about which planets were made of gas.

When the bell rang again, I packed my things slowly so that my classmates—Wade Furr included—had plenty of time to exit before me. I approached the teacher's desk, where Miss Spears had her hands on her forehead, and just stood there for a minute.

She looked up once she realized I was there. "Everything all right, Junie?" she asked.

"Yessum," I said.

"Good deal. Have a nice rest of the day."

I walked closer to the door and turned around. "Miss Spears."

"Yes?"

"Is the eclipse a bad thing?"

She seemed puzzled that I'd asked. "No, Junie," she said, and smiled a warm smile. "It's not a bad thing."

I departed from the room and shuffled past the lockers, feeling a little better. But I should've known what was waiting for me. Wade Furr cut me off right there in the middle of the hallway before my next classroom. I was a runt in every sense of the word, except for my large feet. Wade Furr was a big ole boy who'd already been held back a few times. And he was meaner than a snake. Mama said she was shocked he wasn't old enough to drink. He smiled at me with his surprisingly tiny teeth and three mustache hairs. He had one of them shaggy mullets that would be considered stylish by today's standards, but not back then.

"Let me by, Wade," I said.

"What was you talking to the teacher about?" he asked.

"Nothing."

"Didn't sound like nothing to me," he said. "Was it just girltalk?"

I hugged my books to my chest. "I asked her about the eclipse."

He laughed and puffed out his chest. "Scared, are you?"

"I ain't scared."

"You should be," he said. "If this really is the end of the world, it ain't gonna be good news for you. My daddy says Judgment Day is gonna be rough on queers. But at least you'll be with your dead daddy. And your drunkard uncle. Probably your mama, too."

Wade Furr's father didn't have much room to be talking. Aside from the fact that he was Klan, he sold pain pills and stolen copper wire for a living. I don't remember much about my own deddy, I just know he made me feel real safe. Sometimes when I was little, maybe four or five, I'd pretend to be asleep so that he'd carry me to bed and tuck me in. I wished he would've been there at that moment.

Wade stepped closer to me.

"Wade Furr," the school resource officer hollered from up the hall. "Keep it moving."

Wade smirked at me and mouthed, "Later." Then he pulled a booger from his nose and wiped it on my shirt.

I was dreaming about the wild horses. Them bounding across the countryside with soft thunder in their hooves and through the backwood wallows that evaded the light. How a place could be a mystery to the sun was beyond my understanding of the world and its perfect machinery. They stood two-legged, playing, a harras of them, bumping and whickering, back and forth. Everything swelled with color, the ryegrass and the mud and the blackjack oaks beyond. Like they would bleed if you cut them open.

My deddy was standing there at the edge of the chickenwire fence, saying, "Look at 'em, Junie. Look at 'em go."

When school let out that afternoon, I walked down to the general store to see Mama. It was one of only a few buildings in the middle of town, flanked on either side by a gas station and a movie theater which doubled as a church for what Preacher Mills called "off-brand denominations." Right across the street was where Missus Winderman lived, an old Carpenter Gothic house with gingerbread trim and the previous year's Christmas decorations still up. Mr. Errol was out in front, kicking up a storm on his bicycle, those two great flags wrinkling in the windless summer day.

A middle-aged man and woman were at the entrance of the general store, handing out pamphlets that had "Are you ready?" scrawled in bold font over the top of a brooding black sun. I took one of them just so they'd leave me alone, but I didn't look either of them in the eye. Mama had a line of customers at the front counter when I went inside, so I made my way over to the candy aisle to see if there was anything good on sale. There wasn't. But there *was* Wade Furr tucked behind an end cap waiting for me.

He jumped out and put his arm around my shoulders. "Told you I'd be seeing you later, June Bug."

"Turn me loose," I said, trying to wrestle free from him. I thought about hollering, but then I remembered what Uncle Dipper had said. There wasn't nobody going to come and save me and pull me out.

Wade seized the pamphlet I'd slid into the outside flap of my bookbag. He struggled to read the words at first, but once he understood them, he started to cackle. "I knew you was scared," he said. He eyed the candy on the pegs and shelves before us. "I reckon you come in here for a last meal. Sweet tooth for a sweet boy?"

I gritted my teeth and squirmed some more, tears hot in my eyes.

"I can do you one better," he said. He reached into his back pocket and came up with a can of soda. He cracked the tab and tilted it toward my head.

I closed my eyes, expecting to hear the fizzy pop of cola running over my ears, but all I heard was the faint jingle of the bell at the store entrance instead. I opened my eyes and turned to the front of the aisle. Wade Furr froze and turned, too. Missus Winderman, the blind widow of a former tobacco executive, was shambling her way toward the back of the store. Her guide dog, a useless fat lab named Julian, led the way. Sort of. About halfway up the aisle, the dog halted in his tracks and sniffed a bag of caramel hard candies.

"All right, Julian," Missus Winderman said politely. He started moving again, paws dragging on the carpeted floor, only to flop down a few feet in front of us after a couple of labored steps. He panted and licked my foot, an unsuspecting grin on his goofy face.

Neither me nor Wade Furr moved a muscle.

Missus Winderman sighed. "Who's leading who here?" she asked, gently tugging on the dog's leash. He didn't budge. "Come on, fella," she said. Then she whispered, "Dammit." Finally, he rose to his feet and moseyed around me. Missus Winderman snuffled at the air. "Oh, Julian," she said. "Did you make water?"

I didn't know if he had, but I didn't care. I took that opportunity to wriggle away from Wade Furr. I peeled off his arm and made a run for the front counter. When I got there, Mama was checking out one customer, so I filed in line behind them and waited my turn. I watched as Wade exited through the front door seconds later, his eyes set on me all the while.

Mama smiled when she saw me. "Hey, darlin. You come in for a snack?"

"Yessum, but I didn't find nothing good," I said. I didn't want to worry her with talk of my bully. She had enough on her mind as it was.

"Well, what're you gonna spend your allowance on?"

I shrugged.

"How about these?" she asked, holding up a funky-looking pair of glasses.

"What're those?"

"We're selling 'em for the eclipse," she said. "You cain't look at it with regular sunglasses or you'll hurt your eyes. That's what the news said."

I took them from her and considered them. Then I slid her the dollar and change. She deposited it in the cash drawer and smiled again, less cheerful this time. She looked like she hadn't sat down, let alone slept in days. "Everything okay, Mama?" I asked.

She placed her palms on the counter and took a deep breath. "Your Uncle Dipper got locked up last night for being drunk in public. He was tore plumb out of frame."

I put the glasses in the side pouch of my bookbag and stood there quiet for a moment. "Is he gonna be there for good?" I asked. I wasn't sure of how all that worked.

"No, it was just for the night. But he probably should be."

I didn't know what to say.

"Just pray for him, Junie," she said.

"Okay, Mama," I replied. "I guess I'll see you at home."

"I love you."

"I love you, too."

You can probably guess who was expecting my company out in the parking lot. Wade Furr was standing there, glaring at me with that can of soda, and I was starting to realize that he just wasn't going to be denied. I unshouldered my bookbag so that it wouldn't get splattered, cast my eyes to the pavement, and began the slow, shameful, inevitable march of doom. But as I got within a few paces, I heard a quick scraping sound that nearly caused me to jump out of my shoes. I glanced up and saw Mr. Errol, wedged in between me and Wade Furr on his bicycle. I couldn't see his face, but I saw Wade's, and before that moment, I don't think I'd ever seen him scared. He eased away, picked up a skateboard that was propped on a parking block, and rolled off up the road, peering back only once.

Mr. Errol turned and stared at me, a stoic, rough-hewn face beneath his ball cap. Then he faced forward again and pedaled away.

The Sunday service before the eclipse was tense, even by normal standards. I reckon anxieties were running high over the uncertainty of what would happen the next day. The weekend had been a flatout mess. J.R. Clawson, the star quarterback of the high school football team, had wrapped his deddy's sports car around a utility pole and thrown a quarter of the town into darkness early Friday night. Saturday, a rookie police officer had made the biggest pot brownie bust in county history, only for the evidence to vanish into thin air on his way back to the station. Later that evening, a security guard from the jewelry store had spotted a rare pack of red wolves chewing at the Christmas lights on Missus Winderman's front porch. Mama said she hadn't heard of such strangeness outside a full moon.

The choir belted "When We All Get to Heaven" as Preacher Mills shimmied uncomfortably outside of the pulpit like nature was calling, but he needed to hold it. When the singers finished their last note, he assumed his normal stance at the lectern and dabbed the sweat along his hairline with a handkerchief. "Boy, if you think it's hot in here, imagine how Hell's gonna be for these sinners," he said.

A few members shook their heads. Mr. Tuttle's stomach squelched. I looked around for Wade Furr, but he was nowhere to be found.

"First order of business is to get to the prayer requests and praise reports," the preacher continued, "but I don't wanna spend too long on 'em because I need to get to the message this morning. It's weighing heavy on my heart. Who wants to start us off?"

A woman in the front pew stood and asked us to pray for her sickly mother. A man directly behind her thanked the Lord for a new job.

Mr. Tuttle rose to his feet, tucking in his shirt tail as he did so. "Yeah, um, can we pray for the poor soul on this row who clearly has digestive problems?"

Mama's eyes rolled back in her head so hard I thought they might fall out of her ears.

Preacher Mills nodded.

A couple more people gave their problems to God. Then we all bowed our heads and listened to the preacher petition the Holy Spirit. I prayed for Uncle Dipper like usual—asked the Lord to create in him a clean heart. I might've thrown a little something in there for me, too. Something or another about being able to see my deddy again someday.

As soon as the final amen echoed through the sanctuary, Preacher Mills cracked open his Bible. "I'm gonna jump right into this thing, folks, and I ain't gonna sugar coat it," he said. "That ain't gonna do nobody any good at this point. I spoke some about signs last service, and I reckon after all that's happened this weekend, a lot of you are starting to see why. I know I've said it a bunch recently, but I'll say it again: The signs is all around us. And I don't think it's a coincidence. After all, you cain't have signs without sins."

Some of the congregation really had to think about that one before they conceded.

"Why don't we turn to the book of Revelation, Chapter 12? Bible says, 'And there appeared a great wonder in heaven; a woman clothed with the sun, and the moon under her feet, and upon her head a crown of twelve stars: And she being with child cried, travailing in birth, and pained to be delivered.' Now, just in case some of y'all wasn't here for that sermon earlier this year—the woman in God's word is Mary, the moon is the church, and the child is Jesus."

The toothless woman in the second row squinted at the ceiling, trying to connect the dots.

"Bear with me," Preacher Mills went on, each word carefully measured. "This black hole sun is set to happen tomorrow, right? That'll be thirty-three days after the woman clothed with the sun from the Revelation 12 prophecy appeared in the stars last month."

That much was at least somewhat true. The photograph of a constellation resembling a woman had been on the front page of the paper in July.

"Lemme ask you something," the preacher said. "Where's this thing supposed to start tomorrow?"

"Where?" the congregation asked.

"Oregon."

The crowd looked puzzled.

"That's the thirty-third state. Where's it gonna end? On the *thirty-third* parallel in South Carolina." He paused. "Starting to see a trend? What could the Lord be trying to tell us?"

Nobody answered.

"Well, how about Ezekiel 33:6?" Preacher Mills asked as the panicked flipping of pages tore through the room. "Bible says, 'But if the watchman see the sword come, and blow not the trumpet, and the people be not warned; if the sword come, and take any person from among them, he is taken away in his iniquity; but his blood will I require at the watchman's hand.'" He skimmed the room with his bulging eyes.

I'd never heard the place that quiet. The uneasiness was so thick you could've put it in a gravy boat and served it with biscuits. Dozens of sets of eyes fell on Preacher Mills, desperate for answers.

His lips parted to speak again, and he pounded the Bible in front of him with his fist. "Friends, I've gotta call it like I see it. The Lord's about to throw in the towel on this thing. You heard me right: The Rapture is nigh. The sword is about to come. And there ain't no way I can hold my tongue and not blow the trumpet to warn you." He got teary-eyed and his voice cracked. "I cain't have your blood on my hands. Now's the time to save souls before it's too late."

Members, young and old, were already starting to get up when Preacher Mills opened the altar early. One of the deacons began to hammer on the piano—a number I wasn't familiar with that sounded more fit for a deranged circus than a church. A lot of people had crouched over where they sat and dropped their heads toward their laps, so I followed suit. I'd never seen such a darkness as the kind that was behind my closed eyelids, and the sickness I felt in my chest was enough to make me retch. Mama clutched my wrist.

"You feel that?" Preacher Mills squalled between grunts. "That tug of war happening with your heart strings? That's the fight for your soul. Don't let that thing get won by the wrong side."

Someone shouted, "Glory!"

I opened my eyes and looked straight ahead. A line of parishioners had formed along the wall of the sanctuary like animals awaiting slaughter. One by one, they approached Preacher Mills, who stood in front of the pulpit with his suit jacket gripped tight in his hands. He swung it like a baseball bat at each of them as they came up. Once the garment touched them, they spilled onto the altar with their arms hoisted, some speaking in tongues or carrying on in equally outlandish ways.

I pulled my hand free of my mama's grasp and went up to join them as the music blared. My heart was going a mile a minute, but I didn't know what else to do. When it was my turn to take the dive, the preacher reared back and heaved the jacket toward me. But before it hit me, Uncle Dipper sprang out of nowhere and snatched it from his hands.

Preacher Mills, red and startled, grabbed hold of one end and wheezed. "You better gimme that thing back, Dipper! This don't concern you."

"The hell it don't!" Uncle Dipper hollered, ripping the jacket away completely and falling with it buried in his arms.

Preacher Mills tumbled to the ground next to him, an unfortunate noise that sounded like a burp slipping from his mouth as he hit the floor. Multiple cries reverberated throughout the room as the deacons dogpiled both men and punched at Uncle Dipper's arms.

Preacher Mills wailed.

"Don't you listen to these crazy bastards, Junie!" Uncle Dipper yelled. "Follow your head! Free your mind!" He threw his sharp elbows at the deacons. "Turn me loose, damn you."

I slowly backed away. Then I took off running through the fire exit. I ran through the dirt parking lot, into a road that was so ill with the fever of the sun you'd think you were standing on the floor above Hell's basement. I ran and ran. Ran until my wind gave out, and it was just me, alone with the land and all its sprawling quiet. Or so I thought. To my right, in the weeds just off the shoulder of the road, was a wild horse, watching me with uncanny patience. It was a mare, earthy brown with a sandy mane, eyes cut from an amber gemstone. A miracle or a curse, I couldn't tell you which. To this day, I wonder what crossed her mind as she found me there, torn and tired. A funny-looking animal. Shouldering the guilt of a whole world for no other reason than that's what I'd been told to do. The horse remained there, breathing with me for an indeterminate amount of time, and as much as I wanted her to stay with me always, I knew she couldn't.

She had been gone for several minutes when my mama picked me up crying, some half a mile down the way from the church.

Miss Spears's mind seemed to be on everything other than school when she handed out pop quizzes on Monday morning. Most of the class groaned, but I didn't care so much because it was simple matching and I'd stayed read-up on all the material. But my head was elsewhere, too. I couldn't help but think about Uncle Dipper and how his tomfoolery the day before might have cost me my eternal salvation. I also started questioning Preacher Mills and his magic coat altogether. I thought about Wade Furr—felt his evil smile falling on me, even though my back was turned to him. A profound sadness overtook me, and I left a couple of answers blank because I didn't see the point if the world was going to end in a couple of hours anyway.

The timer on Miss Spears's desk went off. "All right," she said. "Y'all know the drill. Pass 'em up."

One by one, the quizzes went over to the left and then up to the front of the room. Miss Spears collected the sheets of paper and put them in her bag. Then she walked over to the closet and wheeled out the television cart. The class cheered at the first sight of it.

"What we watching?" somebody asked.

"Porno," Wade Furr blurted in front of a fake cough.

Everybody giggled.

Miss Spears popped a tape into the VCR, and a woman with heavy bangs and a colorful scarf appeared on the screen. She was seated at a desk, and behind her, the stock photo of a half-occluded sun hung in the top right corner. "The moment we've all waited for is here," she said with an aggressive smile. "Let's go live to Montana for a view of the first contiguous solar eclipse since 1918." The image switched to a still shot of a black circle suspended in the sky, a glowing silver ring encompassing it.

"My goodness, would you look at that?" a man's voice joined in the telecast.

"It really is something," she said.

"I can only imagine what it was like for those who last witnessed this magnificent event," he replied. "A world at war, years away from broadcast television."

I looked around the room to find twenty faces, each of them ranging from blank to enthralled.

The man droned on for several more minutes until the moon began to peel away from the sun, exposing a burst of light. "Now you can see it coming to an end here, and if we can get a wide shot, we'll see if things are returning to normal." The camera slowly panned out to show a metropolitan skyline, gaining brightness by the second. "Son of a gun," the man laughed. "And we're right back to where we were before the eclipse. Just a normal scene here in Mountain Standard Time. Heather."

The shot cut back to the anchorwoman as she stacked papers on her desk. "Well, there you have it—the last solar eclipse we'll see on this continent for quite some time. The good news is that we won't have to wait another sixty-one years for the next one. The next eclipse will be visible from North America on August 24, 1998. And when it is, may the sun show its brilliant face on a world in peace and harmony. Here's to bringing you the next one, nineteen short years from now." The screen faded to black, and credits began to roll.

Miss Spears hit the power button on the television, folded her arms, and leaned on her desk. "Questions? Comments?"

It was crickets at first. Then the scrawny boy in the first row said, "It don't look like much to me."

"Well, I'm sure the technology of the time doesn't do it justice," Miss Spears replied.

"My daddy says this thing is gonna throw off the alignment of the stars and send Planet X barreling toward us like a bull in a china shop," the girl with the bow in her hair said. She shoved her finger in her nose. "Kill us all and whatnot."

Miss Spears sighed. "No, Ellen Anne. The only danger an eclipse poses is to your eyes. Unless it's at the point of totality, you'll want to make sure you're not looking at it without glasses that have solar filters. Regular sunglasses won't do."

Ellen Anne made note of this in her little book.

"Anybody else?"

"Miss Spears," I said.

"Yes?"

"Do you believe in God?"

Her eyes danced around the room from one face to another, and I immediately regretted putting her in that spot. Just when it seemed as though she would answer, the bell rang. Everybody grabbed their books and hustled out into the hall, except for me. I walked toward Miss Spears's desk, wavered for a moment with my eyes to the ground, and tried to decide if I should apologize or wait for an answer. I chose to make for the door instead.

"Junie," she called.

I turned. "Yessum?"

She spent a good bit of time thinking about what she was going to say before she said it. "I believe in what I can see and what I can feel. I hope that answers your question."

I considered that for a second. It did. "Yessum," I said.

School let out early that afternoon since most parents were going to come and pick up their kids anyway. It seemed like everyone in town was gathered in front of the general store or else in Missus Winderman's yard. She sat in a rocking chair on the porch, Julian belly-up and chewing at his chunky black nails a few feet away from her. All of the roads were blocked off, just like they were for the annual Christmas parade. Mr. Errol weaved in and out of groups of people, sweating and undeterred by all the hoopla. The whole police department lined the side of the street; if anyone wanted to rob a house elsewhere in town, that would've been the time to do it.

I stood by Missus Winderman's mailbox with my bookbag still strapped over my shoulders, and Mama flanked my right side. Her boss had told her she could have a break long enough to see everything happen. Pretty charitable for him. Preacher Mills had a considerable flock of people an earshot away, and they were all praying like crazy. Invoking Yahweh. At the mere sight of them, I felt the lingering queasiness from the day before start to return. The baseless contrition.

Mama touched my forehead with the back of her hand. "You all right?"

I nodded because I knew I was going to throw up if I opened my mouth.

"I don't know what's gonna come of all this," she said. "But I'm not gonna let nothing happen to you."

I looked at my mama, a willowy yet strong woman who beamed so much light, though all the world had ever dealt her was darkness. I imagined my deddy on the other side of her in one of his work shirts, a quiet grin on his face. In that moment, I felt an overwhelming sense of serenity. I didn't understand it then, but I know now that it was unconditional love.

"Look!" someone hollered. "It's starting."

I was fixing to look up before I remembered what Mama and Miss Spears had said. As I fished in my bookbag for my eclipse glasses, I felt a tap on my left shoulder. I glanced over and saw Uncle Dipper at my side, his eyes clearer than normal. They must have just let him out of the jailhouse.

He didn't say anything, and neither did I.

I don't know if I smiled then, but I smile now, remembering it.

In a matter of seconds, the world had taken to an unusual dimness; it was still light outside, but it was like the sun was a lamp bulb and someone had thrown a bed sheet over it.

I put my glasses on and looked up. The eclipse itself didn't appear like much to me—just a golden chunk of half-eaten cheese on an otherwise black canvas. Then, over the course of a few minutes, it waned until it reached the point of totality. I lowered the glasses. It was dark all around us, like it was blowing up a squall, but there weren't any clouds in the sky. The sun was now a bottomless dot with a radiant halo. If only for a split second, we were all a collective heartbeat, floating on a blue marble through time and space. Standing in awe of the universe's design.

Just as the alignment began to shift again, I heard a familiar voice say, "Out of my way."

I removed my glasses just in time to see Wade Furr shove through the crowd and stumble in front of me. "What's up, girlfriend?" he said, pulling out a pair of 3D glasses—the kind you get from the theater.

I opened my mouth to warn him, but Uncle Dipper looked at me and shook his head. So I swallowed my words.

A red bird scampered across Missus Winderman's yard. A lady, hands on what must have been her granddaughter's shoulders, said, "Ooo. Lookit, darlin. A cardinal means a special visitor from Heaven."

She had barely finished the sentence when a Christmas angel plunged from Missus Winderman's roof and into the yard, the impact decapitating it.

The little girl screamed.

Wade Furr cast his eyes to the sky. Smirking at first, he started to grimace after several moments. Then he hollered something awful. Rubbed his eyes and rolled on the ground like he was on fire. Some people came over to tend to him.

Preacher Mills stood with his arms extended upward. Expecting to hear a ram's horn, I reckon.

A couple of cops giggled uncontrollably, their eyes as red as the fire hydrant they stood by.

Miss Spears sat on the hood of her car, and for the first time, I saw a sense of wonderment on her face.

It was then, watching her, that I thought about it. The fight for my soul. I wondered if my immaterial spirit was Mr. Errol, just wandering around with no rhyme or reason on the surface. I wondered if it was Missus Winderman, being led by people who were sweet and cared about me but weren't really qualified on the matter. Was it an untamed, dancing thing, made to roam until the Earth ran out of road? Or was I being taken astray by Pharisees? Was I like my Uncle Dipper? Would I have to figure everything out on my own? For a time, I thought it might be a combination of all those things. Day broke once more, slowly but surely, and the world didn't end. And after the darkness there was light again, stretching its fingers over everything with a warmth and mystery I'd never seen before.

queen of thorns

Whenever Hazel looks at plants, she sees endless possibilities: the promise of growth, the crush of disappointment, proof that life can end and start again. The offerings at the Midway Garden Supply call out to her in sweet, green songs. There are the Zanzibar gems and the fiddle-leaf figs and the golden pothos vines, each possessed of its own particular quirks. Like her.

She is a belladonna.

Beautiful.

Full of poison.

It wouldn't take much for her to get lost in this store for hours, browsing amongst the aisles, all of them crowded and vibrant. Buzzing with energy. She has done it before. She's a regular here, has been for a while. Especially since that day. As her grief grows, so does the number of plants back at her house. It started with a few succulents and snake plants, a showpiece monstera. Now her townhome is its own nursery.

Marjoe had never been crazy about all of it. It just wasn't his thing. He loved her, of course. But could he have loved her as much as he loved heroin? Could he have loved *anything* that much? Every night, in her diary, which sits on an end table next to a jade plant in her office, she writes down things that she would say to him if he weren't dead.

With each trip to Midway, it is becoming increasingly difficult for Hazel to find something that she doesn't already have. The endeavor generally takes her a while, but today is different. She's perusing the flowering plants when she spots it, sitting there in a black plastic planter in the corner, a watchful guardian for this section of the store: It is waist-high and columnar, with tiny, acicular thorns riddled through smooth, bluegreen flesh. Slanted and narrowing toward the top. Imperfect. Gorgeous in its ugly simplicity.

"Wow," Hazel can hear herself saying. Or maybe she just imagines it.

A friendly, college-aged girl in a Midway Garden Supply t-shirt under overalls approaches. She must be new on account of Hazel hasn't seen her in here before.

She says, "Anything I can help you find?"

"What is this?" Hazel asks, gesturing toward the bristly obelisk before her. "I've seen them online, but I can't think of the name."

"That's a Peruvian apple cactus," the employee says.

Hazel crouches to get a closer look. "Right, right. Know anything about them?"

"Not much," the employee admits. "Just that it only blooms once a year at night, and only for a few hours. Has to be in the right place, too, especially if you're keeping it indoors. So, unless the conditions are just right, you'll miss it. It's still a pretty plant without the flowers, though."

"It sure is," Hazel says, and something catches in her throat. She brushes a fingertip across one of the prickly spines, feels the scrape of it against her skin. A tingling sensation crawls the length of her neck, the same way Marjoe's hand once did. A great seed swells in her chest, hard. If she can survive it, she thinks, there will be Heaven. There will be Heaven where there is currently so much Hell.

"What do you think?"

"I'll take it," Hazel says.

Sometimes it was like you were never really here.

Lester Judd likes to think he's full of heart and can-do—what the old timers call gumption—but the only thing he's ever been full of is shit. He's holed up at the Lazy 5 Suites, the dingiest motel on the Mudcat Holler side of Glass, belly full of gas station wine and a pepperoni pizza he only lucked into because some delivery boy had left it in his car overnight and was going to throw it out unless someone claimed it. Lester Judd has a knack for being Johnny-on-the-spot. It is the only way he survives.

Yesterday, he laid an ill-advised bet on the wrong car. Then he blanked on five scratch-offs in a row. That's the nature of the game, as far as he's concerned: Sometimes you're up, sometimes you're bust. It just so happens he's never been more bust than lately. Once upon a time, he had been a promising young boxer, rising through the ranks with an effortless natural ability and two cannonballs for fists. But his moneygrubbing manager had tried to send him up the ladder before he was ready. After a string of lopsided losses, Lester Judd was out on his ass. Now he's a gambling junkie. Whole life gone faster than a ten count.

He fishes his prepaid phone from the greasy pizza box, calls a guy he knows. "Any action tonight?" he asks. "What about the drag strip? Naw?" He hangs up. He's not from here, only has a few plugs in this neck of the woods. He's on the run.

He dials a contact he met just last night. A degenerate who has conned his way into a job at the local drugstore. "Hey, what's the word? What do you mean, 'it's dead'? What happened to them jokers you said was fighting dogs last week? All right, thanks for nothing." He pitches the device back onto the soiled cardboard. "Sorry sonsofbitches."

It's a bad time for the well to run dry. He owes the Morrison brothers big. The Irish twins from the Peach State, who made their nut running creekwater all over Appalachia, helped him get back on his feet when his career went into the shitter. But he borrowed too much, dug a deeper hole than he could climb out of. Now he's into them for fifty large, and they may be damn near three hundred miles away, but it's only a matter of time before their people track him down. He would prefer to have more than twenty bucks in his pocket when that happens.

The southpaw paces the room, shadowboxing. An old habit. Part of him still thinks, as long as he has those capable hands of his, that he could mount a comeback once he gets himself out of this mess. Right jab. Left straight. Right hook. Left uppercut. Right hook.

What sounds like a domestic dispute vibrates through the walls. Or maybe it's sex. Hard to say. Two bottles of fortified wine sit empty on the dresser. Like two people who are alone even though they're together. He swirls one of them, curious to see if he can muster enough backwash for one last pull. Nothing doing. All he's got to show for the five dollars he spent at the gas station is a hangover. It throbs atop visions of better times. Of champagne flutes and steak dinners and ring girls and battle scars. So distant to him now, they may as well have happened on Mars.

Lester Judd reaches for his gym bag on the bed. He pulls out the gun.

You wanted your ashes spread, but your parents wanted you buried. So I took the sand we brought back from Acadia and scattered it in the park where we had our first date.

Hazel has found the perfect spot for her newest addition: right next to the bookcase in her first-floor home office. From across the room, a window spills honey-colored morning light onto the Peruvian apple cactus, which Hazel has set into a woven pot she made in an arts and crafts class. The shades of dawn remind her of Marjoe's curly hair and lazy smile, how sometimes he wouldn't even be in bed until first light. He would come in, eyes made of hot wax, lying to her about where he had been, who he had been with. He would sleep until dinnertime. Not that he actually ate anything when he got up. It was always the same song and dance.

They had met in college, back when all he did was drink too much, smoke a little weed. He didn't touch the hard shit until grad school. Coke, then Oxy, then Ron. He said the needle beat the hell out of anything any doctor had ever prescribed him. Said he had demons that sprouted through the pavement of his soul like weeds, that heroin was the only way he knew how to kill them. Six months after dropping out of his degree program, he was fired from his job teaching elective classes at the community college up the road. He died on their bedroom floor on an otherwise unremarkable winter day.

The plants have given Hazel a new lease on life. Each morning, as she's drinking her coffee, she visits them, one by one. Never for more than a second or two, but it's an important ritual. She needs to watch things grow instead of wither.

"Another one?" she can hear Marjoe say. "Goddamn, Blue." Her pet name. Sometimes he would hurt her feelings, even though he was mostly kidding around. If he had the presence of mind to realize it, he would make a small gesture of apology. A hug around the waist. A kiss on the forehead. Signals of affection that grew coarse and perfunctory toward the end.

If only he could see her now that nobody's here to give her a hard time. The collection she has amassed.

Hazel takes time to admire the cactus, how it stands proud, if slightly askew. A whimsical side to its serious facade. She touches one of its gray thorns, as she had the day before in the store, only this time, she does so a little too hard. She pulls back. Blood surfaces on the tip of her pointer finger in a tiny red blossom. She shakes her hand, curses, sticks the finger into her mouth. The coppery taste, the sting—they remind her that she is alive. That this is a place of the living, if only she would let it be.

She hops onto her laptop to start her day. Hazel is a food science consultant at an out-of-state research firm. She does one hundred percent of her work remotely. When she's not finding responsible and cost-effective ways for her clients to increase the shelf-life of their products, her calendar is jampacked with meetings. Her first call of the day is with a coworker, Talia. A project they're doing for ketchup and boxed mac and cheese.

"Is that a new plant?" Talia asks, forty-five seconds into the conversation. She'll do whatever it takes to talk about anything other than work.

"It is," Hazel confirms. "A Peruvian apple cactus."

"Fun!" Talia says. She always acts like whatever she has just heard is the most exciting information in the world. Whenever there is a company email about a birthday or a wedding, she's the first to Reply All, without fail, and in all caps. Hazel has never met Talia in person, so she only exists to her from the clavicles up. A floating headneckshoulder figure of impossible positivity.

"I've had my eye out for something like it, so it was a stroke of good luck."

"That's great," Talia says. "Gosh, I wouldn't know the first thing about taking care of a cactus. It seems hard!"

Hazel shoots a glance at the window that displays her webcam feed in the bottom right corner of her laptop screen. In the background, the cactus flanks the bookcase, comes about three-quarters of the way up it.

"That's strange," Hazel finds herself mumbling. "It looks even bigger than it did a few minutes ago."

"What's that?" Talia asks.

"Nothing," Hazel says.

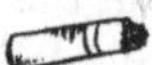

I forgive you for your sickness. I don't forgive your sickness for you.

Lester Judd bursts through the minimart's rear fire exit, out of breath, blood cooking. He jerks his head left, then right, like a bird, as the alarm cries out behind him. Coast is clear, but it won't be for long. He ditches the nitrile gloves, the blacked-out American flag ballcap, and the long-sleeve camo shirt, because that's what they'll be looking for. He lifts the back of his wifebeater, stuffs the gun into the waistband of his cargo shorts. He figures he has a minute, tops, in a town this small, to put as much distance as possible between himself and the minimart before the law shows up.

But he doesn't want to be caught running, either, doesn't want to draw unwanted attention. So he walks, quick but not too quick, to the lunch counter up the way.

These are peak hours for Chic's Grill. Patrons are too busy chowing and going about their day, and staff are too worried with getting people in and out the door, to pay much mind to Lester Judd. He orders a cola and a hot dog all the way, takes his time with them at a two-top table in the corner of the restaurant. Through the window, he sees just about every cop car in town whip by, sirens firing, over the course of five minutes or so. He feigns concern, trying to blend in with everybody else. But on the inside, he thinks, *too slow, dipshits.* On the inside, he wonders *how big was the haul?* He'll have to wait until he's back at the Lazy 5 Suites to count it out.

With his meal finished, he busses his basket and makes a quiet exit, falling in behind another group of customers. Only one bus goes out to Mudcat Holler, and he catches it just as it reaches the stop outside the train station, a quarter mile down the road. He slips into a seat next to the air conditioner at the back, where he can keep everything in front of him, but it's just a precaution. There are half a dozen people on this bus, and not one of them cares enough to acknowledge his presence. He lets loose of a deep breath. A successful heist is a lot like good boxing: You get in, you hit without being hit, and you get out. That simple. He isn't trained to do anything else.

Lester Judd is feeling halfway decent about himself as he deboards the bus into the corner of town where trucks sit on blocks in lawns gone to seed. But the sensation is short-lived. When he gets to his room, there's a note pinned to the door. His heart falls off a cliff before he even knows what is written on it.

He removes the piece of paper, reads it aloud: "You didn't seriously think we wouldn't find you, did you? We have eyes and ears everywhere. If you want to keep yours and those million-dollar hands, you'll have our money by a week from today."

The note isn't signed, but it doesn't need to be. Lester Judd is well aware of who wrote it. He pans the motel's exterior walkway and, finding himself alone, enters his room. He withdraws the plastic grocery bag from one of his cargo pockets, spreads the cash onto the unmade bed. When the first ten bills come up as ones, he knows he's in trouble. He wipes his face with his left hand, keeps counting. Runs through all of it twice. He plops down onto the bed, next to the money.

Seventy-three shittinass bucks.

That ain't gonna cut it.

He needs a bigger score, and he needs it yesterday. Otherwise, the Brothers Morrison are going to have someone take a hammer to his hands, a knife to one of his ears—or both. Something gross and savage, anyway. He has heard the stories.

He's racking his brain for some kind of solution, anything, when, as if by divine intervention, the prepaid phone rings from its place atop one of the pillows. He accepts the call.

"Yeah?"

"Still looking for a dog fight? Coupla boys are putting something together for this weekend."

It's the degenerate drugstore tech.

"Afraid I'm gonna need something with a little more juice now," Lester Judd says.

"Got it. Just thought I'd let you know."

"I appreciate it. Say…you know anything about the Glass Community Savings & Loan?"

There's a pause from the drugstore tech, like he's considering hanging up. Then he proceeds, speaking low: "Worth a look, I reckon. I hear they keep ten or fifteen thou on hand. Minimal security. Some joker hit it five or six years ago. Never got collared. Could be a sweet take for the right person."

"I need more than that," Lester Judd says.

"More than *that*? Hell, partner, I don't know if I can help you there."

"I'm in a tight spot here, man. I don't care how big the job is, I'll knock it down."

Another pause. "I might know of one thing that could earn big, but it's a stretch."

"I'm listening."

"Been thinking about it for years. It's totally untapped."

"Spit it out."

"A lot of money in that drug store."

"Cash?"

"Naw. But our cabinet of Schedule II controlled substances is a goddamn treasure chest, and nobody knows it."

"I ain't looking to take anything I've gotta move later," Lester Judd says.

"I can understand that. But think about this: We've got two bottles of oxycodone, 40 milligram. Hundred count. Now you take that to the street, you can easily get a dollar a milligram from the fiends. It'd take you a while to move it, sure, but you could milk two bottles for eight grand. Or you could flip it in bulk. Won't get as much, but you'll still fetch a good price. And that's just one drug. We've got twenty-five other kinds in there with it. You do the math, brother."

Goosebumps prickle Lester Judd's skin. "Let me think about it," he says.

"Ten-four. You wanna move on it, gimme a holler. We can talk cut."

"All right."

The boxer ends the call. A headrush comes over him, the kind he only used to get before fights. It is the electrical hum of danger, of possibility. This could be big. A six-figure score. It might be hard to sell the Morrison Brothers on anything other than immediate payment, but it's worth a shot. Lester Judd doesn't have the luxury of being picky. He's running out of options. He's running out of time. In his head, he can hear the ding of the final bell.

At night, I would ask God to give me a skin of thorns, so that when you curled up next to me, I would remind you of something you couldn't live without.

When Hazel lumbers into her home office on Tuesday morning, she nearly drops her mug of coffee. The Peruvian apple cactus, which didn't even come up to her belly button forty-eight hours ago, now closes in on the ceiling, its thorny crown poking at the textured white drywall above the bookcase. The plant has gained three new stem segments overnight. It appears more robust, too, its ribs thicker, its bluegreen flesh bulkier, more intense in color. And those spines: Have they doubled in length? They could go into your hand and come out on the other side, Hazel thinks.

Would that have been what it was like for Marjoe?

This is exactly the type of thing that would have griped his ass. She can almost hear him now: "Really, Blue? Didn't stop to think about where you were gonna put this thing, huh?"

His sighs, always tempered with an undertone of wryness, still reach for her across time and space. She can see him standing next to that keg at the house party freshman year, cross-buzzed, nodding his head to the music. Looking goofy and harmless with those dimples of his.

"What's your name?" he had asked her.

"Hazel," she said.

"But your eyes are blue."

"Yes, they are."

"Yeah. I think I'm gonna call you Blue."

"All right," she laughed. "You got a name?"

"Marjoe."

"*Marjoe?*" she asked, before realizing her tone was kind of rude.

He went with it: "Dad's name is Mark. Mom's Josephine." He shrugged. "What can you do, am I right?"

"Okay," she said. "Marjoe. Yeah. I think I'm gonna call you…Marjoe."

He flashed her that easy smile for the first time. "Works for me."

Hazel logs on for the day. She's got a touchpoint with the ketchup and boxed mac and cheese people first thing. In the virtual meeting room, it is her and Talia before anyone else. Her coworker looks like she has been up and at 'em for several hours. Hazel imagines her, sitting in her home, wherever that is, watching the shopping channel at all hours of the night, never blinking. Possibly, probably, smiling.

"Holy cannoli!" Talia shouts so loud that it makes Hazel jump. "Can I just say your cactus is *thriving*? I mean, look at that bad boy."

Hazel does. If she didn't know any better, she would say the plant is getting larger in real time. The thorns, merely scraping the ceiling minutes before, are firmly embedded into the drywall. A detail the HOA would probably deem less than ideal. She'll have to re-pot it outside, and the very thought makes her hands sting.

"Didn't count on it growing this fast," Hazel admits.

"Well, you know what they say about miracles," Talia says. "They come when you least expect them!"

"Right."

Hazel can't deal with the optimism right now, especially the kind that is spiritual in nature, and there isn't enough caffeine in the universe to bring her up to Talia's level. Never will be. But she has no choice. She has to put on her face, has to get through it. This meeting and then one more after it. Then she can take a break. Grab an early lunch, run some errands. She's got some prescriptions to pick up at the drugstore.

You were the funniest person I've ever met.

Lester Judd stares from across the street at the Purdy & Sons Drug. He's in a phone booth, the last one standing in all of Glass, dressed in a hockey jersey and warmup pants, gym bag at his feet. He has just put in a coded call to his contact in the pharmacy. To make sure everything is copacetic. He's been watching the door for about twenty minutes, keeping track of who goes in and out. He figures there are three people in there—at most—along with a front cashier, a manager, the tech, and the pharmacist on duty. He can handle that many. More than that, probably not.

He steps out of the phone booth. Looks both ways, crosses the street. He digs the ski mask out of his bag, pulls it over his head. Snaps the nitrile gloves onto his hands. Then he slings the front door open, slams it shut again, and turns the lock. The cashier, an elderly lady, is ringing up a Western-hatted man not much younger than she is. The shock on their faces is so total it could pass for indifference.

"Hands up," Lester Judd barks at them, gun raised.

They comply.

"All right, back to the pharmacy. Let's go. Get the sand out of your ass, Meemaw."

He follows the pair to the back of the building. Much to his relief, there is only one other customer on the sales floor. The manager is helping her find an item in one of the aisles between the front door and the pharmacy. Lester Judd points the weapon, orders them to join his gaggle of hostages. They do, the woman showing her best poker face, the manager, not so much. Over him comes a wash of Venetian white fit for sixteenth-century royalty, and he looks as though he could have a coronary at any moment. There is one last person to check off Lester Judd's mental list, and he locates her at the pharmacy counter. She is a short woman of her mid-twenties, with butt-length brown hair and an anxious posture. Once she comes into view, unaware of what is going down, he ramps things up a notch.

"Everybody on the goddamn ground!" he hollers, kicking a spinning rack of eyeglasses to the floor. It crashes, and cheap readers scatter all over.

Every person on this side of the pharmacy counter drops like bowling pins, several of them shrieking.

"Y'all move so much as a finger, and I'll turn you into Swiss cheese!" Lester Judd says. "Lord as my fucking witness. And no noise, either. So if you're thinking about boohooing, think again."

He makes eye contact with the tech, angles toward the counter in a way that keeps everything before him. He's both deliberate and light on his feet, a deadly combination. He's a wild dog.

"Don't hurt me," the tech says. Mediocre acting, but it'll do.

"Get your pharmacist."

A sharp-featured woman in a white coat approaches slowly, hands above her head, eyes down. Lester Judd sits the gym bag on the counter.

"Every controlled drug you got, I want it. Understand?"

The pharmacist nods, grabs the bag, makes for the bays to her right.

"No, not them!" Lester Judd shouts, nearly sending her jumping out of her skin. "The ones in the case behind you. The Level Twos. Come on, get with the program. Chop, chop."

She takes a deep breath, digs a key out of her pocket with a trembling hand. Visibly fighting tears, she opens the case and begins to pack the bottles into the bag. Lester Judd uses the opportunity to monitor his other hostages. He moves the gun from one to the next. Everything is still shipshape. He tries to not get ahead of himself, tries to not think about how he's going to get the Morrison brothers to go for this. None of that matters unless he secures the bag first. He's almost there. As the pharmacist loads the last of the drugs, Lester Judd spots a driver's license off to the side of the counter. Hazel Moss. The person in the photo matches the woman on the floor closest to him. She lies on her belly, eyes closed, trying to talk herself through this. She is in the wrong place at the wrong time.

The pharmacist pads back over to the counter, extends the gym bag toward Lester Judd. A beautiful thing. But he barely shoulders it before the shots ring out. Three of them. There are screams, and there is a wet grunt. To Lester Judd's right, the pharmacy tech, his partner in this score, staggers backward, stunned, two rosettes budding on his gray scrub top at the chest.

"Well," he says. "Fuck." He collapses.

A split second is all Lester Judd has, but it's all he needs to see that the Western-hatted man has taken it upon himself to be a cowboy. He has drawn a snub-nosed revolver from his boot and fired a set of rounds from the prone position, two of which have gone into the wrong target, one of which has missed altogether. Lester Judd acts before the man can get off a fourth. He seizes Hazel Moss, sticks his gun to her neck. She gasps.

"Drop it, hillbilly," the boxer says. Adrenaline floods his body, fear with it, and he feels like a dynamo. A human train, speeding through a railroad crossing with cars still on the track.

The cowboy, rattled by this threat, or perhaps shaken from putting down a presumably innocent man, does as he is told. Lester Judd knows he doesn't have much time, but he hadn't planned for this contingency. He's still drawing a blank when the first siren announces its presence about thirty seconds later. Someone must have heard the gunshots from outside and phoned the police.

"Godfuckingdammit," Lester Judd says. He whips around, scouting for an out, holding Hazel close. "Open the door!" he orders the pharmacist, who is shaking, no longer suppressing her cries.

She does, and Lester Judd drags Hazel by her into the pharmacy. He backs Hazel past the bays, to the rear of the room, where an emergency exit beckons him in all its red-and-white-striped glory. The captor and his hostage barge through the crash bar, into the late morning. The alarm goes off, but it doesn't matter. They're already on him.

"Take me to your car," he tells Hazel. She leads him around the building to a green compact. The sirens are getting closer. "You're gonna drive me to your place," he says to her.

You said I had the bluest eyes, but nothing could be bluer than the way you made me feel when you left.

When they pull up in front of the townhouse, black and whites hot on their tail, Hazel is so distracted that she doesn't notice it at first. But when the robber circles around to the driver's side, yanks her out, and hurries her through the yard, she sees it: The Peruvian apple cactus has burst through the roof, its spiky head protruding out of the shingles like a groundhog from a burrow hole.

"Inside," the man says, adjusting the strap on his gym bag. "Move."

They enter the townhouse and shut the door as two units screech to a stop behind Hazel's car. The robber twists the deadbolt home. He grabs her by the arm, and her reaction is instinctual. With her other arm, she swings upward, tearing off his ski mask. He parries the attack and shoves her toward the next room, and it takes every bit of balance for her to stay on her feet. They're in her office now, and he is pissed.

"You try that again, I'll shoot you dead," he says. He motions toward the futon with his gun. "Sit. Over there."

She plops down, appraises him. He's built like a scrapper, lean but broad-shouldered. Strikingly handsome, it bemoans her to admit, if prematurely bald, which would be all right if he had a normal-shaped head, but he doesn't. There is a dip in the crown, and his brown eyes are severe. Like they've seen people hurt, and it hasn't phased them. But there's something else about them, Hazel thinks. Like if you were to scoop away the top layer, really get to the root, it wouldn't all be barren.

He unshoulders the bag. There is a lot of movement outside. What can only be more cars, and with them, more cops. The voices are muffled but purposeful.

The robber paces, clearly trying to plot an escape route. Coming up empty. After several back and forths, he stops, sets his sights on the corner of the room. "That's a big ass cactus," he says.

Hazel turns toward the plant. It must be two feet in diameter, its spines as long as siding nails. She imagines what Talia would say about it, hears her coworker's voice in her head: "Jumping Jehoshaphat!" Hazel pictures Talia's big, perfect teeth, beaming at her via the magic of the information superhighway. Insufferable, well-meaning. Her stream of thought is interrupted by the boom of a megaphone outside. The voice on the other end of it calls out a phone number, directs the hostage taker to dial it.

"Phone," the robber says, holding out his hand.

Hazel obliges.

"Yeah," the man says, sitting in her desk chair, phone to his ear. The gun is in his lap. "Who's this?" A pause. "Don't matter who *I* am, who's *this?* Well, *Sergeant,* here's how it's gonna go: You're gonna get me a car out of here, and then a private plane after that. And if I don't get what I want, somebody's gonna get hurt."

Chatter on the other end of the line.

"I ain't interested in hearing your yinging and yanging. Don't phone me back til you're serious about my demands."

He ends the call, tosses the phone back toward the couch. He buries his face into his still-gloved hands. The ridiculousness of the whole ordeal finally sets in for Hazel. Her racing heartbeat levels off, but it is replaced by a sickening dread that starts in her stomach and radiates to her throat. She has been kidnapped by a stranger with a gun and potentially thousands of dollars worth of pharmaceuticals. Brought back to her own home, where she is being used as a bargaining chip. All for minding her own business. Her boyfriend not even in the ground a year. A man likely dead back at the Purdy & Sons Drug. Hasn't she been through enough?

"Look, I'm not really gonna hurt you," the robber says through his fingers.

"What?"

"I'm not really gonna hurt you," he repeats. His tone is much softer, but she's not falling for it.

"You expect me to believe that?"

"Naw. Naw, I guess not."

In her experience, the ones who have to say they won't hurt you inflict the most pain.

"I'm in deep shit, Hazel Moss," the man admits.

"What's your name?" she asks. She doesn't know what else to say.

"Don't matter."

"You know mine."

"Saw it on your I.D. at the drugstore."

"Well?" she says, crossing her arms, waiting.

"Lester Judd," he says. "Lester Judd Brackett."

"That man in the pharmacy. He probably had a name, too."

"He wasn't nothing but a piece of shit, trust me."

The lack of humanity in the words disgusts Hazel. "That's not your call," she says. "You don't get to make excuses for the mess you create."

Lester Judd scowls at her, face puffy with scar tissue. Then his expression slackens into something more pliable. Something like shame. It gives Hazel deja vu.

He walks up to the cactus, fists balled at his sides. As though he wants to punch it. But he unclenches them. "I wasn't always this way," he says.

"Fair enough."

But what kind of excuse is that? Hazel hasn't always been the way she is now. Marjoe hadn't always been the way he was. That day, when she walked in, new jade plant in her hands, and found him cold and blue, slumped on the hardwoods upstairs. When she thinks about it, she realizes the Peruvian apple cactus is growing through that very spot. Through the room where their life together began and ended. She wonders about Lester Judd, if she can save him. If there is anything left to save.

I wish you had the same look in your eye when you saw me as when you saw dope.

It might appear that Lester Judd is looking at the cactus, but what he's really looking at is life. With a capital 'l.' Armed robbery, holding someone against their will. Murder. Not at his hands, but he doesn't expect a jury to consider the nuance of such a situation. He's facing twenty-five and up. That's if he even makes it to the courtroom without getting got first. For a brief moment, he considers it: forfeiting his weapon, turning himself over to the cops outside. Pleading out. Contrition for these sins and all the ones before them. It's not too late. The Morrison brothers have him on the ropes, and so do the police. But, goddammit, he's used to being there, and he only knows two ways to fix it: fighting his way through the barrage or getting knocked out. Worse comes to worst, he'll run out the back door and go down swinging.

Maybe it was always going to end this way. Every time he has tried to be a good person, it hasn't felt right on him. Like a t-shirt that fits too tight. He ambles over to Hazel's desk, picks up a framed picture there. Her and a pretty boy on a mountain overlooking a lake.

"This your man?" he asks.

"Was," she says.

He nods, puts the photograph back.

He understands, even though he doesn't. How strange and uncomfortable, how humbling, it is to stand at the window of someone else's world. All he has ever thought about is what's on his side of it. Suffering, imposed and received. There is a whole garden of heartache out there, all the time. Far as the eye can see.

I loved you.

Hazel doesn't know how long they've been there in her office. Maybe an hour. Maybe ten minutes. Time has no dominion over such situations. The police have tried her phone no fewer than five times. Over the bullhorn, they've implored Lester Judd to talk this thing out. To reason with them. But he just sits there at his hostage's desk, rubbing the barrel of the gun against his hairless temple as though he is scratching an itch. What's going through that mind of his? Is she going to make it out of here? Are either of them?

Under another set of circumstances, it might have been different. Perhaps they would have passed each other on the street, shared a smile. Never met at all. But that's not how the chips fell. She doesn't pretend to know his life, what led him to this, though she can imagine. He doesn't pretend to know hers. And yet they're forever entangled, regardless of how this plays out.

"When you get your car and your plane," Hazel says, "I imagine you're gonna want to take me with you. Use me as an insurance policy until you get wherever it is you want to get."

Lester Judd doesn't confirm whether he will or won't. He looks at her, wordless, and there is no masking it this time. There is no hard-boiled gaze, no unforgiving death stare. There is only the man and his brokenness, and it is almost too much for her to bear. How many more will expect her to fix them?

"You can make this right, Lester Judd," she says. "You know how. I can see it."

"I do," he replies. "But I can't."

The cold finality of those words is suffocating. A thief of oxygen. Hazel feels like her throat is closing. She feels that grief poison, rising, welling, curling throughout her body, and she's got to bleed it if she wants to survive. She's got to lop off the rot before it spreads all over, degrades her to nothing.

She reaches for her diary on the end table, opens it to a random spot.

"Hey," Lester Judd says. "What are you doing?"

"Sometimes," Hazel says, her voice shaky, "it was like you were never really here."

"What?"

She flips the page: "You wanted your ashes spread, but your parents wanted you buried. So I took the sand we brought back from Acadia and scattered it in the park where we had our first date. Do you remember that little cove by the bridge?"

"What the fuck are you doing?" Lester Judd repeats.

Hazel gets up from the futon. She flips the page again. Her voice is becoming clearer by the word. It is aching, full of strength and pain: "I forgive you for your sickness. I don't forgive your sickness for you."

"Stop that."

She has begun inching toward him. "At night, I used to ask God to give me a skin of thorns, so that when you curled up next to me, I would remind you of something you couldn't live without."

Lester Judd covers his ears, shakes his head wildly.

"You were the funniest person I've ever met."

He is backing up now, retreating, slowly. So slowly that it is hard to tell if he even realizes he's doing it.

"You said I had the bluest eyes, but nothing could be bluer than the way you made me feel when you left."

"I said stop that, goddammit!" Lester Judd hollers, and he is pointing the gun at her.

For the first time since she can remember, Hazel is not afraid. She acknowledges the gun but doesn't stop walking toward the man holding it. She leafs through to another page. "I wish you had the same look in your eye when you saw me as you did when you saw dope." The last four words leap from the top of her lungs: "That joy. That hunger."

"I'm warning you, Hazel Moss," he says, flicking the safety.

"I loved you," she says, closing the diary, tears waterfalling down her cheeks. She is close enough to touch him. "I loved you."

Lester Judd brings both of his hands to his face, presses the gun flat against his forehead. From someplace that neither of them can see, he howls. It is an animal hymn. One of great loss. If she were to press her ear to the mouth of the world, Hazel thinks, she would hear a hundred million howls back. But in this room, there is only space for his.

The tortured robber, Lester Judd Brackett, wheels around, has a mind to make a run for the door like a scalded mutt. But before he can get there, he trips over his own two feet. Drops the gun. He reels across the room, hands searching for purchase along the floor. They don't find any. In a last-ditch effort, he uses his momentum to swing around, tries to fall on his ass, to reset. What he falls on, though, back first, is the Peruvian apple cactus. Hazel doesn't cover her eyes in time to shield herself from the gruesome sight. The spines make a slimy, shucking noise as they enter his flesh all at once. A scream lodges itself in his lungs. He stills for a moment, body in a lazy crucifix, before he goes to twitching, a human pincushion, the needle points emerging from his neck and chest and abdomen and thigh, where one particular offender has severed the femoral artery. Blood spurts in places, trickles in others. Through the agony and the shock, his darting eyes beam bright with realization. He has mere seconds for any last words before the lights go out for good.

They come from Lester Judd in gentle, choked whispers. "Okay," he says. "Okay."

All around him, glimmering, fat pitayas, violet-red and the size of tennis balls, begin to swell from the ribs of the cactus.

It is three o'clock in the morning when Hazel rolls over, squinting into the light from the lamp on her office desk. For the past week, she has been sleeping on this futon, bound to this room, on leave from work. No calls or meetings. No Talia, though her coworker has somehow acquired Hazel's address and sent no fewer than three I'm-thinking-about-you popup cards and one edible bouquet. No ketchup and boxed mac and cheese. Just late nights and trying to make it through. She's been thinking about Lester Judd a lot. The boxer. The gambling addict. The bank robber. A degenerate for all seasons. How much of his life must have been spent on timing—of punches and bets and holdups? Yet in the end, timing was the thing that brought him here, that did him in. Now the only evidence of his existence is a bushel of pitayas, which Hazel has picked from the cactus and piled into a clay pot on her desk. She doesn't know what to do with them.

"Fuck it, Blue," she can hear Marjoe say. "Eat 'em."

"Isn't that a little morbid?" she would ask, to which he would shrug.

The fruit of the Peruvian apple cactus is said to be sweet. But Hazel has spent enough time subsisting off the dead.

She sits up on the edge of the futon. By the warm wash of the lamp, she notices something on the cactus that she hasn't seen there before. Flowers. As many as a dozen of them have bloomed up and down the plant. The employee at Midway was right.

There haven't been many changes since the medical examiner's team pried Lester Judd loose. This must have happened as Hazel slept. She pushes off the futon and shuffles over to take a closer look. The blooms are as big as her open hand, with cream-colored elliptical petals and delicate yellow stamens curling from their centers. She imagines they would glow a milky white in the dark, but she doesn't attempt to find out. She knows this is fleeting enough as it is. A miracle, Talia would say. Hokey as that sounds. Hazel doesn't want to move too much. She caresses all the flowers within her reach, half expecting one of them to draw blood, but none of them do. They simply embrace her touch as though she were one of their own. A burst of grace amongst the thorns. If they can grow here, now, Hazel thinks, they can grow anywhere.

see if it hollers

You watch the boy from a distance. He is tall and floss-thin, brushing his curtained hair out of his handsome face as he talks to his friends. You haven't forgotten about the time in third grade when you brought a two-liter of soda to the class party and he called you poor because it was Dr. Perky instead of Dr. Pepper, but you still love him anyway. Just because you are both in middle school does not mean you don't love him.

He rolls away from his favorite spot by the claw machine, not in a hurry (because, you know, it's whatever), and hits the rink running, spinning on the hardwoods. You love the way he skates. Forward, backward, side-to-side at will under the blacklights, which make everything glow like sea jellies. You're not saying he could be in the Olympics if it had such an event, but you're not *not* saying that. He has his own pair of shoes because why wouldn't he? They are a deep black with fiery turquoise wheels.

A song hemorrhages through the speakers, and it is probably "Jump Around" by House of Pain.

You walk over the smelly black carpet that should have been replaced years ago, counting the neon shapes within. Last weekend you were a rectangle, but tonight you feel like more of a rhombus. The girls' room mirror is striated into a thousand pieces, but it is still intact enough for you to see your reflection, if you push your layered bangs out of the way: thrifty pink shirt with short, ruffled sleeves, the white skirt you got for your birthday. Your mom even let you wear makeup. So what if it's not really covering up the acne? You have acne. Your friends have acne. Your enemies. Everybody in this place has acne. Toilets flush behind you, and you feel cute. He will think you are cute.

On your way out of the bathroom, you run into the boy. You nearly collide, and for a moment, you forget that you have a circulatory system because you can't feel anything. You open your mouth to speak but swallow spit at the same time, and it chokes you. He wipes his hair out of his face, watching you cough like an idiot.

When you finally get your breath back, you say, "Hey."

Do you bat your eyes in an attempt to recover? There's a chance.

He takes a sip from his soda cup and says, "Hey."

You do not have a contingency plan for this scenario (typical you), so you do this weird nod thing. He does it back. He skates off, you walk the other way.

Some kid is standing next to the quarter toy machines, judging you.

The same lady has worked the Skate Return since your brain first unlocked the power to create memories. She is the type of person who begins to look old when she's young but stops aging by thirty. She is heavy-handed with the eye shadow, and she may have been beautiful once if not for all the cowboy killers. She is a little intimidating, but you are not so much scared of her as you are of what is behind her. The world beyond the rack of rental skates is total in its darkness. Cavernous. There are only rumors of what it holds. Last week, two boys got into a fistfight out in the parking lot over something stupid, and their punishment was to clean the returned skates back there for the rest of the night. They haven't spoken to anyone since.

The lady asks, "One pair?"

You say, "Yes ma'am."

The lady asks, "What size?"

You say, "Seven, please."

She peers down at your enormous Keds.

"Okay, nine," you say, embarrassed.

She reaches for a pair of beat-to-shit quads, sits them on the counter, and says, "Five dollars."

You give her the bill.

She says, "Bringum back like they are by ten o'clock. No funny stuff."

Behind her, you see a pasty hand emerge from the black. It replaces the empty spot on the rack with a clean pair of rentals, and suddenly, you can't be sure it was a hand at all. It could have been some kind of tentacle. Some kind of leafless vine.

You lace up with your back against the fuzzy orange wall next to the beginner's rink in the corner of the building. Planet Skate is alive with the colors of outer space, the odor of feet and the cheese pizza that's so greasy you could style your hair with what remains on the wax paper. High hold, high sheen. Across the room, you see your friend and wave her over. Your parents don't like you hanging out with her ever since they caught the two of you trying to spark one of your grandmother's cigarettes with a candle lighter behind the shed, but she's all you've got.

She says, "Hey."

You say, "Hey."

She looks pretty. She is skinny, and you are still holding on to some of your baby fat, but you're not bitter.

She asks, "Have you seen him yet?"

You say, "Yes."

She says, "Well?"

You say, "I'd rather not talk about it. I blew it."

Okay, she could totally be a Spice Girl.

"Why do you even love him so much anyway?" she asks.

"I just do," you say.

"I mean, have you even passed him a note yet?" she asks.

"I'm working on it," you say.

There is a break in the song, and a kid you don't know, scared whiter than jasmine, leaps from behind the counter at the Skate Return, bunnyhops the railing at the edge of the main rink, runs onto the floor waving his arms above his head in exaggerated squiggles. He latches on to an older boy, bares his teeth like an angry chihuahua. Sounds like one, too. God knows what he is saying.

The lady who works Skate Return calls "Get him" over the PA system, and tonight's security detail, a local police officer with a race car driver's mustache, wrangles the boy up. He drags the boy kicking and screaming back to Skate Return as the next song starts.

Your friend says, "Only here, man."

You were at church camp two years ago when you fell in love with the boy. It was the last day, and each of you was to recite Bible verses you had been assigned at the beginning of the week. Being the diligent student that you were (and still are), you rattled yours off without missing a beat. When he got up in front of the rest of the group, it was a different story. He was no star pupil to begin with, and he had not yet grown out of his stutter. He stumbled through Galatians 6:5 well enough, but when he got to the next verse, he froze.

He said, "'Be not deceived. Um. Be not deceived; God is. God is, uh…'"

You put the Dr. Perky incident aside and joined him at the front. You looked him in the eyes, deep-set in his red face. You walked him through it. Together, you said, "'Be not deceived; God is not mocked: for whatsoever a man soweth, that he shall also reap.'"

Everyone clapped because it was a sweet moment.

Later, down by the lake, you sat on a rock across from his. He gave you a tender smile and said, "Thank you."

You felt worthy.

Where else would you want to be on a Friday night? The mall? The high school football game? Yeah, right. Everything you need is right here for you beneath these lights, an ocean bathed in ultraviolet. Fun and games, mystery. Your future.

You kick your friend's ass at the coin-op Tekken machine for the third straight time, and she rolls her eyes.

She says, "This is boring. Let's skate."

The two of you hit the floor as "Macarena" begins to play. You're a decent skater, but not good enough to do the moves while you're in motion, so you just race around the rink, holding your skirt, letting your hair fly. After a few laps, you turn to find your friend skating with a high school freshman. It figures.

You look over to the other side, and there's the boy. His hands are behind his head and then crisscrossed over his hips and then they are on his skinny butt and then he is shimmying. You saw him on a four-wheeler once while you were running errands with your mom. It was so exhilarating. Now, every glimpse you catch of him harkens back to that moment. A spinning multicolor strobe ball catches you just right, and you are blinded. In that burst of light, you see all manner of foolish things. Wedding bells, the boy older and even handsomer, a little girl with your eyes, a sensitive little boy with your big heart. He looks like his dad, of course.

As the afterimage of the strobe melts away, you realize that you are right beside the boy.

You say, "Hey."

He says, "Hey."

You want to tell him something, anything. You really like this song, or you think his shirt looks nice. But you don't. You chicken out again. Bock, bock, bock. He skates ahead.

You sit in on some random birthday party, staring straight ahead. The theme is dinosaurs. Nobody bothers to ask you who you are or why you're here, though you're obviously much older than the other guests. The kid who was judging you earlier by the quarter toy machines is also here. He is wearing a glittery cone hat, and his mouth is oily with potato chip residue.

He says, "I don't know you."

While "Happy Birthday" is being sung, you think about bashing your head against the lime-green exposed brick of the party nook. You feel a whisper at your shoulder, maybe even a grazing touch, and when you glance back, you see a pale, lithe appendage retreating into a utility closet. Your body registers a slight increase in heart rate.

When the parents pass around the single-serve cups of vanilla ice cream, you find comfort in the artificial smell, the oversweet flavor. The fibrous taste of the little wooden spoon.

Staying around for the presents is probably too much, and so you take your leave. Out on the main floor, the limbo competition is winding down, and off to the side, the lady who works the Skate Return is sharing a smoke with the police officer. A crazy thought crops into your mind, and for a split second, you entertain the idea of going up to the unmanned counter and exploring behind the rental racks. But you think better of it.

On a bench ahead, your friend is making out with the high school freshman. Frenching.

The police officer, cigarette still in hand, says, "Hey, no hanky-panky."

The lovebirds separate, but your friend is moonstruck and the boy wears a cool smirk as he wipes his lips with the back of his wrist.

That tears it. You suck in the belly pooch underneath your pink shirt and roll off toward the claw machine in a march. The boy is there with his friends, staring absentmindedly at the stuffed animals through the glass, jiggling the joysticks, though he hasn't put any money in to play. He doesn't see you until you are right up on him.

You say, "Hey."

He says, "Hey."

You ask, "Have you won anything?"

He says, "No. But only because I haven't tried."

You say, "Oh. Do you wanna skate?"

He asks, "Now?"

"It's whenever," you say.

"Sure," he says, throwing shrugs at his friends. "I'll come get you?"

"Cool," you say.

You glide back to the wall by the beginner's rink, pulling your hair into a scrunchie. It feels like there is a little person inside of you, a smaller you, bursting to get out and jump and jump and jump.

You try to not overreact when fifteen minutes have passed and the boy still hasn't come to get you. He is no longer manning his post by the claw machine, and you don't know where else he could be. Your friend, having given the high school freshman her phone number, is telling you her strategy. She will act like she's not home the first two times he calls. If he tries a third time, she still might pretend she's not there, but at least she will know that he's not a jerk.

Suddenly, someone hits the dimmers on all the lights, and now it is only the disco ball over the center of the main rink, dropping sparkles of white on the floor that scatter like loose change from a tipped over jar. A slow jam starts to play, a hand-me-down song from another generation's prom. The boy strolls over and holds out his hand. You didn't know he would want to skate during this portion of the evening, and it sends your stomach into cartwheels.

Your friend makes a face at you (for some reason you thought she'd look happier), but it's not a big deal. All that matters is that the boy is pulling you out into the main rink where everybody can see that you are together. You are nervous, sure, but so was he when you saved him at church camp, and you know he will return the favor. You interlace your fingers around the back of his neck, he puts his hands on your waist. He is so dreamy.

You say, "I like this song."

He says, "I like *you.*"

Nothing has ever sounded sweeter. Anything can happen from here. Your first kiss, or maybe you'll settle for laying your head on his chest as the two of you sway softly to the music. You turn your cheek to lean into the boy, and you feel something brush against your butt. You don't think anything of it at first, but then it happens again. You touch the area with your hand, and when you inspect your fingers, they are covered with a thick red substance.

People are already snickering when the boy backs away from you, and you see that he is holding an open ketchup packet. You throw a panicked look over your shoulder. The streak on your white skirt is slick and fatty, smeared from the bottom of your cheeks down to the hem.

The song ends as if on cue, and the boy says, "Look, she's on her period."

Planet Skate explodes with laughter, and you are alone in the world. Thrust into a black hole. You hope for support from your friend, but when you locate her in the crowd, she won't look you in the eyes. She seems more embarrassed for herself than she is for you.

A few begin to chant, "She's on her per-i-od, she's on her per-i-od."

The boy shows no emotion when he skates away from you. You are beneath the floorboards, you have never been lower.

Back in the bathroom, nobody is there to share your tears. Save for the skunky ghost of a jay some girls have flushed down one of the commodes. You cry so hard you can't breathe, your mother's makeup running, and the smell of urine and toilet cleaner, on top of the weed, isn't helping. You try to wash the spot on your skirt with a wet paper towel, but it just makes it worse. You are a clown in that broken mirror, a stupid seventh grader with large feet, a fake blood stain on your backside, a paint palette face. Home. You just want to go home.

You have just hung up the payphone when you see the police officer approach the boy by the claw machine, brandishing one of those expandable batons.

The police officer says, "We can do this the easy way, or we can do this the hard way."

The boy squints defiantly.

The police officer bats the stick in his hand. He says, "You choose."

The boy goes quietly, his friends looking on. You don't know if this is all because of what he did to you, but you guess it is. The boy gazes back into the main rink, once, poorly hidden fear in his eyes, before he disappears into the Skate Return. This is what he deserves. So why do you feel so bad for him?

You forego saying goodbye to your friend, opting instead to turn in your rentals. With your chin tipped to the musty floor, you place the heavy shoes on the counter and wait for the lady to dismiss you. Several beats pass, and you have heard everything but the okay to get lost: the dance pop music from the house speakers, the pew-pew from the Space Invaders console, the end-of-night chatter. One last thump of bass. You think that the lady might not be there after all, but when you lift your head, she is, and her eyes are fixed on you, indifferent, budding feet, knowing something that you don't know. She lights a cigarette, and smoke squeezes through the gaps in her teeth, a curtain of it drawn over the top of her unblinking face.

There is a vacant space on the rack behind her, but not for long. A black pair of skates with turquoise wheels slides into the empty slot, easy as the cigarette smoke, pushed by a limb that is too long, too ropey to belong to any person you have ever met.

When your parents pick you up, you reluctantly tell them what happened. Your dad threatens to kick the boy's ass, and your mom has to talk him down because beating up a minor has got to be some kind of crime. Then your dad threatens to kick the boy's dad's ass, and your mother rolls her eyes. From the back seat, you stare at his monklike bald spot. Planet Skate orbits the rearview mirror, a gaudy phosphorescent star suspended in space. A place where your innocence has been left stranded. You just cry and you cry and you cry.

See the boy. He exists somewhere that is impossible to know. In the years to come, you will hurt like this, and you won't know why, but it will pass and you will be glad. You will know that you are worthy. Your dreams will come with your eyes open, and you will build universes for yourself, make them after your own image because you said so. You will have what you desire. You will have the girl with your pretty eyes, the sensitive son with your big heart. If you want. Maybe the boy from this night will have these things, too. You won't be mad if he does. If only he can make it back from beyond the Skate Return.

american bastard

It was my freshman year of college when my boy Larsen hit me up about going out to Red Creek.

"Why, what's going on out there?" I asked through the flip phone. I was hungover, and I'd spent all morning on the teal shag rug of my dorm room, trash can at my side, eating sugary cereal and sticking my finger down my throat.

"Ceegray's gathering the troops," Larsen said.

"Oh."

"I can be there in an hour. You down?"

I didn't know if I wanted to go, I really didn't. But I needed something to distract me from how my blood sounded coursing through my veins just then. Frantic and self-aware. Not to mention my roommate was coming back from a couple of days home that night, and he did weird shit like pick his dead skin and eat it. Masturbate without putting a sock on the doorknob as a warning. Who in their right mind would want to be around for that?

"All right," I agreed. "All right, I guess."

"Heavy," he said, and I didn't hear another word from him until he rolled up to the dorm parking lot in that ancient pickup of his. The same one he'd had all of high school. He leaned out the window, grinning like a possum. Larsen was short and fat. Affable. The kind of guy all the girls treated like one of those big stuffed animals you win at the fair. An accessory. He went to school in the mountains, which at the time was synonymous with being hippie-dippie and granola.

"This thing still runs?" I asked.

"We're gonna find out," he said.

I hopped in. It took me three tries to shut the passenger side door. The shifter was equally fucked, so he had to use a flathead screwdriver to pop it into gear.

"Roll one?" he said, once we were off.

"Where?"

He nodded toward the glove compartment. I pulled out a cigar box. Gutted one of the rillos inside and replaced the tobacco with weed. It was mid. An underwhelming green but with some pretty white hairs here and there. I sparked it as soon we hit the highway, right around the time the lemon drop sun was dipping behind the pines. People will pay money for photographs of such sights, or so I hear.

The blunt wasn't life-changing, but it did the trick. It took us a hot minute to finish it, too. A lot of coughing and eye water. A tribal understanding of what it means to turn to stone in real time. Larsen slotted the roach through the crack in his window, and then it was as if someone had shut off the power. There in the dark, I felt shame. Like the trees we passed, all huddled together, were judging. Not us, just me. Don't ask me why. At home, I was outside the bathroom door, begging my mother to come out. My big sister—who seemed more like a little sister in these moments—was there, too. The sink faucet was dripping. I could live a million years and never forget that sound.

"I'm loading it," she was saying. I could hear the cylinder clicking into place.

"Mama, please. I want you to come out. *We* want you to come out."

"You cain't always get what you want," she was singing.

My sister just screamed and screamed.

Larsen saved me by throwing on some IDM, God bless him. And that's when the high really kicked in. My hangover was gone. Ambient tones bounced around the cabin. It sounded like someone was bending them with a tool made from a material we didn't have a name for yet. Maybe some kind of weird composite. Along the interstate, the overpass lights were fleets of tiny flying saucers. Idling. Horizontal. We were going exactly four miles per hour under the speed limit, but it felt faster. A lot faster. Like zipping through an underground tunnel at warp speed. My mind was a large, membranous engine. Sputtering then firing. Revving toward death. Telling my heart, "Hey. Hey, dipshit. Heads up."

We made the whole trip from Raleigh to Red Creek, about eighty miles, on word-of-mouth directions. Hung a right off the highway. A left, a left, another right. Onto a country backroad and over a one-lane bridge you could spit across. The bridge fed us into a hilly, dead-end neighborhood with five modest houses. Little brick ranches, not unlike the one I'd grown up in. Larsen parked in front of the second one on the right.

"You sure this is it?" I asked.

"Lemme text Mick," Larsen said. His phone rumbled less than a minute later. He chuckled. "He didn't say if it was or wasn't. Just said to come in."

"Well. Shit."

We bumbled up to the front door, surely looking more suspicious than we hoped. I prayed it wasn't a bathroom door. I know how stupid that sounds, but I can't explain the things that go on in my head. I won Rock Paper Scissors, right there on the stoop, so Larsen had to enter first. You didn't knock because that's what the police did. The door put us into a small kitchen, and the first thing we saw was a lady, her back turned toward us. She was dressed in a black kimono with cherry blossoms all over it, even though she was white as wedding cake frosting. An oxygen tank rolled at her side, over the buttermilk-colored linoleum.

I'll always remember the look Larsen gave me. Probably the same one I gave him. The two of us frozen in the doorway. I don't know why we didn't bolt.

The lady turned to the side, but she still didn't acknowledge us. She was older, that much was certain. But she was deceptively built so that you couldn't tell what was skin loosened by age and what was fat.

"Y'all come on in, now," she said. "Grab you a plate, don't be shy."

The smell of food hadn't even registered, at least with me, until she spoke. It was onion-forward, acidic. Coming from a speckled enamel stockpot on a coil burner. I was trying to build myself up to a place where I could talk. Where I could tell her the gesture was awful kind, but we'd made a terrible, terrible mistake. Somewhere between my brain and my lips, the words were interrupted by laughter. It was coming from somewhere else in the house. The next room, as it was.

We scooched past the old lady, and what a relief it was to find Ceegray and Mick parked on a couch in the wood-paneled living room. A game show on the tube. I could have danced to the jingle.

"You dimwits thought you were at the wrong house, didn't you?" Mick said. He was thickset and much too bearded for twenty. Bearish. Forever attired like he was fixing to go fishing. It was funny seeing him next to Ceegray, who was so soft-featured and slight. You wouldn't want him to go out when it was too windy.

"No," we lied.

"It's all right," Ceegray said. "This *is* the boonies."

We'd never been to his spot before. He was a couple of years older than us, though you couldn't really tell. A guy Mick had met through the Big Brothers program when he was in middle school. We'd all buddied up after me and Mick hit it off in a Spanish class first semester of college. It was actually "C. Gray," as in Chase Gray, but I thought the man's first name was Ceegray, and after a while I was too embarrassed to come clean on the misunderstanding.

The old lady dragged her tank to a hallway off the kitchen.

"That there's my mama," Ceegray said.

"Get you something to eat," she called through the wall. Every word for her was a strain. "I know y'all are hungry."

"Don't be rude," Ceegray said. "Take a plate."

"What about y'all?" Larsen asked.

"We already eat some."

It was redneck spaghetti: noodles and ground beef, sweet onions and watery canned tomato sauce. Each of us doled out a polite amount, carried our portions to the living room. The pasta didn't offer much in the way of flavor, but it was still good and filling. I'm sure having the munchies had something to do with our standards. We both went back for seconds, anxiety giving way to giddiness, as Ceegray and Mick tried to guess how most Americans would respond to "Name things you bring on a camping trip." Halfway through that next helping, a grown ass man tore through the front door and plopped down onto one of the stools at the bar that separated the kitchen from the living room.

"What's up, fuckboys?" he said.

Mick shook his head.

"Who're these j-holes?" the man asked.

"Larsen, T—meet Bud," Ceegray said.

We nodded.

Bud had things other than pleasantries on his mind. "Any left?" he asked me, eyeballing my plate.

"Yeah. A ton."

"Right on."

He disappeared and returned with a mound of the stuff. The man ate like an animal. You could hear every wet mastication. He finished his food around the same time me and Larsen did, even though we had a big head start. Licked his fork clean.

"So, how do y'all know each other?" Larsen asked.

"He's my cousin," Ceegray said.

I knew that was bullshit. They looked nothing alike. But nobody questioned it. If you said someone was kin, they were kin. The guy was at least forty, maybe a hard thirty-seven or thirty-eight at the youngest. It was in the eyes. He wore a t-shirt that depicted a screaming eagle, pissed off and covered in flames, clutching the handlebars of an ape hanger motorcycle in its massive talons. A ballcap with a bill bent into a skinny upside-down U. His cowboy boots were filthy.

A new show started.

"What's the plan for tonight, anyway?" I asked.

"We're gonna go out yonder a piece," Ceegray said. "Back in the woods. Have ourselves a fire. Maybe do a little muddin."

"Maybe?!" Bud hollered, lurching forward, smacking his thighs. "Ain't no 'maybe' about it. We're gonna let 'er rip, you pussies! What do you say?"

I nearly jumped from the abruptness of the response.

"All right, all right, don't blow a gasket," Mick said.

Bud ignored him. "Well, don't just sit there," he said. "Let's party."

"This is gonna be classic," Larsen whispered as we stood.

On the way out, we sat our dirty plates on the Formica bar. In the dim hallway off the kitchen, a halo of yellow light delineated a closed door. I shut my eyes. For how long, I don't know. I wasn't sure, to tell you the truth, which side of the thing I was on.

We piled into Bud's sandblasted Jimmy, Mick in the passenger seat, me, Larsen, and Ceegray on the bench in the back. It was one of those early-model SUVs with the hardshell convertible tops. A path led out of the back yard and into the towering pines. Bud gunned the Jimmy about a mile into those woods, until they opened up on a vast clearing where trees had long ago been knocked down and hauled off to make room for something that wasn't yet there. We parked on the edge because the deeper you went, the craggier the terrain became. It looked like some miniature desert that had been delivered to the wrong place but couldn't be returned.

Me and Larsen were tasked with unloading the cooler and busting down the blunts while Ceegray and Mick built a fire in a makeshift pit that was already out there. I guess Bud felt like he'd done his part in bringing us to our destination, so he contributed by taking a piss on a rock. Told us there was some lighter fluid in the wheel well if we needed it.

"I don't know about this guy," I said, to where only Larsen could hear.

"Relax, T," he replied. "He's just insane. It's harmless."

I supposed he was right in a way. I'd met dozens of Buds before that night, and I'm sure I'll meet plenty more before the end credits roll. Well, at least a few. I tried to not sweat it. Took a lighter to the seam of one of the rillos. I always used too much spit. The first one was ready to be put into rotation by the time Ceegray and Mick had the fire going. The flame danced in a two-dimensional, sawtoothed bulb of saffron, chest-high on a teepee of tinder. It felt good. It was mid-March, the time of year when spring is itching to get out from underneath winter's thumb. Soon enough, everything would be hot and sticky with life. It wasn't fair, in my opinion, to the things that wanted to stay dead.

We convened in a pentagon around the pit, passed the blunt. Everybody else had cracked a light beer—hell, Bud was on his second— but the thought of drinking alcohol made me want to lose my spaghetti. I stuck to the weed. Pillowy clouds of it evacuated our lungs and hung in the air. Gray strati above the blaze. Etiquette said that two hits was about right, but Bud was taking three or four per turn. It was the third time before anybody said anything.

"Quit chiefing that thing, man," Mick said. "What are you doing?"

"Hey," Bud coughed. "I need this, all right? Got a lot on my mind. There's plenty to go around here."

"Just make it last, okay?" Ceegray said. "We got all night."

Bud frowned. Handed the blunt to Mick with an expression of indignation.

Larsen and Ceegray had started a side conversation, but I couldn't make out what they were saying.

If God had fingers, He snapped them. I felt warm around the ears, hollowed out below the neck. If I focused, I could hear my hair growing, little by little. Everybody but Bud was sitting on the ground, myself included, but I couldn't remember how we'd gotten there. The trees were closer than they had been half an hour before. Taller. Into the fire, the roach went screaming. You know how they say if you lose an arm or a leg, it still itches? I wonder if that happens with your brain, too. I typed out "You ought not have done that, we were just kids" into my phone, then deleted it. A white crust was growing on the logs of the fire. I wanted them to melt me to nothing.

Ceegray burped. Lit another blunt.

"Thinks she's gonna take my boys from me," Bud was muttering off to the side. Other things, too.

"What is this place?" I asked.

The question was directed at Ceegray, but it was Bud who answered. "What do you think?" he said. "They're gonna turn this whole area into one of those gated communities with a name like Dogwood Acres or Willow Downs or some shit. You know the ones where all the McMansions look the same, and they're built shitty, and they're so close you can smell whenever your neighbor lets one fly."

He hadn't specified who "they" was, but I knew who he meant.

"Same damn thing they're doing everywhere else," he continued. "They're gonna ruin this place, but not before I've had my kicks, by God."

Mick laughed.

"It's not funny, asshole," Bud said, crushing his beer can. He reached into the cooler for another.

Mick kept laughing anyway.

Larsen threw on two more logs.

Ceegray presented me with the blunt, a needlessly round sonofabitch. A brown torpedo. I toked it, gazed across the land with a face full of blood. The pale clay begat a kingdom of two-story newbuilds, all of them at least five-thousand square-feet and stacked right on top of each other. Made of fancy cardboard. Three-quarters of a mil before options, easy. Maybe more. There were cul-de-sacs and comically small lawns. People pulling into their driveways in cars that didn't rely on the rain for a bath. Returning home after a long day at the office, which was forty-five minutes away because this was the middle of nowhere. Back to the ol' humble abode. I never realized they built mausoleums that big.

Who knows how long I would have gone on thinking about it if Bud hadn't started firing the thirty-eight at the sky. The maniac emptied the clip, roaring, but I only heard the first one. It was a colossal crack. Lightning clapping a dead tree. My sister keened with such power, it brought me to my knees. Birds don't even die that violently. My mother opened the door. She had made the noise by slamming a cabinet as hard as she could.

I turned to Ceegray, who was looking into the fire. Blankly. His eyes were half open, and you could skate on them. Have a cute date night.

Larsen lifted his head toward Bud. "Why do you have a gun?" he asked, nonchalantly.

Asking why we were out there was like asking why a bear shits in the woods. It's just the nature of the thing, you know? Another blunt came and went, serving no purpose. I could already smell every pinecone falling within a quarter mile. I wasn't going to get any higher.

"I'm fucking bored," Bud said. Then, hiccupping: "Can we go muddin already?" I counted no fewer than seven crumpled beer cans at his feet. Nobody knew where the gun had gotten off to.

"Hell yeah," Ceegray said, as if snapping out of a trance. "Let's get it."

Mick dumped a jug of water on the fire, used a stick to stir the wood coals together until there was only steam left. Bud pissed again. Staggered over to the Jimmy, fell in. Everyone else just followed along, on autopilot, resumed the same seating assignments as before. We buckled in, except for Bud. The air in the cabin suddenly tasted mildewy.

"What about the cooler?" Ceegray said.

"We'll scoop it later," Bud slurred, waving him off.

"You sure this rig can handle it?" Mick asked. "Fucking bumpy out here."

"You kidding me? This thing ain't got a dick, but if it did, it'd be big!"

Larsen laughed, but it was only because there was nothing else you could do in that situation.

I wanted to say something but didn't. I've spent my whole life, as it happens, trying to say something but not knowing how.

Bud cranked the ignition and switched on the Jimmy's brights. Without further warning, he goosed the accelerator. Bounding over the dirt we went, Larsen hanging onto his Oh Shit handle. Mine was missing. I braced myself on Mick's headrest in its absence. Ceegray sat wedged between us. We were shipping toward the ground, then the sky, and Bud was yippeekiyayying and Ceegray and Larsen were howling with laughter, and I think I was trying to laugh, too, but not having much success. I sometimes forget how to be a person.

The whole thing felt like a deranged carnival ride, all of us jostling in our tightening belts, elbows and knees knocking. Gravity suspended. It was a wonder the Jimmy was still upright. Clay was peppering the windshield, and Mick was shouting.

"Slow down, you idiot!" he said.

"No," Bud said.

"Well, at least wear your seatbelt. Jesus Christ."

"What for? You cain't stop this red-blooded American bastard! I'm a goddamn winning machine."

In the blinding jumble of bumps and bends, it was hard to know whether we were coming or going. At one point, Bud seemed to bottom out and stall, but right when it appeared that he was in real danger of getting stuck, he dug his way out of the jam and rocked on, whooping. It had rained recently enough that the dirt was sticking to the glass, and visibility was failing by the second. We pitched across the future housing development, unsure of where the other side of the woods started, but still knowing it was there. The engine cried out for mercy.

"Man, I'm serious," Mick said. "I can't see shit. Take it easy."

"Winning machine," Bud was saying. "Winning machine. Winning machine. Winning machine. Cain't stop, won't stop."

Larsen and Ceegray joined his chant:

"Winning machine."

"Winning machine."

"Winning machine."

Bud started pumping his right fist in the air, and Larsen was laughing so hard I thought he'd throw up.

Mick was saying fuck.

There was a beat before it happened in which Bud seemed to know what was coming. Or maybe he thought that bigass eagle would leap off his shirt and carry us to safety in its divine, patriotic claws. I don't know. I don't pretend to understand someone else's pain. I can't even come to terms with my own. I just know that, for a split second, he stopped chanting. He wrapped both hands around the wheel, stared ahead with nothing left in his heart. He grunted animalistically.

In the same breath, the treeline came out of nowhere. Alakazam.

"Bud!" we all hollered.

If he made any effort at all to avoid the longleaf before him, it was the bare minimum. He swerved just enough to where, when he went through the windshield, the tree stopped him from coming all the way out. He lay across the dash, everything from his waist down still in the cab, his upper half sprawled on the hood of the Jimmy. Smoke whispered from the car's front end. I still don't know what it said. Everything inside, all the space, felt shrunken down. Cut in half.

"Holy shit!" Ceegray yelled. "What the fuck?!"

Mick, so vocal moments before, was speechless.

We unhooked ourselves and exited the vehicle. The skin along my collarbone burned from where my seatbelt had caught me, but I was no worse for wear. I can't speak for everyone else. We circled around to the front of the Jimmy, but once everyone got a load of Bud, they all walked away. Cursing or else not saying anything at all. Mick interlaced his fingers behind his head. Only I stayed up there, examining our ill-fated captain.

Bud's left cheek was pressed to the hood. He was dead, all right. As dead as a person can be. Blood jellied down his face, over his open eyes, in a medusa of purple. I never knew blood to be a color other than red, but it was what it was. I'm no doctor, I'm just telling you what I saw. Maybe the night makes things more dramatic than they are. Crueler and more beautiful at the same time. Bud's right arm was broken at an angle that also didn't seem possible. I stared at him for a long time, wondering if his brain would do any of the funny shit that brains do. Make his eyes twitch or his fingers spider up or something. But none of that happened. Somewhere close, I heard a whimper. You could have told me it was Ceegray or a woodland animal come to pay its respects to someone who didn't really deserve any. I would've believed either.

Nobody spoke on the walk back to the house. You got the impression that Ceegray wanted to, but his throat would lock up every time he started. Inside, Ceegray's mom was passed out in one of the living room recliners, nasal cannula wrinkled across her upper lip and cheeks like a catfish's barbels. Her snores came in at least three distinct octaves. The TV was playing one of those nature programs. The one set deep in the ocean. It always amazed me how bright everything looked down there.

Ceegray helped himself to another plate of spaghetti. The pot was still on the stove, but I can't imagine it was warm. It's not my place to judge.

It wasn't long before Mick was asleep, and Larsen was nodding himself. I guessed I would have to drive us back to Raleigh when the time came. Typical. Outside the bathroom, we hugged at our mother's waist. She walked right through our ghosts.

I was beginning to wonder about the developers. Would they simply build their McMansions over the tomb of the Jimmy out there, off in the pines? Would they make it a landmark with its own plaque? Or would they call someone in? Someone who takes care of such things. But then Bud came in the door, as he had earlier. It felt like forever ago. It *was* forever ago. Perhaps you really couldn't stop him, after all. He was busted up and splattered and none of his bones fit right. Galumphing over the linoleum in a bestial locomotion. And yet down he plopped onto that stool at the bar, his boots somehow cleaner this time around. I don't know whether it was him or not. Maybe it was, maybe it wasn't. Maybe he was the only one who survived.

rider, on the storm

It just ain't natural, he thought.

The wind outside screamed. Bloody murder. He looked at the boy in the rearview mirror. Rider sat in the back seat, staring at the tablet in his lap, his eyes washed a pewter blue. Somewhere between longing and boredom. Jarrell shook his head and tightened his grip on the steering wheel. What could possibly be more interesting than this? Unless it was Doppler radar, of course. Doppler radar was always neat.

His wife could tell something was bothering him, even if he didn't say so outright. He never did. "What's got you ill?" she asked from the passenger seat.

"I'm just focused, is all," he said. "I'm ready for this thing to put up or shut up."

"Sure," she said, turning back toward the window.

"Don't start, Erda."

Rider tapped at the tablet with his fat fingers.

They had been following this supercell for forty miles now, and while it had seemed juicy at first, it was starting to look like a big fat nothing burger with no toppings. The sky to the east was still an ominous gray, textured over by a wall cloud that bloomed black-green flowers of death. But they had learned not to get their hopes up before.

Jarrell let loose of a nasally sigh. "We shoulda stuck with the one in Kolomi," he said.

"The one I suggested?" Erda asked. "Oh."

He opened his mouth to fire back when a bark issued from behind. The corgi leaped onto the back seat from the floorboard, his tiny nub twitching side to side on his straw-colored bottom. He spilled over Rider's lap, propped his stumpy forelegs on the armrest, and commenced to howling.

Jarrell and Erda squinted ahead as raindrops pricked at their windshield. The heavy wall formation to the east, ever-lowering, began to rotate. Almost gently, a funnel cloud appeared to sweep downward. Winding, deliberate. Like the stirring finger of God Almighty.

"Atta boy, Fujita," Jarrell said. He smiled thinly beneath his wiry mustache, flipped on his emergency flashers, and punched the gas.

"Still the best warning system this side of the Mississippi," Erda said.

Rider nudged the dog by his bandana-covered chest until the goofy animal moved into the other seat. "Get down, Fuji," he said. The corgi responded by licking him on the cheek.

Rain stung the car like a swarm of horizontal bees as the family headed north on the highway. Then came the hail. The radio began chopping in and out. Only random snippets of sound got through.

"We've gotta get farther ahead of it," Jarrell said. The same fizzy feeling he always got bubbled in his stomach now. He looked back at Rider, hoping the score was the same with him. The child's now-gleaming eyes stayed glued to the tablet. Jarrell hoped he was watching Doppler radar. He hoped he wasn't watching what he thought he was watching.

Little marbles of hail pinged the hood as Jarrell whipped the wagon onto the shoulder of the road. He reached for the duffle bag at his wife's feet and pulled out a heavy-duty camera. Then he shoved his narrow head into his old football helmet. Erda snapped the strap on her dented motorcycle hat. The one she had acquired from a yard sale many, many chases ago.

"How far in front of it are we, Rider?" Jarrell asked.

The boy gushed at the screen before him with a dreamy smile. Fuji lay next to him, grinning and panting.

"Rider."

The boy's eyes jumped from the tablet and met his father. "Um," he said.

"Gimme that," Jarrell said, snatching the tablet. He turned it right side up. Members of the Paris Opera Ballet paraded across the screen in a wide looping formation, the women in their pancake tutus and bodices, the men in their gold-trimmed tunics and tights. And they were smiling at him. In on some joke he had been left out of. "I knew it," he said.

"I can explain," Rider said.

"There's nothing *to* explain," his dad replied.

"Jarrell," Erda said.

He waved her off. He was still collected on the outside, but under the surface, he was fit to be tied.

"I wanna take dance lessons," Rider mumbled.

"What was that?"

"I just wanna take dance lessons, Dad."

"Well, you're not gonna dance," Jarrell said. "You're gonna chase tornadoes. You're gonna chase tornadoes because that's normal!"

For a moment, there was only the whistling of the wind, the spattering of the rain, and the low growling of Fuji. The dog was unamused by the tension. Jarrell breathed in and out. Then he flung the door open and jumped into the storm.

Erda turned toward her son with a soft, pensive expression as if she wanted to say something but didn't know how. Then she followed her husband, wielding her handheld. The last of the hail peppered them and tapered off as Jarrell steadied the camera on his shoulder and aimed it toward the east. The funnel cloud churned more dramatically now.

Jarrell slipped the eyepiece through the open slot of the football helmet. "Come on, now," he said. Manifesting. Willing the whole production into existence.

A wispy line extended from the base of the funnel cloud like the needle on a spindle. Swaths of earth twisted and slipped upward until the ground met the clouds in a slender spiral.

"Touchdown!" Erda shouted.

Jarrell adjusted the focus on his camera and followed the condensation funnel, a formidable, ropy sidewinder, as it bent left to right. They were miles away from the twister, and thankfully, from most everything else. If anything was taking a hit, it was crops or else pastures. Still, the tornado's funnel twirled and wheeled almost rhythmically—a curving brown-gray lash against the pale sky, graceful yet violent. Jarrell glanced at the back-seat window of the car, only to find Fuji's smiling face where he wished Rider's was.

"Are you getting this?" Erda asked.

"Yeah," he said, swinging back toward the twister again.

The tornado tore on for another five minutes before it lost most of its tight shape, and eventually, fizzled out altogether. Thunder clapped overhead in its wake. The pulse of the world throbbing adrenaline.

"Never gets old," Erda said, giddy, kicking sparkling hailstones as she approached her husband.

"Let's try Channel 4 in Flathead first," Jarrell said, something in his eyes duller than usual. "I reckon they'll pay the best price."

"What's the matter?" Erda asked.

He bit his lip and scoffed. "I just don't know how to get through to him, Er."

"Who?"

"The boy."

"For God's sake, Jarrell."

"Chasing is in our blood. It's what we do. I don't understand why he can't see that."

Erda shook her head. "After Carpenter, do you blame him?"

Jarrell didn't have anything to say to that.

He returned to the car to find Rider sitting there with his legs folded and his droopy cheeks angled downward. Like a road sign knocked sideways by a microburst. The boy didn't say it, but he looked like he wanted to be anywhere but there.

It was an unusually humid night in December of the previous year when Jarrell, Erda, and Rider filed into the Fairview Civic Center for a showing of *The Nutcracker*. They had been winding down in their highway motel room following coverage of a rare offseason outbreak when Rider spotted the flyer on the mini fridge. He had pleaded with his parents to take him, and once they had crated Fuji, they reluctantly agreed.

Jarrell didn't much care for the ballet—he didn't much care for anything other than the weather, come to think of it—but he didn't think it was an existential threat to the family business. Not yet. Now and then, he would catch Rider whirling in front of the produce backmirror at the grocery store, or he would stumble across "dance classes" in the search history on the laptop. He wasn't crazy about it, but he didn't lose sleep over it, either. All right, maybe just a half hour here and there.

Once they were seated in the auditorium amongst a decent-sized crowd, Rider fidgeted with an enthusiasm Jarrell hadn't seen in months. The boy rocked back and forth in his rickety chair, tracing various geometric shapes into the palm of his pudgy hand with his index finger as he often did when he was nervous. Jarrell liked to imagine he was etching invisible tornadoes, but that was wishful thinking. Erda thumbed through the program she had been handed at the door.

On the third page, Rider pointed at the picture of a man with disheveled white hair and a mysterious eye patch. A great black cape billowed around the man like a plume of coal smoke. "That's Uncle Drosselmeyer," Rider explained to his mother.

"Drosselmeyer?" Jarrell said, butchering its pronunciation. "What a silly name. Where'd you learn that, anyway?"

"At a school play," Rider replied. "When I used to go with everyone else."

"That's the type of stuff they were teaching you? Looks like we made the right move when we pulled you out."

Rider's face shrunk inward like a deflated balloon.

Darkness fell on the auditorium, and Jarrell crossed his arms and sighed. The stage curtains drew back, revealing a massive, shimmering Christmas tree festooned with tinsel, candlesticks, and bows. An ensemble of adults, decked in their finest late nineteenth-century duds, stood chatting in a circle around it. The sound of upbeat strings and horns tickled the auditorium acoustics for a moment or two before a gaggle of children made their entrance onto the stage. They reminded Jarrell of a skein of birds.

The little ones pranced around briefly and took a seat at the base of the tree, admiring it for several minutes as the music carried on. It was all so jaunty. But then came the deep, ominous chime of a clock striking eight. The wild-haired man from page three entered from the left, four toylike dancers marching behind him.

Jarrell snorted. "Drosselmeyer," he muttered, again mispronouncing it. He glanced over at Rider, whose face was full once more beneath his bowl-cut hair. It swelled Jarrell with a frustration he couldn't quite understand. So he kept his lips tight. Watched in silence for well over an hour as one song and dance number elapsed into the next to the tune of changing curtains and vigorous applause.

Just before the finale, the curtain unfurled again to display a sprawling red, green, and gold banister. The stage lights, bright until now, were dimmed to their lowest setting. A ballerina and ballerino stood on the tips of their toes, each forming an arc with their arms, each garbed in a crown or tiara and bejeweled outfits.

"I wanna beat the traffic outta here," Jarrell whispered to Erda.

She rolled her eyes. "It's almost over."

He grumbled.

The ballerino took his partner's hand as a harpist began to pluck away in the orchestra. Sorrowful accompanying strings tugged at the air. After a few light-footed moves—Jarrell didn't know what they were called— the ballerino grabbed hold of his co-star and spun her like a stick he was trying to start a fire with. But it reminded Jarrell of something else, too. He closed his eyes, and his mind wandered back in time to April:

They had tracked two storm systems that day and wound up chasing the one that produced a weak, short-lived tornado, which looked like nothing more than a splinter in the sky. Sometimes, this business could be a gamble.

"I shoulda known," Jarrell said when it roped out. "Fuji didn't so much as sniff at this one."

"National Weather Service just issued a Tornado Emergency for the other cell in Grissom County," Erda replied.

Jarrell gazed up the side of the road where Rider was gamboling in his bright yellow poncho, the corgi waddling at his side.

"A Tor-E?"

"Yep," Erda said.

"Dammit."

"I know."

"How far is that?"

"Twenty-five or thirty miles."

"Maybe we can still catch the end of it if we hightail it outta here. Come on, Rider."

They piled into the wagon and headed northeast at breakneck speed, the sky growing darker all the while. Jarrell whiteknuckled the wheel, manning it with reckless abandon. Weaving in and out of lanes, liberal with the blinker switch.

Until they started to see it.

He tapped the brakes. The wreckage was here-and-there at first but grew more widespread with each mile traveled. Route 72 had become an obstacle course of tree branches and power lines. Miscellaneous scraps. It was almost impassable.

"Jesus," Jarrell said as he maneuvered around a downed utility pole, which had amounted to a toothpick in the face of what had transpired here.

They could drive no further by the time they reached Carpenter. Or what was left of it. Normally, a water tower would have welcomed them. There was just one problem: It no longer stood. Jarrell threw the car into Park and instructed Rider to stay where he was. He popped his door open and emerged into what felt like an alternate dimension. The warning sirens, which still blared despite the storm's conclusion, brought to mind an apocalypse. Hell ushered into Earth. Indistinguishable shreds of structures lay strewn amongst mangled cars and trees stripped naked of their bark—spiderlike limbs and gaunt trunks awkward against the ash-gray sky. Curbs impaled by two-by-fours. Concrete foundations sat clean and deserted, cracked in some cases, and entire stretches of pavement had been hulled to reveal a hypodermis of dirt. Remains, everywhere, as far as the eye could see. The putrid smell of natural gas was dense. Inescapable.

Only the world could have made something capable of such cruelty.

Jarrell turned to where a steel truss lay rolled up like a newspaper; a dog limped past it, wet and dirty. Hardly alive. The first thing that came to his mind was the casualty count. It had to be in the dozens if not *hundreds.* "I've never seen anything like this," he said. "EF5. No doubt."

EF5. The stormchaser's white whale. He had always wanted to experience one of these, right? Hadn't he?

Erda stood speechless a few feet away, her eyes weighed down by tears.

Droves of people, most bleeding and sandblasted, stumbled aimlessly in all directions. Zombies. Jarrell grabbed one of them by the shoulder—a man of similar age with a nasty gash on his forehead and a pink tear at the crook of his elbow that went down into the sinew. "Do you need help?" he asked him.

"Naw," the man said. "I just need to set a spell." He plopped down on a pile of rubble.

"What happened?" Jarrell asked.

"Just come up on us," the man said, struggling to catch his breath. "The sirens started to hollering, and it weren't two minutes til it was right on top of us." He rubbed his head. "I think."

The sound of a door shutting behind him caught Jarrell's attention. He looked over his shoulder to find Rider standing there, eyes wide and clear on a face robbed of its color. Broken and peeled down to its slab. Like all he had ever known was horror and darkness.

Jarrell had never felt so helpless. He began to walk toward his boy as the wailing warning sirens of Carpenter melded into the horns of the orchestra pit in the Fairview Civic Center. He found himself seated amongst the audience once again. The horns, triumphant yet tragic, crashed through the aisles without relent. Jarrell glanced at Rider. Stage lights filled the child's glistening, wonderstruck eyes like a cloud of beautiful debris. And everything was simpler than destruction and death.

Jarrell twisted the gas cap off the wagon with one hand as he held on to Fujita's leash with the other; the corgi moseyed off toward the grass, nose low to the ground, and cocked his leg on a "Teddy Moore 4 City Council" sign. Then the dog let out a single yap. That was good enough for Jarrell. He pored over the cloud-cluttered horizon before him. The previous day's footage had earned a respectable sum from Channel 4 in Flathead, but conditions were even riper now. The forecast for storms was good. The forecast for his family, not so much. There was a "moderate" risk of losing his son to foolishness. According to the Storm Prediction Center, that was the second-highest threat level.

Once Jarrell finished filling up, he hopped into the car and rubbed his hands together in a rare display of emotion. "Ready to track down some gnarly mesocyclones, Bucko?" he asked Rider.

"Sure, Dad," the boy answered with an unconvincing smile.

Jarrell frowned in the rearview mirror. He loved Rider, even though he couldn't remember a time he had told him so. But he was starting to doubt that he would ever get through to him.

"PDS Watch in effect for Poplar County until 5:30," Erda said as she scrolled through the feed on her phone.

Jarrell's eyes grew wide. "You thinking outbreak?"

She smirked. "Guess we'll find out."

Poplar County was 130 miles south, but with almost seven hours until the Particularly Dangerous Situation was set to expire, Jarrell had plenty of time to get there. He threw on some bluegrass and headed down the highway at the speed limit. Rider peered out the window at passing copses of cottonwoods along the road, their leaves brimming a deep, late-May green. Jarrell couldn't help but speculate about what was going through the boy's head.

The sky held back its baleful darkness until they were nearly halfway to their destination. Rain sprinkled the face of the car, but in the west, a skinny sliver of sun lined an enormous black cloud. "Devil's beating his wife," Jarrell said. Within seconds, the sun vanished without a trace, and a downpour took its stead. Lightning winked through the windows. And then came the thunder.

Fuji, now clad in his WeatherPro® harness, squinted and snarled.

Jarrell kicked the windshield wipers up to full steam. "I bet the view out in front of this thing is really something."

They punched through the rest of the cell and came out clean a few miles ahead on the other side. A discordant wind whispered as they crawled to a stop in the breakdown lane.

"Oh, wow," Erda said.

Jarrell gaped out the window to where a sweeping shelf cloud stretched thick and grimy-white across a sinister skyscape. Wind turbines, spinning steadily in the foreground, seemed to tickle the dancing purple fringes.

"We've gotta get some footage of that," Jarrell said. He paused. "Rider, you wanna do the honors?"

The boy turned from the window. "Me?"

"I don't see why not," his dad replied.

Erda grinned and extended the handheld camera to her son. He took it and cradled it like some ancient artifact, both wonderment and unsureness in his eyes. Jarrell gave him a go-ahead nod, and the family exited the wagon. Straightline gusts met them outside and stirred through the surrounding trees as rain came in inconsistent drops. The shelf cloud had swelled and contorted into a warped mass. Like a half-finished piece on a potter's wheel.

"Boy," Jarrell said, tracing the leading front of the storm with his pointer finger. "Check out that outflow." He watched in awe for several minutes as Erda captured a panorama with her phone. "How does it look, Rider?" he asked.

There was no response.

"Rider?" He turned around, searching for his son.

Rider, Fuji at his side, had roamed off into an open field a stone's throw beyond the shoulder of the road. The handheld lay propped on the boy's drawstring bag, and in front of it, there he was rehearsing some strange, choreographed boogie while the corgi scampered about and nipped at his ankles. Rider whipped back and forth, opened his arms, and wagged his fingers, a look of intense focus through it all.

"Dammit, Rider!" Jarrell hollered, startling the child. He motioned him over.

Rider collected the camera and bag and trudged over, his head ducked in shame. "Sorry," he said.

Jarrell lifted his arms in exasperation. "What are we gonna do with you, son?" he asked, his voice gaining pitch by the syllable.

Rider remained silent as the corgi slumped backward onto his feet.

His father sighed. "I dunno, maybe we should pray or something."

"Don't be ridiculous," Erda said.

"Look at that," Jarrell said, gesturing toward the shelf cloud in the background. "Not a lot of people get to see something like that."

"It's just not me," Rider mumbled.

"Not you?" Jarrell dug his hands into his hips. "We've talked about this. We've planned this out. You're gonna finish out school on the road with us, then you're gonna go learn the weather up north at Ames." He hesitated, licked his lips. "You're not gonna go around carrying on like some weirdo clown. Don't you wanna make your living like a sane person?"

The boy's eyes met his father and his bottom lip quivered. "Storms are stupid, Dad!" he shouted, before tearing off to the car and slamming the door.

Jarrell kicked a clump of dirt and cursed under his breath. "Unbelievable," he said.

Erda approached him. "You need to let all this go, Jarrell," she said, a calm strength in her lilting accent. "This ain't anything to pitch a fit about."

"But he's supposed to be one of us, Erda."

"He's supposed to be a ten-year-old boy," she replied. "And ten is too young for a boy to feel like he can't do nothing right."

Thunder hummed overhead as the couple gazed at the car. Fuji wallowed in a patch of grass.

"It's just the way he is," Erda said. "A force of nature. You should understand that better than anyone."

Jarrell huffed. He reckoned he should have.

They reached Poplar County shortly after one o'clock. The houses on the outskirts of the county seat, Tulip, had sustained minor damage—roofs missing a few shingles, mailboxes knocked over, broken glass, gutters askew. A line of strong thunderstorms, one on top of the other, had crept northeastward across the radar for the past two hours. One had warranted a Tornado Warning that quickly expired.

"Looks like EF0, maybe low-end 1," said Jarrell as he assessed the impact.

"Yeah," Erda said, fighting back a yawn.

Rider lay sleeping in the back seat, Fuji's barrellike body sprawled atop him.

Three shrill beeps cried out from the radio, followed by an extended tone. Then a robotic voice: "The National Weather Service has issued a Tornado Warning for Central Poplar County until 1:45 p.m. Eastern Standard Time. At 1:07 p.m., Doppler radar indicated a severe thunderstorm capable of producing a tornado near Fremont, moving southeast at thirty miles per hour. If you are in the path of this tornado, seek shelter in a basement or interior room away from windows." The message sounded off in the same way it had introduced itself.

"Now we're in business," Jarrell said.

Erda zoomed in on the tablet. "Turn right here."

They followed a network of backroads for six or seven miles, the outside world eerie in its dark tranquility. The sky beyond the Fremont city limits looked as though green and gray had birthed some strange new color. The sirens at the firehouse sang their portentous song as lightning brightened the sky and backlit a monstrous form in the west. Jarrell stopped in the dirt driveway of an old farmhouse.

"It's radar-indicated," Erda said, nodding to the left. "Distinct hook echo."

Jarrell grabbed a pair of binoculars from the dash and poked his head through the driver-side window. "Damn thing must be rain-wrapped," he said. "What's our position?"

"We're out of the way, unless it switches course."

They made sure that Rider and Fuji were still sound asleep and departed the car. A stiff wind matted the tallgrass around them as they readied their cameras. The surrounding roads were empty. And that was probably a good thing.

"Sometime today," Jarrell said, staring into what other career chasers called the "Bear's Cage."

"Tornado on the ground!" Erda blurted after a few uneventful moments.

Jarrell swung around toward the back end of the cell. The funnel was top-heavy and partially obscured by rain, but it was there, nonetheless. It kicked flecks of debris as it grew in size and visibility. Jarrell shouldered his camera and pointed it at the tornado, now a classic stovepipe shape racing across the rural landscape. It was the most complete formation he had seen all season—a beaut. In years past, he had witnessed dozens like it.

So why was it making him emotional?

Something else wandered into the corner of his lens. Rider had rambled down the bare stretch of road an earshot behind them and now twirled in an unpolished pirouette, side-by-side with the twister, albeit miles away from it. He seemed lost in the wind, an expression of innocence and contentment that couldn't be brought down. The tornado spun with him—equally alive and untamed. A being of sheer energy.

Jarrell lowered the camera and saw his boy. Really looked at him through his own two eyes. Not through a lens or a mirror or a radar screen. The sight of it all pulled at Jarrell, drew him toward this surreal, exquisite chaos. Erda flanked him and rested her hand on her husband's lower back. He watched on, something like sadness, something like pride, blowing over him like a storm.

the gospel according to manfred

There weren't no two ways about it: Meemaw Nutter had been a hoarder, like the kind you see on The Learning Channel. *Had been* because she was no longer anything. "On home" is where she had gone, as they say. To where, Manfred couldn't speculate. Although everybody else in the cemetery seemed to have it figured out. It was him, two of his cousins and their fathers, and an old friend of the family carrying the casket, three on each side, from the hearse to the hole in the ground. The box weighed next to nothing, but Manfred was heavy. Sluggish with dope. Good and warm. Cheap sunglasses to hide his flat eyes, and an ill-fitting ensemble he had gotten from the Goodwill. He wondered if he could crawl into the hole before they lowered his meemaw. Give himself to the dirt. Just start scooping handfuls of it over his britches. Etcetera. Would anybody notice?

The sky couldn't make up its mind between blue and gray, and the sun was a white, shapeless thing. Awful hot for November, and too many bees. Graveside, the preacher from the Pentecostal Church was saying a few words. About Meemaw having a new body. Tapdancing through streets of gold yellower than butter. Wings like a great, luminous eagle. Manfred didn't know about all that.

What was a body, after all, if not a vessel of hurt?

Meemaw had been some kind of woman, sure. She had grown up on a farm with five siblings, taught herself to read and write, and by the time she was in the fourth grade, she was walking three miles both ways twice a week to the only library in the county to check out college-level books. That didn't save her from working forty years in the dye room at the mill, though. She had a reputation for being hardheaded and surly, taken to fighting, and she hadn't had a tooth in her head since her early thirties. She was twice married, twice widowed, once by a drunk with a faulty heart, and another time by a man who held the distinction of being the only North Carolinian to die from rabies in 2002. Raccoon bit him, and he was too damn stubborn to seek medical treatment before it was too late. After he departed this world, she became a recluse. Things started coming into the house, but they didn't come back out.

Manfred stood next to a floral arrangement, a dull ache in his belly and in his groin, thinking about the time she had chased off a door-to-door vacuum cleaner salesman with a machete, only to come right back in and order one of his products over the phone. Then she had fixed Manfred and his cousins tomato sandwiches with buttermilk. In the back of his throat, he could still taste the sourness.

People paid their respects by pitching flowers onto the lid of the casket and somebody played Gospel on a little boombox and it wasn't fifteen minutes before the entire production was over. Whole life up and gone in the time it took to kill two cigs. Like it wasn't ever there to begin with. His obligation fulfilled, Manfred had a mind to execute an Irish goodbye, his preferred method of exit. But a woman who looked like a less weathered version of his meemaw tracked him down before he could sneak away.

"Manfred."

"Aint Honey."

"Appreciate you coming out."

"It was a beautiful service."

A pipit hopped stupidly around on the ground between them. In front of God and everybody. If you listened real close, you could hear the mechanics of the casket being lowered into the earth. The canorous hums of the undertaker.

"We sure could use your help over at your meemaw's house."

"What y'all got going on over there?"

"Toast went and got himself lost. Ain't seen hide nor hair of him in days. Cain't get him to come out for nothing."

"I hate that."

"I know it."

"Yeah."

"So you gonna come help us?"

"What you need me for?"

"To look for him."

"Get Jermy and Little Shane to help you."

"Oh, they coming, too. Don't worry about that."

He looked to where his cousins stood. The giant and the grunt.

"I don't know, Aint Honey. I ain't got time to go digging around in there for no cat."

"I sure would appreciate it if you could."

"Maybe he run off."

"You know better than that."

"Well, I cain't come today. I got a doctor's appointment. I got to go."

"We'll still be over there tomorrow, way things is going. It'd mean a lot to your meemaw. Sure, it would."

"All right, then. I got to go."

He caught the bus and rode it out to the station and walked from the station to the county hospital, and that's where the doctor was. General, specialty, emergency—all under one roof. He got down to his birthday suit, only a thin gown separating him from bucknakedness. The room was the kind of cold that shows up in the tips of your teeth. On the wall was a painting of a masked and scrubbed doctor performing surgery, and over his shoulder peered Jesus, glowing, guiding the doctor's hand, telling him what to do, and Manfred wondered which medical school Jesus had gone to. To be in a supervisory role like that.

Dr. Trout knocked and came in carrying a folder of radiographic images, and the frown on his face told most of the story.

"Well, shit," Manfred said.

It's strange what you can get used to, and in Manfred's case, that was the gritty texture of the lorazepam that crawled up his nostril and gummed up in his sinuses a little and trickled down the back of his throat. There was even something sweet about it. Kindly agreeable. His love affair with the drug had begun with an adoration of the feeling—or lack thereof—its pharmacological properties inspired, but now it was strictly a matter of chemical dependence. He took two a day. One milligram apiece. That's what Dr. Trout had prescribed him, anyway. The other two or three he snorted on any given day came from a gal called Bunny who lived in the other unit of his duplex. Elfin Bunny with her platinum bangs and gauged lobes. He didn't know her real name, but he didn't think it was that. One night, he had himself a dream: Him, Bunny, a picket fence. What would their lives be like? She was a pretty, tragic creature.

He partook of his morning dose and made the twelve-ish minute walk to Meemaw's house. A little mill village cottage. Nearly every home in town shared the same floorplan. Two characteristics distinguished hers from the others on her street: its yellow color and the contents of the front porch. Most of the mess was confined to the house, but some of it overflowed onto the concrete. A burgundy shag rug, three or four gallons of antifreeze, countless empty planters, a cat scratching post or two. A rotary phone. This that and the other. The neighbors had called the City time and time again over the years, but nothing ever came of their complaints.

Jermy was milling about the front yard in the same shit he had worn at the funeral. Dirty polo shirt, bluejeans, shitkicker boots. Manfred's youngest cousin was a nosehair shy of seven feet tall and he had the physique of a lightning rod and he wore his hair in a dumb rattail.

"Jermy."

"How the hell are you, Manfred? Shame I didn't get to talk to you yesterday."

They shook. Jermy's fingers closed around Manfred's hand like an impossible spider.

"I've got cancer," Manfred said.

"You're shitting me."

"Afraid not."

"What kind?"

"Testicular."

"Damn."

"Yeah."

"You mean the kind that's in your balls?"

"Yeah."

"Damn. Bad?"

"Don't know. They ain't staged it yet."

"I hate that."

"I appreciate it."

"It's in both of 'em?"

"Just one, I think."

"Dammit, dammit."

"Listen. You got any weed?"

"Me? Shit no. I'm on the Straight and Narrow. Found the Lord again. He's all I need from here on out."

"Found the Lord again."

"Yessir."

Church as a child was a fever dream. Before Meemaw had become a shut-in. The stink of guilt, strong and rotten as sulfur. God's army lobbing arrows of conviction from every which way. Incomprehensible tongues. Blood and tears. Spit and sweat flying like rain crows running from a storm, and there were King James Versions thumping in the cadence of war drums. You ever held a snake by the throat, then you know that brand of violence.

Jermy was smiling. "He was working on me, all right. All on His time. Remember when we used to watch that show where them vegetables would reenact the Bible? He was working on me then, too."

"Yeah. But I also remember us eating addies and ripping whippits behind the utility shed."

"Well. All have sinned and fallen short of the glory of God, cousin. I've turned from them wicked ways. That's all that matters."

"You were lost, but now you're found."

"So to speak. Say. You still write them essays and whatnot?"

"Not so much."

"That's a shame."

"So you know anybody else that would have some weed?"

About that time, out barged Little Shane with the topheaviness of a toddler. Buzzcutted and mad again. Every breath of the man's life was an advertisement for anger management or else medicinal reefer. Manfred's stepcousin was Little Shane on account of his deddy, Aint Honey's second husband, was Big Shane. Little Shane was on a two-week break between AIT and assignment. He was red in the face. Down to the acne scars that collected around his boyish cheeks and temples. It was his dream to kill and be killed in a foreign war.

"Cain't even walk for all the shit in there," he bitched.

"Any luck?"

"Does it sound like I had any luck, Jermy?"

"I was just asking. No need to be ill about it. God don't like ugly."

Little Shane tugged at his balls and spat into the flowerbed. "Yeah, well I'd like to see Him hop down off His fancypants cloud and come sort through this fuckshit."

"Relax. Manfred here's gonna help us."

"Howboutya, Shane?"

"Manfred."

"Where's your mama and them? She said she was gonna be up here with y'all."

"You know better than that. She rented one of them industrial-sized dumpsters and left us to it."

"Where is it?"

"City should be bringing it directly."

Sure enough, up the way it came on a heavy-duty truck with a great big mechanical arm that unloaded the large green receptacle half a foot away from the curb at the front of the house, and the driver drove off without saying a damn thing.

Little Shane spat again. "I reckon we oughta get a move on, boys. Clock ain't on our side."

"How long can a cat go without food or water, anyway?" Jermy asked.

"I surely do not want to find out."

"I guess I don't, neither."

"But that ain't even the half of it."

"How do you mean?"

"Well, you know the damn thing's got the epilepsy."

"That where it cain't relieve itself without being squeezed?"

"Hardly. It's a seizure thing."

"Damn."

Manfred stood quiet and annoyed. He imagined he would derive quite a bit of satisfaction from taking a shovel upside the both of them, but that had to be some kind of crime.

"Mama says we gotta give the little shit his shaky-shake medicine before he connipts himself to death."

"You sure we cain't just say 'here, boy' and lure him to us with a can of tuna or something?"

"He just won't come out when other people are around. Simple as that."

"All right, then."

They all farted around outside for another minute or two. When they couldn't put it off any longer, they entered the house. Jesus wept! What a sight they beheld! A dioramic empire of refuse, junk stacked in scaled towers across the matted brown carpet from wall to wall. Cardboard boxes brimming with newspapers gone flaxen and puzzle books and black trash bags stuffed with bills and those Sunday ad circulars you get in the mail, all the good deals circled in marker. Microwave ovens and old vacuum cleaners. The ones with the bag attachment. A queen-size mattress and boxsprings lay propped against the far wall, and there were blue-eyed prayer dolls genuflecting in random corners. Camera film canisters in gallon slider bags. A bird cage with no bird. The couch, a halfway decent Chesterfield, housed all manner of items, from VHS tapes and dust-covered encyclopedias to clothes and recyclables. Only a recliner remained unburdened by the clutter, and that's where Meemaw had sat all day, sunup to sundown, watching her programs.

Manfred didn't know why any of them were surprised. It was always going to come to this. Cat or no cat. His eyes watered. His nose itched.

"God Almighty," Jermy said. "What's that smell?"

True, there was a faint odor of piss. And something else. Like rancid cheese.

"Mama burned some sage and patchouli last night, but it didn't take."

"Sage and patchouli? Hell's bells, Shane. Meemaw weren't no demon."

"Well, it stinks like the Devil's dick in here."

There was a roll of trash bags just inside the door. Manfred ripped one off and commenced to rummaging. Little Shane had been right, you had to step over debris just to get from one pocket of clean floor to the next. Every once in a while, one of the cousins would make a trip out to the dumpster and huck a fat bag of garbage into its open mouth. They purged the obvious things first: empty grocery bags and containers, actual litter like wrappers and disposable plates. But after two long hours of work, they had barely made a dent in the detritus. And, of course, there was no sign of Toast. This wouldn't have been a problem with Meemaw's other cat, a tortie named Jelly. Hell, you couldn't keep her inside. She used to lie behind the car when you tried to back out of the driveway, then glare at you like you were inconveniencing *her* when you shooed her away. But she was dead now. Had been for two whole years. Possibly from drinking coolant, but it was hard to say.

Manfred was fixing to set a spell when Jermy hollered, "I got it!"

Little Shane nearly tripped and fell out, he was hurtling across the room so fast. "You found him?"

"Oh. Naw."

"Christ Alive, Jermy. Then why the hell'd you say, 'I got it?'"

"An idea. I got an idea."

"Yeah?"

"The litter box."

"What about it?"

"Where is it? Cat's gotta do his business at some point, right?"

"It's back in the kitchen."

"Well, maybe we can camp out and wait for nature to call."

"It don't matter where the litter box is, numbnuts. He won't come out. Not to meow, not to shit, not to eat, not for nothing. Period. We've already been over this. Stay with the program."

Little Shane hefted one of the microwaves onto his shoulder and lugged it through the front door. Manfred popped a squat on an upside-down bucket. Jermy went back to cleaning as if nothing had happened. Birds pick at dead things in such a way.

The next time Manfred looked up, his cousin was holding a frame and squinting at whatever was inside of it.

"I'll be dogged. 'I Believe in the Blood of Jesus' by Manfred R. McCombs."

"Aw, piss."

"What's the matter? Ain't you proud of it? Looks like Meemaw sure was."

"It's a crock of shit, is what it is."

"Didn't it win best essay at the school?"

"That was a long time ago."

"'I believe in the blood of Jesus. It wraps around me like a blanket.'"

"Are you tearing up, Jermy?"

"It just touches my heart. I musta found it for a reason."

"You found it because you were digging around the pile of crap it happened to be in."

"It's a terrible thing to not give God His glory, Manfred."

"Yeah, well, something tells me He'll get it in the end."

The rest of the day came and went, and the cat never turned up. By dark, the cousins had managed to clear half of the living room, a feat that was more impressive than it sounded. Meemaw was probably rolling over in her fresh grave for all the stuff they were throwing out, but she had no say in the matter. Manfred poked his head into her bedroom. It was arguably worse. An antique wooden rocking horse blocked the door from opening all the way, but you could make out everything well enough. From a waterbed frame poured a fantastic vomit of stuffed animals and bottles of liquor dating back to her first husband and piles and piles of clothes like you wouldn't believe, and was that a football helmet from one of the grandkids' pee wee days? A monitor with no computer or keyboard? There were tabloid magazines and more bills. Some loose, some in bags. A totem of three television sets sat between a dresser and a wicker basket holding enough wrapping paper for a dozen Christmases. More boxes stowed God knew what.

The display aggravated Manfred. He didn't need this in his life. There were plenty of other worries. Like how he was going to pay for the orchiectomy procedure when his insurance through the Griddle Hut covered some of the cost, but not all. Like how Bunny was going to keep getting away with stealing pills from the nursing home where she worked. Pills! Holy shit! Of course! He hadn't medicated since that morning. It was no wonder he was so anxious. He was getting to that point. The point where he wouldn't be able to so much as take a breath without crying.

He said, "He ain't in the living room, y'all."

"It sure as hell don't look like it. Jermy, you seen anything new?"

The giant set the blades of the ceiling fan in motion with a single finger. Gnatlike clouds of dust pulsed in the air around his head. "I ain't seen nothing."

"All right, then."

Manfred rocked back and forth on the balls of his feet. "Well. I got to go."

"Me, too. I reckon if we come back tomorrow, we can split up and get at some of these other rooms. Don't make sense to only do one at a time."

"That's a peach of an idea," Jermy agreed.

"It's what they teach us in White Phase at Basic. Teamwork. Sometimes it's divide and conquer, you know?"

"All right, then, I got to go."

He was walking around the block in a penguin walk, wearing nothing but his gym shorts, and it was three o'clock in the morning. There had been a pill and a half and three-quarters of a bottle of wine. Something red and cheap. Whatever had been on closeout at the gas station. He was trying to remember where he was when it happened. When he realized that he no longer had the capacity to feel joy. That that part of him was dead, but at the same time, he didn't have the courage to make the rest of himself dead, too. Not directly. He did a couple of laps, and not even the cops would arrest him. A flashbeam was trained on his face with the blinding white determination of the Rapture. Lord? Lord! Ain't no Lord. It's the police. Did you know that in Heaven, you won't know nobody? Lord? Ain't no Lord, I told you. Go home, Manfred. Go home.

Sometime after ten o'clock the next morning, the fucked-up rescue mission resumed. A steady rain had come up out of nowhere about an hour before, and it made you feel like you were trapped inside a loose-skinned drum. Manfred waded into Meemaw's bedroom and stood there for a minute. Knee deep, biding his time. He didn't know what the holdup was. Maybe he was waiting for the bric-a-brac to come to life. Talk to him. Oh, how the box fans would sing like a choir. How the candles would burn for this shrine of filth. Tell the story of ten thousand days and ten thousand nights of pain. A wilderness parable.

He was sick. Hurling wasn't out of the question. But even though it was probably just bile, he would make himself keep it down. Out of respect for the dead.

Two things were for sure: This amount of trouble wasn't for the faint of heart, but it also wasn't going to take care of itself. Now, he didn't much like the cat—he was mildly allergic to him, in fact—but he hated the thought of the animal being buried under all that shit with no way out. So he rolled up his sleeves. He trashed the liquor bottles. A lot of cheap vodka and fortified wine. There was a certain amount of guilt that came with discarding the stuffed animals instead of donating them, but they smelled like death itself, and nobody in their right mind was going to want them. Most of the clothes seemed one half-hearted tug away from disintegrating, so into the garbage they, too, went.

Once Manfred had relieved the waterbed frame of its miscellany, he labored his way around the room, sneezing some, stopping every so often to steal a closer look. To see if Toast was hunkered down in one of the many nooks and crannies constructed by the waste. At every turn, he came up empty. Turned out most of the boxes he had seen the day before contained books. Hardcovers and paperbacks alike. Meemaw must have collected close to a thousand of them, even though there was nary a bookcase on the property. He moved the boxes to the far corner of the room until they could decide what to do with them.

Among the odd things about these mill houses was that the fireplace was located in the master sleeping quarters rather than the living room or den. Along the mantle of this one were various items, mostly pictures. The vast majority of the photographs lay loose across the dusty shelf, but there was one in an ornate gold frame that caught Manfred's eye. It was Meemaw as a girl, bestrode the saddle of a pony. In her best Sunday dress. Sometime in the first few years after the Second World War. She was not smiling. It had never occurred to Manfred that he hadn't seen what his meemaw looked like as a child until that moment, but she didn't appear any different than she had as an adult. He found himself wondering if she had ever felt happiness. If she had known what was coming. Not that it mattered now.

Next to the framed picture rested a thin burgundy booklet. Meemaw's hymnal. Her name was printed in faded silver at the bottom right corner: Wanita Nutter. Manfred took the booklet in his hands, closed his eyes. He could smell the cracked vinyl seats of that sedan she drove. They were on the way to church. Her hair was mouse gray. On the radio was a song about Jesus taking someone up to Heaven in a big Cadillac.

Was it possible for a person to run out of breath like a car runs out of gas?

Manfred opened his eyes, returned the hymnal. He was at once drawn to the firepoker stand and, oddly enough, that's where the old machete was, the one she had wielded at the salesman back in the day, corralled amongst those irons, rarely used, if ever, and Jermy was in the adjoining guest bedroom carrying on about something or another.

"Ha! There you are!"

Manfred got there at the same time as Little Shane, who had come from the den across the hall. Their cousin, the stalky dote, was holding a blue disclike device that appeared no larger than a half dollar in his hand.

"Get a load of what I found, fellas. Been looking for it for years. Didn't think I'd ever see it again."

Little Shane's anger was tenfold what it had been as a result of the previous false alarm, and he had the rhubarb-complected face to prove it. "You're telling me that, again, you didn't find the cat but still proceeded to blurt something out of that stupid hole in your face as if you did find the cat? Is that what you're telling me? That there's no cat?"

"It's my PocketPet Possum, Grinnie." Poor Jermy, never particularly gifted in the art of pronunciation, added an unnecessary 't,' and so what he was actually saying was "poss-tum."

"See, this is what I'm talking about. This is the type of thing you could get fucked up for!"

"Aw, shit, Shane. I'm sorry. Honest. I just got excited, is all."

Manfred plopped down on a steamer trunk that was probably one of the only items in the house still worth a hill of beans. He couldn't see himself, of course, but he felt extra white. All fluish. It was Jermy who picked up on it first.

"You all right, Manfred? You don't look so hot."

"Yeah."

"Yeah, you're all right, or, yeah, you don't look so hot?"

"I don't know. Both. What the hell difference does it make?"

"You're awful sweaty. You sure you oughta be out here doing all this?"

"Why wouldn't he need to be out here?"

"He's got cancer in his balls."

"No shit? Damn, Manfred."

"Dammit, Jermy."

"Sorry."

"Bad?"

"Couldn't say."

"Damn."

The air plumb went out of the room, and they all just sort of hung their heads and wandered off. Back to their respective sections of the house. Manfred catnapped on a mound of quilts, and in that catnap he had a dream about Toast, all orange and trapped and convulsing without his shaky-shake medicine, making absurd cat sounds like they do in the cartoons, and he used to have a bell on his collar (didn't he?) but he must not have had it anymore because they'd be able to hear it somewhere in the house, right? Unless he was dead, which, they had to admit, was beginning to look like the case. Anyway, the cat was spasming up one side of Manfred's dream and down the other, as though overcome by the Holy Spirit, and it made Manfred feel terrible. He woke up thirsty. On the verge of tears. The sun had come and left again.

Later, at suppertime, Little Shane ran out and got a great big bucket of chicken and a two-liter of yellow drink from the Colonel. Allowing himself an extra half milligram of his medicine, Manfred sat, again on the steamer trunk, in a balmy, blissful apathy, as his cousins tore meat from bone. Their slimy animal noises turned his stomach, but he was otherwise at peace. As at peace as he could be. Jermy licked the grease off his fingers. He looked at Little Shane.

"Reckon you could spare a swaller of that yellow drink?"

"Hell no. You're lucky you're even getting any of this here chicken after all your bullshit."

"You know, in church, they say to have a forgiving heart."

Little Shane tossed a clean leg bone into the grocery bag that held the other scraps. "You ever actually read one word in the Bible? Plagues and floods and motherfuckers turning into salt. War. I don't know why it's all 'forgiveness this' and 'forgiveness that.' God is a wrathful sumbitch, He is. Don't you forget it."

"That's kindly gloomy, don't you think?"

"You can call it what you wanna call it. I'm just talking facts."

"Sounds like it wouldn't hurt for somebody to read Manfred's essay. I found it the other day, you know?"

"What essay?"

"You know, the one about Jesus."

"Oh yeah. You still write them essays, Manfred?"

"No."

"If I could write essays like that, I might not have joined the Army. Or I might would and then write a book when I got out. But I cain't write essays like you, Manfred."

"Best thing I ever read."

"Oh, would y'all shut up about the damn essays?"

"Christ Alive, who pissed in your apple juice?"

Manfred could hear Jermy say, "I think it's, you know, on account of that cancer in his balls," as he left the guest bedroom, left the house, trudged back to his duplex to see if Bunny had any more pills.

There was this one time that both him and the cat had a seizure right in front of Meemaw. Toast pitched a fit first (they should have known something wasn't right on account of the cat wasn't hiding even though there was company over), then Manfred fell out next to him, and the last thing he heard before the lights went off was aw hell aw hell aw hell. Manfred had been careful about taking his medication at the beginning. Doctor Trout had gone out of his way to caution his patient about the dangers of using the lorazepam more than needed, and Manfred had taken the warning seriously. But somewhere along the way, Manfred's willpower crumbled. Maybe it was when his mama had done that thing the family didn't dare speak of, or after his deddy hit it big on a scratcher and blew town to Florida. Either way, Manfred got to a place where he had to feed his nose—the fastest route to the bloodstream without shooting up—just to get through routine activities. Or anytime any kind of emotion cropped up. Sadness, happiness, anything.

Well, he was withdrawing on that particular afternoon, had been the previous two or three days, too, because he was tired of feeling the way he was feeling, and he did the dumbest thing possible, which was to go cold turkey, and he didn't know how he ended up at his meemaw's house, on the arm of her couch, but he did, and it was going to happen anyway, but something about seeing that cat flopping and jerking with its jaw all locked open seemed to grease the wheels, so to speak. They must have looked a sight to Meemaw, all right. This grown, underfed man and this egg-shaped Tabby cat, writhing next to each other on the floor like they were getting tasered by a haint. Have mercy.

Meemaw was at the side of his hospital bed, enormous pocketbook slung over her shoulder, and Manfred had the notion that she had been running her hand over his forehead, brushing his hair out of his eyes, but by the time he woke up, this was not the case.

"I don't know what you got going on, and Lord knows I don't pretend to know why you do the things you do, why Jermy does the things he does, your mama and them, hell, all my family's fucked up in one way or another, and I know I ain't no prize, neither, but this ain't no way to live. You was my first granyoungin, flesh and blood of my flesh and blood, my little writer, and you ain't never had much, but what you did have was special. I'd wager it's still there, somewhere, stuck under all that darkness. Waiting for somebody to come pull it out. You got to have belief, boy. Belief. That's the only thing that's gonna bring you back to the light."

Under the kiss of the sedative, Manfred drifted off to sleep again. When he woke back up, his meemaw was gone.

The order caller was talking.

"Pull one livermush. Drop one hashbrown, smothered and covered. Pecan cake."

Manfred did his thing on the flattop. His shirt clung to his skin, and his red apron clung to his shirt, and he knew, just about as well as he had known anything all his life, that he stunk. Like meat. The breakfast rush at the Griddle Hut had almost passed, hallelujah, but that meant he was that much closer to having to drag his sorry ass into the manager's office to talk to the bosslady, who wasn't mean by any stretch, but she was still a no-bullshit type of gal. Over the phone, the specialist assigned to his orchiectomy had told him two weeks, minimum, but probably more like three, when Manfred had asked how long he would be out of commission. Manfred realized an icecube stood a better chance in Hell than he did of getting that much time off. His plan was to ask for one week. But when he went that way, toward the tiny room next to the timeclock, and the bosslady flashed that gold-toothed smile at him, he changed his mind. He would ask later, perhaps after his next shift. For now, he had to return to Meemaw's. No rest for the wicked, and all that.

It was now, in Manfred's case, day three of the search, day five or six in total. He knew that, at least in cases of human abduction, the odds of rescue drastically decreased after forty-eight hours. Hadn't he heard that on TV? He didn't know if the same statistics applied to animals. Besides, Toast hadn't been taken by anyone. Still, the outlook wasn't so good.

Manfred hadn't even set foot in the house yet when he heard Little Shane. The grunt was hopping mad about something. Inside, the cousins were at the end of the hallway that led to the kitchen. The giant was scratching the back of his head above the rattail, and the shorter man was letting him have it.

"Didn't I tell you you could get fucked up for this? Ain't that something I said to you?"

"I thought I found him this time, Cuz. Honest."

"What now?" Manfred said.

"Shitforbrains here cried wolf again."

"Looked like him to me, is all I'm saying."

"What looked like him?"

There was something of an anteroom, which, in these homes, served as a housing unit for the residence's gas water heater, between the hallway and the kitchen. Wedged in a crate next to the tank was a furry orange bathmat that, in fact, looked nothing like a cat.

"Oh, Jermy."

Little Shane was marching for the deep end. He had that look in his eye. "I swear. Whole week down the commode looking for a shittinass cat with the dumbest, ragtagginest sumbitch on God's Green Earth. Another afflicted and useless. Lord, I don't know what I done to you. I truly don't."

"Well, it ain't all been for nothing."

"What did you say to me?"

"It ain't all been for nothing. I did find Grinnie."

Jermy had barely retrieved the blue device from his pocket before Little Shane snatched it and threw it against the wall.

"To Hell with your PocketPet, you freak!"

The device exploded, and for a second or two, you could hear every mechanism of the house. The ticking and tocking of the stock racecar wall clock in the hallway, the air coursing through the HVAC system, the old pipes click click clacking behind the sheetrock. Little Shane stormed off, past Jermy and then Manfred, muttering about how they'd been warned, hadn't they been warned, how it was three strikes and you're out, and when he reappeared moments later, he had Meemaw's machete, and Manfred was inching toward the guest bedroom while Jermy's face contorted like a drama mask.

"Whoa, now. Easy, Shane. What in the blue fuck are you doing?"

"I'm gonna chop you down to the stubs, you birdnoodled, bamboosticklooking motherfucker!"

Jermy was already making a run for it as the last word was uttered, and Little Shane chased him out the back of the house, leaving Manfred by his lonesome. God Almighty! It was always something!

There wasn't really much else to do after all of that, so Manfred sat out on the front porch for what must have been forty-five minutes. Waiting, staring at the flowerbed. Thinking of all the ways he had destroyed his body. Which was a temple, they had said. But shit. Even temples weren't built to hold up forever. They were just buildings, no matter what you called them.

Little Shane returned through the front door, sweaty and defeated, about the same time Chief Clu Scofield himself showed up in his cruiser. Some kind of earlier-model widebody, not department-issued. It was anybody's guess who had called. There wasn't a lot of urgency in the whole deal. The lawman didn't even have his lights or siren fired up. He parked behind the dumpster, took his time getting out. Tugged at his service belt, spat some brown juice to the pavement. Little Shane turned loose of the machete, and the weapon went clanging to the porch.

"Chief."

"Boys."

"What brings you out here?"

"I gotta arrest you, Shane."

"Yeah."

"All right, then."

The chief opened the back door and Little Shane got in without protest and they were off. Manfred was sure that his cousin would wind up in prison, maybe not this time or the next, but sooner or later. He would not kill and be killed in a foreign war, but he very well might kill and/or be killed in the state penitentiary. Shanked by somebody gunning for revenge out on the yard. Who knew?

Anyway, as soon as the cruiser was down the street, Manfred went into the bathroom and ripped a whale of a line off the sink.

The whole reason Manfred had written that essay in the first place was on account of a quack who had guestspotted at the church one Sunday. Prophet Horst, he called himself. He had hair like a helmet and one of those profound chin dimples and he wore better clothes than anyone within at least a fifty-mile radius and he talked funny. A bizarre fusion of Midland Southern and some kind of German that nobody was qualified to identify. He came waltzing in there, silk necktie knotted in a perfect triangle. This was years before he filed for Chapter 11, mind you.

Well, it just so happened to be the same morning another fellow showed up—nobody had seen him before, nor did they see him after—complaining about the most hellacious back and leg pain anyone had ever heard of. He couldn't have been more than four and a half feet tall, and he walked with an unfortunate limp that, according to him, was the result of being born with one leg shorter than the other. Prophet Horst preached the message and a few got saved at the altar call and then they got to the healing and wouldn't you know it, the stranger was the first to hobble up the aisle, nearly wiping out a woman in a wheelchair.

"Prophet Horst, I cain't hardly walk for the pain in my back and legs."

"One of this boy's legs is shorter than the other."

"Yessir, I knowed you'd know it."

"Sit in that chair."

"Yessir, glory to God."

The stranger fell into a chair that had been placed in front of the altar and Prophet Horst said, "Leg, I command you to grow," and the stranger was crying and Prophet Horst removed a tiny bottle of his miracle water, which he sold for ten dollars a pop after the service and he unscrewed the cap and flicked the bottle at the stranger and he said, again, "Leg, I command you to grow," and he asked the stranger if he believed and the stranger said that he did believe and Prophet Horst said, "Leg, I command you to grow in the name of Jesus," and damn if that afflicted bastard didn't spring up out of that chair and take off running back down the aisle, talking about how it did grow, hot damn, would you look at that and people, Manfred's Meemaw included, were hollering words that didn't exist in any language.

Prophet Horst was flinging whatever was left of that miracle water on the rest of the congregation.

"Do you believe?"

"I believe!"

"Do you believe?"

"I believe!"

The stranger was doing laps around the room. Prophet Horst was looking right at Manfred.

"Do you believe?"

"I believe!"

"Do you believe?"

"I believe!"

Jermy poked his head through the front door around lunchtime, stirring Manfred from his nod-out.

"He gone?"

"Yeah."

The giant took a long, clodding step into the living room, and it put Manfred in mind of how a string puppet would walk. Jermy breathed a sigh of relief. He had with him a brown paper bag, the contents of which were unknown to Manfred, and he held it half-tucked behind his hip as if that would hide anything.

"Whatcha got there?"

"Aw, this? Nothing."

Manfred nodded. He recognized Jermy's lying face/voice better than most, but he decided against pressing the issue. What business of it was his, anyhow? The man had been chased with a machete, which was probably not normal. In any event, with Little Shane out of the picture, Manfred figured he would have to be the one to keep things moving.

"Wanna get in there and knock out that kitchen with me?"

"Shit. I reckon we better."

"If he ain't in there, I don't know what to tell Honey and them. Other than he up and abracadabra'd his ass out of here."

"Well, they do say we won't know the mysteries of God's ways until we meet Him."

"Sure."

They went down the hall. Stood at the threshold of the anteroom, looking into the kitchen. One might think the cousins would become numb to the mess at a certain point, and while it didn't have the same effect on them as it did at first, it was still mind-boggling. A landslide of dishes and utensils, many with food still caked on them, spilled across the linoleum floor in various receptacles. Laundry hampers and plastic storage tubs and wash bins. On the counter sat one of those deep fryers like you see at diners, the oil old and stinking. Also, for some damn reason, there was a labeless tin can of solidified grease on the lip of the sink. Manfred imagined the roaches and mice had a field day in this place after dark. And the inventory wasn't limited to what you would normally find in a kitchen. No, there was one of those portable toilet chairs that looked as though it had never been used (thank God) and there was a full body mirror with a decorative frame and atop a stack of pizza boxes on the dining table was a camcorder from the 80s, one of those unwieldy contraptions that weighed about as much as a small child. Plus, Little Shane had been right: Beside the refrigerator, with no fewer than a dozen long-dried turds in its litter, was the cat's box. It all might have been tolerable if not for the stench.

Jermy gagged, pulled his shirt over his nose.

"You all right?"

"I don't think so."

"Well, then we better make this lickety-split."

There was, as it turned out, nothing particularly quick or urgent about their efforts that day. After propping the front storm door open to air out the odor, Manfred and Jermy chipped away at the refuse until an hour before sunset, and in that time, they hauled only one bag of garbage out to the dumpster. They moved about, poor Jermy retching, as if their assignment was now recovery rather than rescue. And it probably was; they just didn't have the heart to say it out loud. For whatever reason. Maybe it was because admitting defeat would mean all their work was for nothing. Or maybe, just maybe, on some level, they felt like Meemaw was still in the house, and if they said Toast was dead, she would hear it.

Eventually, as Jermy fooled around by the alcove that contained the washing machine, Manfred decided to try his luck in the walk-in pantry. He pulled the cord attached to a fixture in the ceiling, and the single bulb flickered to life. The cans on the shelves had to have been twenty years old, if not more. Many of the labels, he knew for a fact, had undergone at least one rebrand. All in all, though, he was surprised at how uncluttered the space was. It wasn't perfect, but compared to the rest of the house, it was immaculate. Here and there were stray items that didn't belong, of course. An Easter service program or else a flower vase. But the one that stood out to Manfred most was an unmistakable 3x3 square. A Polaroid. It had been snapped on the porch steps some two decades prior, Meemaw with nine-year-old Manfred and five-year-old Little Shane and four-year-old Jermy. In the white space, written in black marker, was: Meemaw and her granboys. Manfred ran his fingers along the coarse edge, and he didn't know why, but the waterworks started. He was crying, all right. His nose scrunching up and his lips puckering. Jesus, Mary, and Joseph! What a sad sack he was! He needed to get a grip before he went back into the kitchen. He couldn't let Jermy see him like this.

Turning the photo over, Manfred noticed writing on the back as well. But he didn't have time to read what it said because he heard a rustling in the corner of the pantry. His heart did a few jumping jacks. He crouched next to the bottom shelf, rifled through what appeared to be a tangle of those reusable tote bags. He pulled one out, pushed another to the side. He almost didn't believe what he saw. By God, there he was. Loafed up, snug as a bug. The Tabby cat peered out at Manfred with disinterested, chartreuse eyes. Tears still running, Manfred reached into the nook and took Toast into his arms. He held the animal toward the light. The cat was oblong and fat as ever, even after days without food. But his fur was matted, and he smelled awful. Had he been seizing and drooling and messing on himself? Manfred didn't want to think about it. He just wanted to bask in this victory. This life reclaimed. The cat meowed weakly. Manfred choked on his breath. He was sobbing.

"I found him."

He emerged from the pantry.

"I found him! I found him!"

He lifted the cat outward like a pagan offering.

"I found him, I found him, I found him!"

Toast dangled from Manfred's hands in the same fashion as the cat in those "Hang in There" posters that became so popular in the 70s and Jermy's mouth yawned open as though Christ Himself had come back and somewhere Little Shane was in a holding cell telling anyone who would listen about how he couldn't wait to go to war with China and Meemaw? She had been trapped in the purgatory of this place, but witnessing this final act of salvation, she was allowed to leave. To where was nobody's business but her own. Oh, what an experience it must have been! To be rid of the world!

Manfred made to turn Toast back toward him, but the cat began to kick and Manfred told him, easy, boy, easy, now, but the words didn't take and the cat scratched the shit out of his face. Ouch. Toast landed on all fours and then the little asshole took off in an orange blur and he was already gunning it down the hall by the time Manfred and Jermy were falling all over each other, saying no and shit, and they weren't even in the living room yet when the cat slipped through the cracked storm door, to uncharted territory, to freedom, but they were screaming like a couple of scared kids, no, shit, and they made it to the porch as the cat was running into the street, behind the dumpster, and for fuck's sake, a car was coming at just the right time and the cousins turned their heads before it happened.

Later, after Manfred had scooped the remains into a pillowcase, he went back into the house. Down the hall. The bathroom door wasn't shut all the way, so going in there didn't give him any pause. But when he pushed the door the rest of the way open, what should he see other than Jermy, straddling the pot with his head practically on the tank. The giant's gangly arms swung to either side, one of his hands clutching the paper bag from earlier, and in the other was an aerosol can of spray paint. He rolled his head and gazed up at Manfred, eyes feral, breathing short and heavy through a mouth and nose caked with white paint.

"Yeah," Manfred said.

There they were at the diner in the mall. Well, what was left of the mall. It had lost two businesses a year for the past decade until it dwindled down to one department store, a jeweler, an electronics shop, and a two-restaurant food court. Following a day away from Meemaw's house, they had returned to lay Toast to rest next to Jelly, under the bloodgood in the backyard. Jermy had read from the Gospel of Matthew. Aint Honey said that Meemaw sure would have appreciated it.

Manfred stared at his cheeseburger. Every now and then, he dabbed at the scratch on his cheek with the tip of his finger. The four lines were red and even. Classic Toast. The Polaroid Manfred had found in the pantry lay facedown on the table next to his napkin. He had finally gotten to read what was on the back of it after the cat's graveside service: Mix one tsp. grease into kibble. Perhaps long, long-ago directions for a catsitter. Useless now.

Jermy eyed the photo. "You mind if I have that?"

"No."

"No, I cain't have it, or no, you don't mind?"

"You can have it, Jermy. I don't have no use for it."

"Awful kind of you. Won't be long til Meemaw's house is cleaned out and sold. Reckon I should have something to remember her by."

"Yeah."

"About the bathroom…"

"Don't mention it."

They sat in silence for several minutes. Their waitress took a smoke break.

"You know, a few years ago, me and a buddy of mine were out in the sticks past Planerville. We's supposed to be buying addies off a feller out there, but he ghosted us. Truth be told, we was gonna rob him. So it probably served us right. Anyway, we're driving around in his Stang. Man, he loved that car. I was in the passenger seat, and he had his dog, some kind of mutt that was probably about eight different things and older than Methuselah to boot, in the back. Not sure why. Poor thing hated to ride. So we're in the boonies, right? Storm come up out of nowhere. First rain drop ain't even started sliding down the windshield when there's this crazy flash. Bam! A bolt of lightning hits the car."

The diner's only other two patrons threw glances over their shoulders.

"I ain't never been that scared in my life, Manfred. My buddy slams on the brakes. We check ourselves, pat ourselves up and down to make sure we're still in one piece. When we realize we are, we just kindly look at each other and laugh. But then he starts to sniffing, and we go straight-faced. We look in the backseat, and that dog back there has blowed shit all over the leather. I mean, it's *everywhere*. Windows, floorboards, you name it. He's shaking and panting like there's no tomorrow. Tail tucked, ears down. My buddy don't even say nothing. He just lets off the brake and drives away. Five under the speed limit the whole way back home."

Manfred waited for the punchline, but it didn't come. Jermy faced away, toward the window next to their booth.

"What's the point of that story?"

"Don't know."

"You don't know."

The giant took a sip of his drink. It made the sound that good ice makes in a styrofoam cup. "Hold on, it's coming to me. Maybe it's that you might feel like you're unlucky now, but you can always be unluckier."

How they explained it to him was that, once removed, the diseased testicle would be prepared in a solution—he couldn't pronounce the technical name of it—and staged by a pathologist. Even if the cancer had spread beyond the point of origin, it would have a high degree of treatability. There were, of course, aggressive cases, and he should be prepared if the news was less than ideal. Funny: He had wanted to be dead plenty of times, but it had never felt like a real possibility until now.

It was a quarter past six in the morning, and Manfred lay in a bed in the pre-op room, sporting nothing but a stupid gray gown and stupid pale green compression socks. Everything was so cold. He was told he could have one person with him until it was time to go back, but he didn't ask anyone to come. Bunny would pick him up on her lunch break. He hadn't even told her what they were doing to him. On the mounted television, someone was talking about the weather with the sound off.

A masked nurse entered the room through a curtain that could have been on anyone's shower.

"You ready to rock and roll?"

"Yeah."

The nurse began to wheel him off. Through the stations, down a hall. Next stop: OR.

"Nervous?"

"A little."

"Don't worry. We're gonna give you a little drip of something for that."

He had lied to them on the form he filled out pre-surgery. About how much of his anxiety medicine he took. They needed to know so that they could dose the anesthesia just right. But he was ashamed. So he lied. He hoped he would wake up. If not, it was what it was. The nurse juiced his catheter. Thirty seconds later, they were going through some double doors, and the dope hit him like a jacked-up truck. There were three others in the room, and they were beautiful. The whole place shined.

"Mr. McCombs, we're gonna have you start counting backwards from one hundred, and we'll see you on the other side."

He nodded, or maybe he just imagined nodding. In his mind, thoughts were coming fast and slow at the same time. He couldn't keep up. He was taller than Jermy and shorter than the man Prophet Horst had healed. Looking up at the sky through a pair of binoculars. Somebody was taking his meemaw, Wanita Nutter, up to Heaven in a big fucking Cadillac, Toast on her lap, a plume of smoke corkscrewing from the tailpipe, and angels wrapped Manfred in their blinding, velvety wings. Told him it'll be all right, it'll be all right. With their celestial, nonsensical tongues.

When he was a child, he believed in the blood of Jesus. He wished he still could. The room went dark. Like before the world was born. He wished he could believe. He wished he could.

Believe. He wished. He wished he wished he wished. Do you believe. I believe. Do you believe. I believe.

I was to report to Joyner's Crick Park at 7 a.m. on March 2, and so that's what I've done. It's cold as all get out. The kind that hurts. The three of us—me, another man, and a lady—are waiting at the park ranger's office, a considerable amount of personal space between us. The smell is a blend of morning dew and sewage water.

"What are y'all doing just farting around out here?" the park ranger asks when he pulls up in an old rustbucket.

"We haven't been given our orders yet," the lady says, softly. "Just to be here at 7."

"Well," the park ranger says. There are old people, and then there is Melvin. Park Ranger Melvin has *both* feet in the grave; he just hasn't remembered to shovel the dirt over himself yet. Face like one of those pug dogs—the grumpy ones with breathing problems. Swearing under his breath, he opens the door to his office with more keys than any one person should carry. They bring to mind sleighbells.

We try to enter behind him, but he discourages us.

"Wait out there, dammit," he barks.

So we do.

After a minute, I mosey over to the vending machine at the corner of the building and peruse the soda options, even though I know I won't be able to do anything but window shop. The DWI depleted my CitizenPoints™. They'll go back up after I complete my hours, but for now, I'll just have to suffer the consequences. When the points took over as the national currency, most people were cool with it. Especially the conservatives (no more lazing around on John Q. Taxpayer's dime, you know what I mean?). These days, the arrangement isn't so popular. What with people not being able to do normal things like buy a soda after a moderate fuckup and all.

I return to my place by the office door, lean against the wall next to the doorjamb. Melvin is inside making some kind of fuss. The other man approaches me. He has a braided goatee on his chin and a tribal tattoo on his upper arm. A muscle shirt, sweatpants. "I'm G-Bird," he says, extending a hand with a ring on it. State champions, '04.

"Clay," I say.

"Clay," he repeats. "Like dried dirt?"

"Sure."

G-Bird turns toward the tight-lipped, sandy-bobbed lady. She could be as young as twenty-five and as old as forty. "What about you, miss?"

She doesn't answer.

"All right."

Park Ranger Melvin fumbles through the doorway, the handles of three orange buckets in one hand, three sticklike apparatuses in the other.

"Okie dokie," he coughs, dropping them to the ground. "For the next two days, this is how y'all will start your morning. Go around the grounds and use these grabbers to pick up trash. You can drop it in these here pails. I don't care where you go, just don't walk together. House rules. And no smoking. If I catch you lighting up on park property, that's a 250-point fine and a trip to the courthouse."

"What about you?" G-Bird asks him.

"I'll be around directly."

We grab our buckets and our pick-up tools and march toward the greenway.

Joyner's Crick is your average American park: running trails, volleyball pits, basketball courts, playgrounds, and shelters tucked into the woods and spread across a thirty-acre lot. Poorly maintained, underfunded. I had a birthday party here when I was in elementary school. If only little me had known young-adult me would drink and drive and wind up here doing sixteen hours of court-ordered community service. I got off easy, frankly, but it doesn't feel like it.

"What're you in for?" G-Bird asks me.

"DWI," I admit. "You?"

"Driving While License Revoked," he says. "My fourteenth." I can't tell if he says this proudly or not.

"Oh."

"How about you, miss?" he asks the lady.

She has a kind, unassuming face, but her hesitance is palpable. "Unregistered plants," she concedes.

"What kind of plants?" G-Bird asks.

Something tells me it ain't geraniums.

She tenses up. "You heard what the park ranger said," she snaps. "We're not supposed to be walking together." She sashays off in a different direction.

"Real piece of work, huh?" G-Bird says to me.

I know his assessment isn't fair, but I don't agree or disagree.

G-Bird sighs as we cross over a bridge. Water dances in the creek underneath. The grass on either side of the paved path ahead is just beginning to look healthy again, and some of the trees have been reborn, but not many. The sun is rising, but the temperature isn't.

"Look," G-Bird says, like he's about to get down to brass tacks. "I don't believe that no-walking-together bullshit. Or the no-smoking business. My money's on that park ranger sitting his fat ass in that office all day. So we can work together if you want." He pulls out a wrinkled pack of cigarettes from the pocket of his muscle shirt. Government Menthols™. "You smoke?"

I take one, and we both light up. We make a U-turn at the south entrance and start to work our way back, picking up cans, brown paper bags, napkins, and cigarette butts. Our buckets are already half-full after a quarter mile's walk.

"DWI, huh?" G-Bird says. "Been there, done that. I got me one when I was about your age, fifteen, twenty years ago. Judge made me fold clothes at the Donation Station™. You wouldn't believe what people'd bring in." He shudders. "I unfolded this pair of short pants one time, and doodoo rolled out."

I grimace.

"I'd take this over that any day of the week."

We burn through another cigarette in the time it takes us to top off our buckets. We're emptying them into a large trash receptacle when Melvin comes humming up the way on a green and yellow UTV, his right leg cocked across the passenger seat.

"Mr. Park Ranger," G-Bird says.

The old man throws his cart into Park. "I thought I told y'all no walking together." He looks at me. "Go on, now. Scram."

I walk away, but as soon as Melvin starts off, G-Bird calls me back. I return, reluctantly.

"Old cooter's as useful as fartdust in a hurricane," G-Bird says as Melvin disappears.

We're about halfway back to the park ranger's office when I notice the odor. It's faint, putrescent. But this is the park, and critters die out here all the time. The smell grows stronger as G-Bird leads us to a playground off the greenway. I pinch my nose, but he doesn't bat an eye. The equipment is small and colorful. Monkey bars. A geodesic dome and a slide. G-Bird crouches down next to the latter, shoots his eyes in every imaginable direction.

"What are you doing?" I question.

"You like to party?" he asks, sprinkling a tiny white pill onto the blue slide.

"What is it?" I bury my nose into my shirt. The stench is almost unbearable.

"Oxy," he whispers. "You done it before?"

"A few times."

"Here," he says. "You can have a bump." He crushes the pill into a fine powder with his CitizenPoints™ card and separates two lines, one much thicker than the other. He wiggles a piece of a drink straw from a fold in his wallet—like he's done this many, many times—and snorts the thicker line. Then he hands the straw to me.

I get down on my knees like I'm praying. Do my line.

"To the face," G-Bird grunts in celebration. I imagine a caveman standing around the first fire.

Within a few minutes, I can't feel my legs. Angels have kissed me with their cold, blue lips. Inside, there's a war going on between feeling nothing at all and this wonderful, pulseless euphoria. Pain is impossible. Funny. I could take off running and end up in Forever™.

But not even the high can mask the surrounding smell.

G-Bird sparks a cigarette and pops a squat on the slide as I wander off to investigate.

At the edge of the playground lies the woods.

At the edge of the woods lies a body, sprawled flat on its stomach at the base of a tree. It's bloated and gray, maybe green. There's an imperfect hole in its head above the right eye, brain matter curling around it like expired chuck squeezing through the grate of a meat grinder, and I can't tell if it's a man or a woman. But there is a smile. Something tells me that's a coincidence. Involuntary.

I cup my hand over my mouth. Then I jolt away and vomit. A hot, biley broth.

G-Bird casually walks up beside me. "Ooo-wee," he says, dragging on his cigarette. "Ain't he ripe?"

"Christ on a cross," I gasp.

"Poor sonofabitch," G-Bird agrees.

"What—what do we do?"

G-Bird doesn't flinch. "What do we do? *We* don't do nothing. I ain't touching him. I'm doing my two days, and I'm getting the hell out."

"We can't just leave them here, man."

"We sure as shit can."

My head is swimming, and someone is shaking my guts like they're fluffing a pillow. "I've gotta tell Melvin," I say.

"I wouldn't do that, Clay," G-Bird says, turning. If I didn't know any better, I'd say there was something threatening in his eyes. He smokes his cigarette down to the filter. Stamps it out with his foot. "Let him be. Let's finish up this trash and see what Park Ranger Melvin has for us next." He walks away.

I start to follow, and the body watches me as I go.

When we return to the park ranger's office, I'm sure that I look sick as a dog. Kite-high and vaguely traumatized. But he doesn't notice.

"What now?" G-Bird asks.

Leaning in the doorway, Melvin presents as disinterested. Sounds like he's got something lodged in his throat. "I've got something for y'all, all right," he says. "Come with me."

G-Bird hops into the passenger seat of Melvin's UTV, and I jump on the bed. The old man drives us out into the middle of the greenway, and we all get off.

"We already walked this over," G-Bird says.

Melvin ignores him. Spins around with a shaky pointer finger. "Your job is to pick up sticks." He pats the bed of his cart. "Put 'em in here. When you've filled it up good, just wait for me. I'll be back directly to drive 'em off."

I scan the immediate area. You can't put one foot forward without stepping on a stick.

G-Bird looks baffled. "Pick up sticks?" he asks. "We're in the fucking woods, Melvin. It's nothing *but* sticks."

"Then you should have plenty to keep you busy," Melvin responds.

"What about me?" I ask.

"I got something different for you. Walk with me."

I hear G-Bird cursing at the wind as we leave. Melvin leads me back closer to his office at the north entrance, his hook and loop shoes scraping the asphalt all the while. I want to tell him about the body, but I don't. We stop at the volleyball pits, and Melvin hands me a rake that's propped against one of the posts. Then he shuffles off toward his office without further instructions.

"Thanks," I say, and it might as well be into the void.

In the distance, families are beginning to show up in the parking lot.

I drag the rake over the sand for what has to be an hour and a half, putting a lot of effort and detail into something I'm not even sure I'm doing right. On the edge of the volleyball pit is a set of spring riders, those animal-shaped playground toys that rock back and forth. The little girl staring at me is on a horsey. She is all head in a heavy coat.

I force a smile at her.

"Whatcha doin?" she asks.

"Raking the court," I say.

"Are you here because you made bad life choices?" she asks.

"Yes," I say.

❧

I figure I've raked all over creation before I finally call it quits. I return the rusty tool to its post, careful not to create too much of a disturbance in the even sand, and stroll off toward the park ranger's office. I knock on the cracked door, it inches open. Melvin sits at a desk in front of an ancient desktop computer in nothing but an off-white undershirt and a pair of boxer shorts. Dylan is playing softly. There is a glassful of unidentified brown liquid next to the keyboard.

"Sorry," I say, backing off.

"No trouble," he says. He nods toward a chair on the other side of the office. "Come set a spell before lunch."

"No, I better—"

"Come set a spell."

I do as he says, folding my hands to hide the discomfort. The office is a dump. Food containers, stray papers, miscellaneous equipment like baseball bats and helmets. I catch a glimpse of what's on the desktop screen. An article. Headline reads: "17 Arrested in CitizenPoints™ Protest."

Park Ranger Melvin shakes his head. "This world is going to shit, you know? Right. To. Shit. Ain't enough TP on the planet."

"I guess."

"First, they wanted a meritocracy, now they don't. People are so goddamn wishy-washy. But I think," he says, turning toward me and wagging a finger, "that it was bound to happen once the younger generation lost their respect for the ones who come before. Look around you. People used to stop for funeral processions in this town. Now they just keep fucking going."

Thoughts of the body crowd my head once again. "Speaking of going to shit—"

Melvin holds up a hand, shushing me. He turns up the volume on the music and sings along. It's "The Times They Are a-Changin.'"

"I love this song," he says.

Dad brings me lunch at noon. It's my mom's vegetable soup, the same recipe every mother has. Ground beef and canned green beans, corn, carrots, new potatoes. Tomato juice. Dad's dressed like he's going to church, even though it's Saturday. She's not with him.

"We're disappointed, Clayton," he says as he hands me the Tupperware in a tied plastic bag, his eyebrows wrinkled into a rictus of hurt. Clayton. My grandfather's name. "There's no way around it. But we're proud of you, and we still love you."

"I know," I reply as he pats me on the back. Yes, I'm in my twenties. Yes, I live with my parents. Yes, I've heard this spiel several times over the last six months.

"I hope today shows you that we raised you better than that," he says.

"Yeah."

"See you tonight, son," he says, and then he's off to the races in his electric minivan.

I spend most of my lunch break on a tree stump, stirring my soup with a plastic spoon. I don't have the stomach to eat any of it. G-Bird is on the stump next to me. He's wolfing down a tomato and mayonnaise sandwich. The lady—she never told us her name—is nibbling something under one of the shelters. A skink with an electric blue tail skitters over my foot. On to better things.

It's still chilly, but it's turning into a nice day outside. On any normal afternoon, I might be reminded of how it felt to be a small child swinging on the Joyner Crick Park swingsets. But this is no normal day.

I consider telling G-Bird about walking in on Melvin, but I don't. Instead, I ask him a question: "Why do they call you G-Bird?"

He sits his sandwich on his lap and lifts up his shirt. His chest wears a massive, janky chickenhawk, a kingsnake ensnared in its talons. "I didn't choose this life," he says. "This life chose me." He resumes eating his sandwich. Doesn't say any more about the tattoo. I guess he doesn't have to.

I scoop broth, let it fall back into the bowl. "Have you thought about the body?" I ask.

"What body?"

We finish out our day at the softball field on the west side of the park. Church leagues will be underway soon. I pick up dog turds, and G-Bird drags the infield. We smoke a cigarette behind the equipment shed, and he says he'll see me tomorrow.

That night, I dream about the body. I dream about a poor man or woman, backpedaling through a playground, woodchips stuck in their shoelaces, and no, and please no, and don't. I dream about a bullet zipping through the air, exploding through a skull, brainsplatter on tree bark, a sickening wretch of a sound that makes my mouth water.

I wake up, and I don't go back to sleep. When you're falling, you never forget the feeling.

Bodies used to be breaking news. Strings of them popped up all over the place for no good reason. But now, we don't hear about them.

It's Sunday, and I've got a sunburn. I'm trying to focus on the one good thing: My CitizenPoints™, at least some of them, will be replenished once this is all said and done, and I'll be able to save up for that liquorsickle I've had my eye on. The morning is much warmer than yesterday, and the dew is twice as heavy on the grass. Me and G-Bird have reported to Park Ranger Melvin, but the lady with the plants is nowhere to be found.

"I guess it's just the three of us today," Melvin says, insinuating that he *actually* does anything. He hands over the buckets and the pick-up tools. "Make sure you do a better job than yesterday. The grounds was uglier than homemade sin."

We nod.

G-Bird chainsmokes on the way to the south entrance. His pupils look like pissholes, and the skin on the back of his neck is red. "He's full of shit," he blurts after a time.

"What?"

"Melvin. He's full of shit. We picked up all the trash yesterday, and I musta cleared four bed-loads of sticks outta here."

"That's just how he is," I say.

G-Bird scowls ahead, and the sunlight glitters in the grays of his hair.

There are a few morning joggers and bikers as we comb the greenway and pack our buckets with treasures of garbage. Today's haul consists of chip bags, tissues, foam cups, a few articles of clothing, and of course, cigarette butts. G-Bird steams through an entire pack of smokes before we get back to the park ranger's office. As we sit our buckets next to the door,

Melvin pops out, and if I didn't know any better, I'd say he was drunk as a skunk. He's in his undershirt, but at least he's wearing pants this time.

"What's on deck, Melvin?" G-Bird asks.

The park ranger digs into his pocket and palms his ludicrous set of keys. It takes him a minute or more to find the one he wants. Then he hands it to G-Bird.

"What's this for?"

"Go around yonder and wrangle up all the bags from them trashcans," Melvin slurs, tossing us a pair of gloves apiece. "Huck 'em in the dumpster out back the office when you're through."

"You don't care if we take the cart?" G-Bird asks.

"Naw. Ain't nothing to it."

"All right," G-Bird says.

We saddle up in the UTV and putter off. We make our rounds, G-Bird driving decidedly more reckless than Melvin had yesterday. Most of the bags in the receptacles are ripped and spilling trashjuice. There's a puddle of it in the bed after a few stops. As we work our way toward the playground off the greenway, G-Bird glances at me and sniffs.

"You wanna do a bump?" he asks.

"Not today," I say.

He frowns. "Suit yourself."

I see the slide to my right, the monkey bars, the jungle gym. "I'm gonna go get the bag from the playground," I say. My nose picks up the scent of what my eyes can't yet see.

"All right," G-Bird says, withdrawing a pill bottle from his pocket.

I tell myself that the body won't be there, but it is. The look of it isn't much different from yesterday, but the miasma of decomposition is tenfold. I have to plug my nose with my fingers just to be able to stand there.

I turn away, then back again. On second glance, there are some changes in appearance. It looks more sunken into the ground, the body. The skin is somewhat greener. The eyes are deader. The bundles of brains have dried around the hole in the head, which looks like a third eye. The smile is droopier. The body itself nearly gives off the impression that it's moving. As I get closer, I realize that's because maggots are squirming around it.

I gag this time, but I don't throw up. I remind myself that the body belongs to someone's mother or father. Someone's son or daughter or sister or brother or friend or cousin or lover. The guilt that's gnawed its way through my gut works its way to the top, breaks my skin, and finally shows itself. I can hold out no longer. I phone the police.

When they show up, there is little sense of urgency. There is a man cop and a woman cop, the man short and the woman tall. They have the same haircut, and their belts rest at about the same distance above their hips.

"What seems to be the problem?" the woman cop asks.

"Didn't your dispatcher tell you?"

"That's not what she asked you, sir," the man cop says.

"I reported a dead body," I say, gesturing toward it.

"Let's take a look," the woman cop says, bathing the body with her flashlight, even though it's ten o'clock in the morning.

Neither of them gets too close. They squat, mumble something to one another.

"That's a body, all right," the man cop says.

They rise to their feet.

"That's a body?" I repeat.

"Yeah," he says. "A body. A perfectly normal one, if you ask me."

The woman cop is uncomfortable, and she shows as much by rubbing the back of her neck. Then she nods like she's in total agreement.

"That's it?" I ask.

The man cop squints at me. "What's it?"

"Aren't you going to investigate?"

"What for?" he asks. "Everything seems to be here and accounted for."

I feel like pushing forward, but I'm uncomfortable with how his hand is hovering over his pistol. I fear that I'm coming off as too disgruntled.

"What's all the fuss about?" a voice calls from up the way. Melvin duckwalks toward us, fully clothed in his park ranger uniform. He's got a bag of something in his arm.

"Can you answer for this, sir?" the woman cop asks, tipping her head in the direction of the body.

"I'm the park ranger, ain't I?" Melvin says.

The man cop and the woman cop look at each other.

"I think that about covers it," the man cop says.

"Y'all have a good one," the woman cop adds.

Melvin salutes the police officers, and they drive off as I stand there, dumbfounded. Some power walkers tear by and wave with yearbook smiles. The park ranger plods right past me and plunges a hand into his bag. He sprinkles a dark brown substance onto the body like he's feeding geese.

At lunchtime, I take a seat next to G-Bird, but he cuts his gray eyes at me and moves four tree stumps down. When I give him a strange, questioning look, he whispers, "The G-Bird don't hang with worms," and drifts even farther away.

Those are the last words he will ever say to me.

I remain sitting for a moment, and then I go to the park ranger's office. Melvin is facedown in his own arms. There's an empty bottle next to him. I clear my throat, hoping it will wake him. It doesn't, so I nudge him. He snorts himself awake and winks to life.

"What the hell do you want?" he asks.

"What's the deal with the body?"

"What body?"

"Don't 'what body' me. The fucking dead body by the playground, Melvin."

He coughs.

"Did you kill it?" I ask.

His face folds like I've just asked him the stupidest question in the world.

"Did you?"

"Naw, I didn't kill it," he grunts, rubbing his eyes.

"Then what are you doing with it?"

He gives me a long, hard look. "Look," he says. "I didn't put it there, but it's my responsibility. It's my responsibility, goddammit. People got no sense of responsibility these days. It ain't my doing, but it's my mess to tend, by God, so I'm gonna tend it. And it's nobody's damn business but my own."

He gavels his fist on the desk.

I don't know what to say, and so I don't say anything. I'm angry and confused and conflicted. I storm out of the office and spend the rest of my day picking up sticks.

That night, I skip dinner. That night, I don't dream. But I do think. Lying in bed, I think about the DWI. The front end of the car pitched over the curb of the road. My mouth tasting like dirty ass. How fucking stupid I felt performing a field sobriety test at seven o'clock in the morning while commuters made their way to wherever the hell it was they were going. The whole thing was a formality, of course. I'd already blown into the breathalyzer thing. Nearly twice the legal limit.

I think about Joyner's Crick Park, all the patrons and their flesh. The flesh that will someday return to the earth. The lady with the illegal plants. G-Bird, the former state champion and fourteen-time Driving While License Revoked ticket recipient. With his prison tattoos. The body and its caretaker, both of them withering away until there's only dry remains…

And a world that was there before them…

And a world that will be there long after they're gone.

By tomorrow, my CitizenPoints™ will have been restored. But my humanity will have nosedived through the flats of my feet and into the ground, and after enough time, it will sprout ugly flowers of what we lost. You can see them from the playground. Opening toward the swallowtail butterflies. Oh, how poisonous, how sweet, is that nectar.

lazarus home

They put me up in this place between Perch and Bayfort. Name of Lazarus Home. It's half rehab, half long-term care, though I'd wager it skews a lot more toward the latter than the former. Me myself, I broke my femur coming out of the Fryer Family Steakhouse. It was a stupid thing to do. My poor, useless son, Butch Jr., had took me out to lunch, and on the way to the car, I misjudged the steps. Thought I'd made it to the bottom, but there was still one more to go. So I tripped, and down I went, screaming Holy Hannah, Lordy, Lordy, Lordy. At least I landed on my hip and not my head, but I was in too much pain to be grateful in the moment. I lay there on the concrete, on the verge of passing out, listening to the nuthatches chirp. Thought they might sing me home, but they didn't. By the time the ambulance come, Butch Jr., who had been walking ahead of me when it happened, was working circles around the parking lot, saying dammit and what was he gonna do and oh, Mama, Lord, carry her now. Tears in his eyes. He was always the kind to make it about himself.

I got toted up to Bayfort General for the surgery, and when I woke up, they had a cast on me. One of those deals that starts above the waist, goes down the whole of the hurt leg, and a quarter way down the othern. After about a week of overnights, they shipped me here. Lord, was I red-assed about it. So you can imagine how I felt when the doctor told me it would probably be four months before we could even try real physical therapy. And that was *if* I responded well. All the same, I remember thanking God it was just a temporary arrangement. That I'd be back home once I did my time. Back to the little house with the sunroom and the garden, the crape myrtles and the Bradford pears. Where wouldn't nobody bother me.

I'd heard tell of this place before. A few folks had referred to it as "transitional living," though, outside of me, I wasn't sure what anybody was transitioning *to* other than the Sweet By and By. Bless their hearts. There were twenty-two residents, about half of them in memory care, another five or so with physical needs they could no longer attend to. I was one of only a handful rehabbing from an injury. I had my own room with a TV and an en-suite bathroom, so at least there was that. Otherwise, it kindly felt like a prison. All white walls and bad smells that no disinfectant could mask. You know the kind. But, at the end of the day, I had something of a countdown to look forward to. Not many there could say the same.

Naturally, my first day at LH was the hardest. I got there at the crack ass of dawn, for starters, and Butch Jr. had to leave before I was good and settled in on account of he had to take his daughter, Nevaeh, which, yes, is Heaven backwards—and I thought that was just about the stupidest thing I ever did hear—to school. I just sit there for a while til the doctor come in. Squat young gal, hair in a long braid, smart as a whip.

"Hi, Missus Hill," she said. "I'm Dr. Calvert. How are you today?"

"Dale," I replied.

"I'm sorry?"

"Just call me Dale."

"Missus Dale. How are you?"

"Well, I been better. But I was about your age."

She laughed. "You'll be fixed up and good as new before you know it."

"I ain't holding my breath."

She took my vitals, then said, "I have to ask you a few questions. Just standard procedure."

"All right."

"What year is it?"

"Let's see. Twenty and…nineteen?"

"And can you tell me who the president is?"

They'd pulled this mess at the hospital, too. Like I was some kind of loony-tune. I squinted at Dr. Calvert. "Tony the Tiger," I said.

She give me this look like she knew I was shitting her. But there was a smile in there somewhere. "Not quite the answer I was looking for."

"Well, he *is* orange."

About that time, a hoss big enough to be a linebacker come in. Had a shiny bald head and an expression on his face that I couldn't peg as boredom or defeat. Maybe it was some combination of both.

"Missus Dale, this is Edgar. He's gonna take you to the cafeteria for lunch."

I said, "Lord, what the hell for? It ain't but 10:30."

The good doctor shook her head and grinned. "You'll get used to it."

Edgar, the orderly, excuse me, *caregiver*—I've been told "orderly" is demeaning by the P.C. Police—wheeled me down a long hallway that I thought was much too narrow. I imagine Edgar felt like a golf ball traveling down a garden hose.

"You used to play football or something?" I asked him.

"No, ma'am."

"Basketball? Wrassle?"

"No, ma'am."

"Well, Hell's bells, son. What did you used to do? I know you ain't always been here."

"Cheerleader," he said.

"Lord God."

The original building had been an ugly, single-story mansion for some kind of peanut tycoon before it was turned into a hotel, and then a televangelist bought it in a state of almost total disrepair, slapped it back together with prefab and paint, and made it into a special care facility. About the only trace that was left of the old house was in the cafeteria, which had once upon a time been the dining room. It had these grand archways and crown moldings on the ceiling and baseboards. If you tried real hard, you could picture the pretty wallpaper, maybe a chandelier. Edgar rolled me up to one of the two rectangular tables, where the other residents had already congregated. A few eyeballed me, most others paid me no mind. Nobody said a word, which was all right by me. I didn't want to look any of them in the eye, nohow.

The staff brought out the plates and placed them on chargers before us. Much too fancy, if you ask me, considering the quality of the food:

bland chicken à la king, an overdressed Caesar salad, and a baked sweet potato that was more dried up than the people trying to eat it. They hadn't even finished serving lunch before this tall drink of water at the other end of my table slammed his fist next to his silverware. He had a bandage on his nose from where they had recently removed a skin cancer.

"I ain't eating this goddamn slop again!" he said.

"Now, Mr. Barbee, the faster you finish that, the faster you can get back to your programs," said one of the gals dishing out the food.

The man huffed and proceeded to lick his plate slap clean. I shook my head. Wasn't even afternoon yet, and they were already talking to us like children. I poked at my food but didn't really eat nothing. It was all I could do to keep from bursting into tears. Some of the staff were floating around, helping residents butter their sweet potatoes or what have you. Nobody asked after me. Looking back, I think there was a reason for that. I reckon it's because they realized how hard an adjustment it was. Can't say I blame them. If there's one thing I've learned in this life, honey, it's that you have to let people work things out in their own time.

So, Lazarus Home. The name is an obvious nod to the Good Book, to the story of Jesus and the dead man. But He ain't raising nobody from the grave in there, that's for sure. Plumb helpless would be how I'd describe most of the residents. Take Mr. Barbee, the feller who was complaining about his lunch, for example. His daughter showed up to take him to breakfast one of those first Saturdays I was there, and he come out of his room wearing a striped shirt with plaid pants. Can you imagine that? Then there was Missus Gibson. She'd whip her teeth out with no discretion. During Sunday Praise Hour or bingo. Didn't really matter. It was just whenever the mood struck her. Not to mention she was known to shack up with one of the menfolk from time to time. I know what you're thinking: That stuff don't happen in a nursing home, but trust me, it can and does. Mr. Ernie would try to eat things that weren't food. Chinese checkers and magazine inserts. Even the leaves off the fake plants. Then you had Missus Hunsucker. There wasn't nothing wrong with her at all, and she was just happy as a lark. Didn't have no place else to go, I reckon. I remember thinking that was the damnedest thing, that someone would choose those circumstances. Far as I was concerned, if I had to be in there with them people forever, I wouldn't have made it.

There was no shortage of "senior activities." Walking clubs (for the residents who *could* still walk), puzzles, board games, painting classes, yoga, something called tai chi. But the one I was most leery about was what they referred to as pet therapy. Basically, they'd bring in these dogs. Three or four of them at a time. They said the interaction was good for us, but I couldn't see how at first. Now, I didn't have much of an opinion on animals one way or the other. Don't get me wrong: I'd had me a cat or two growing up, but they weren't particularly keen on me, and the feeling was mutual. I kindly let them be, and that seemed to work out for everybody.

The first time they pushed me off down the hall for pet therapy, I passed Lazarus Home's seniormost resident—ninety-two, I believe— Missus Ruby Lee. She, too, was in a wheelchair, only she was there for good, and she was holding a blonde-haired doll in her crepe paper hands.

She said, through a dreamy smile, "This is my baby. Would you look at my baby?"

I said, "That ain't no baby. That's a damn doll."

That smile of hers evaporated, and there was a hurt around her eyes and cheeks the likes of which I've only witnessed a couple times in my day. She looked into that babydoll's face and stroked its hair.

"Missus, Dale, you cain't do that," Edgar said.

"Cain't do what?"

"You cain't say things like that, especially to someone like Missus Ruby Lee. She's delicate, if you understand where I'm coming from."

"Somebody might as well do it," I said.

"Not everybody's operating at the same speed around here. Just be mindful of that. All I'm asking."

"Well."

I felt a little bad, I did, but I still stood by it.

The activities room had been a study of sorts, I think. There were these floor-to-ceiling built-in bookshelves, but they were stripped of all their character by at least two coats of haint blue latex. One of them long, fold-in-half banquet tables sat in the middle of the room, and two of the dogs were laid out right on top of it, if you can believe it. That particular day, it was a golden retriever and a three-legged scruffy thing whose breed escapes me, though I'm inclined to say it was some kind of mutt. About half the residents were gathered around in chairs. Some were content to simply watch—hell, even Mr. Barbee had a smile on his face—but most were fixed with hairbrushes, combing through those dogs' fur, and let me tell you, them critters were as happy as pigs in shit. Except for one that I hadn't even noticed at first. It was some kind of stubby border collie or another, and it was just standing there in the corner, facing the wall, panting up a storm, nub tail twitching. It looked like it wanted to be there about as much as I did.

Edgar parked me between Missus Gibson and Missus Hunsucker. Missus Gibson took a break from grooming the scruffy dog long enough to frown at me through that sunken mouth of hers.

"This one's mine," she said, real hateful. Even though others were brushing it, she didn't seem to mind all that much.

"Shitfire," I shot back, blowing a raspberry. "See if I care, you toothless bitty."

She pursed her lips and carried on.

Cheryl, one of the other caregivers, giving a nod to the golden retriever, said, "Why don't you brush Jackson, Missus Dale?"

"Well, I don't wanna brush him," I said.

"Why not?"

"Because I ain't some witless old coot, that's why."

"All right."

I sit there for a spell, extra ornery on account of the pain pills. They always made me worked up and grumpy and itchy. Enough time had passed to where I'd forgot about the border collie shepherd thing in the corner, and wouldn't you know it, here it come my way in these quick little half steps, that nubby on its bottom wagging left to right, up and down. I tried to not make eye contact with it, hoping that would send the message for it to go bother someone else. But it didn't take. The dog lowered its head and started sniffing my feet.

"Shoo," I said, under my breath. Enough to where the caregivers wouldn't hear it. "Git on, now. Git."

Damn thing ignored me, kept sniffing.

"That's Dodger," Cheryl said.

"What the hell do I care what it's called?"

The dog sit back on its hind legs, and its floppy ears stood up. It started to panting again, and I could smell its breath, and let's just say it wasn't like sticking your face in a rose. The dog turned its head toward Cheryl, all expectant-like, and then back toward me. This went on for a while, us staring at each other, neither knowing the other's intention. I wanted it to leave me be; Lord knows what it was after. I was fixing to tell it to skiddoo again when it took one step closer and laid its head on my leg. The one that wasn't afflicted. Gentle as a lamb.

"Oh, my goodness," I could hear Cheryl saying. "He's taken with you, Missus Dale."

He was purdy in his own way, sure. I had to give him that. He gazed up at me with sad, nervous eyes—one ice blue and the othern brown as dirt— made even more striking by the fact that he was white from his muzzle to his shoulders. His wavy fur was jet black the rest of the way down, except for white accents that made his legs look like little boots. And how could I forget about the coal-colored dappling on those droopy ears? I had never seen such markings on a dog. His name may have been Dodger, but he didn't appear to dodge or dance or do much of nothing at all, for that matter, far as I knew. Save for resting his head on the legs of strangers.

"He don't care much for being brushed, dear," Missus Hunsucker chimed in. "But he'll let you pet him from time to time. It ain't often he comes up to any of us, though. I'd wager somebody hurt that dog at some point."

"Anybody tries to hurt these dogs, I'll take my forty-five and blow 'em to Kingdom Come," Missus Gibson said. "Damn right, I will." She kissed the scruffy tripod on the nose.

"I know it, dear," Missus Hunsucker said. "I know it."

"They don't live here, do they?" I asked.

"Naw," Missus Hunsucker said. "They stay over to the Bethesda Ranch. It's a rescue off the highway. Come out here for a couple hours about every two weeks."

"From Heaven is where they come," said Missus Gibson.

Some of the other residents nodded as though they'd been listening all along. They brushed tenderly at Jackson and the other pooch, and Dodger didn't move his head from my leg for the rest of the afternoon. I considered petting him, but I thought better of it. No use in getting attached to something I was gonna be leaving behind, though I've got to say, it was hard. That boy would melt you if you were ice, all right. When Edgar come to take me back to my room before supper, Dodger finally lifted his head. His eyes opened real wide, his ears perked up, and then he did the damndest thing. He burped. A tiny croaking sound. Lord, I laughed so hard I almost fell out. It was the first time I'd laughed, or even smiled, since the fall.

"Take the wheel, Edgar," I said, wiping my eyes.

As we made our leave, I stole a glance over my shoulder. Dodger, ears down, watched me go the whole way.

Time is shaped different in a place like LH. It ain't a straight line like it is on the outside. Or even a crooked one. I reckon a circle would be the best way to describe it, for lack of a more creative geometric figure. Wake up with the sun, take pills, ache, go to breakfast, put up with nonsense, watch TV, try to nap, ache, go to lunch, take pills, go to activities, put up with nonsense, watch TV, go to supper, take pills, put up with nonsense, watch TV, try to go to bed with the sun. Did I mention all the nonsense you have to put up with? Having to ask for help to do your business through a hole they cut in the tail of your cast? Lap after lap, you spin on the Merry-Go-Round of misery. That might sound dramatic, but you try it on for size.

The monotony is bad, don't get me wrong. The physical pain, the emotional stress. But the realization that you've lost your independence is the worst part. It kept me up nights that first month. Tossing and turning. I didn't have me a lot of distractions to get my mind off it, either. Nary a visitor a one. My husband, Butch Sr., run off to Texas. Not that we ain't been divorced since the nineties, though. And Butch Jr. always had some excuse. I gotta take Nevaeh to someplace or another, or I'm in this bowling league, or the car's in the shop again. He finally did darken my doorway two weeks to the day after I met Dodger.

"Well, Hallelujah," I said. "Look who decided to grace us with his presence."

"I missed you, too, Mama," he replied, plopping down in one of the uncomfortable sled chairs in the corner of my room. He was skinny everywhere except for the paunch above his belt buckle, where he folded his hands into a steeple.

I studied him a spell. "You know, you may have your deddy's name, but you're the spitting image of me. Except for that mustache."

"That's what I hear."

"Well, don't sound *too* enthusiastic about it."

"So, they treating you good in here or what?"

"Or what."

He rolled his eyes. "Come on, now. I know it ain't that bad."

I huffed. "Yeah, ain't that bad if you ignore the terrible food and the stink of piss and the fact that most of your neighbors have lost all their marbles. If you don't mind people coming up in your room asking the most foolass questions. What year is it, and who's the president? Like you don't have a damn lick of sense in your head."

"You gotta give it a chance."

I waved him off.

"You never give nothing a chance. That's your problem. Your mind's already made up from the word 'go.'"

"I ain't used to this, is all," I said. "Being laid up and pitiful. I used to run circles around every Tom, Dick, and Harry at the tobacco factory. Look at me now."

"Hell, Mama, that was almost twenty years ago you retired from that place."

"Fifteen."

"Whatever. Point is you ain't the same person. Things has changed."

He stopped short of blaming the fall on my stubbornness, even though I knew he was dying to. In the Fryer Family Steakhouse parking lot, he was all tore up, but now it was like I had asked for my misfortune. Classic Butch Jr. I raised the boy as best I could. Me and Butch Sr. both. Fed him and clothed him, tried to teach him morals. Sent him off to school, but he got in some trouble. Ended up coming back home to be an electrician like his deddy. Not to say that's not a decent trade, but it's not what I picked out for him. I don't think that's what he'd had in mind, either. A kid out of wedlock with a gal who works the desk at the tanning salon to boot. You'd think I was responsible for all the grief he had over not living up to who he was supposed to be, what with the way he talked to me sometimes and all.

"Your leg feeling any better, at least?"

"Hardly. It's still sore as all get out. And this damn cast itches like ants."

"Well, you heard what them doctors said. It's gonna take some time."

"Yeah."

We watched TV for a few minutes. Some soap opera or another.

"I don't mean to gripe," I said when the show went to commercial. "I'll just be glad when this is over with, and I can go home."

Butch Jr. didn't say nothing back. I knew what that meant. Better to change the subject, I figured.

"How is my house, by the way?"

"We taking care of it," he said, though he wouldn't look me in the eye. "Don't worry."

I thought about my tomatoes. How I'd give anything to pick one right off the vine and take a big ole bite. Let the juice run down my chin. Sun on my face. The smell of earth. Moments like that were too perfect for forever.

The soap opera played on. A detective feller was coming out of a coma and getting it on with a nurse right there in the hospital bed. Butch Jr. started to fidgeting, but it wasn't because he was uncomfortable so much as that's just what he always did when he was about to hit the trail.

Sure enough, he said, standing, "Well, I hate to run, but I gotta go pick up Nevaeh."

"She doing all right?"

"You know her. Little Miss Extracurricular."

"That's good. I'm proud of her."

"I'll have to bring her up here soon," he said, and I immediately knew he had no intention of any such thing.

"All right. Well, I love you, honey."

"I love you, too, Mama."

Butch Jr. hugged my neck and was on his way. Whole visit over in the matter of half an hour. He wasn't through the door five minutes before Mr. Barbee come out of Missus Gibson's room across the hall, adjusting his mismatched clothes. All I could do was shake my head and reach for the channel changer.

Later on, both Mr. Barbee and Missus Gibson were grinning ear to ear at pet therapy. With their rotten selves. The golden retriever was there, as was the scruffy tripod and some heavy-set, spaniel-looking deal. All getting brushed. And lo and behold, there was that weirdo, Dodger, milling about. Have mercy. I had been convinced the time before was a one-off, but Lord God, the minute that dog spotted me, he was like white on rice. He come hustling, making these high-pitched whining noises, nubby working overtime. He planted his head on my leg, tried to break me down with those multicolored eyes. I could tell Missus Gibson was jealous, and that gave me a certain sense of satisfaction. She glared at me as though she had sucked on a lemon. Removed her dentures, set them next to the scruffy mutt, who sniffed them.

Dodger sighed. The residents combed as Caregiver Cheryl supervised. Wordless, feel-good music filled the room. Out in the hallway, Ruby Lee was babytalking that doll of hers.

I squinted at the dog dead-on. "All right," I said. "Let's get some things out of the way. You and me can be friends, but it's only temporary. You got that?"

He just stared at me, and I imagined a fat tangle of static between his floppy ears.

"My name's Lou Dale Hill, and you're Dodger. We've got that far. What else?"

He said nothing.

"I'm seventy-eight. How old are you, anyway?"

Nothing again. They'd later tell me he was twelve or thirteen, which would mean he should have had white face. But he didn't because he was already white from snout to collarbone. I didn't know what twelve or thirteen was in dog years, but I knew it wasn't no puppy. When you stacked our ages against one another, they really weren't all that different.

"I come to be in here because I broke my femur. How about you?"

With this question, he was suddenly alert. He shifted his focus toward the far wall, occasionally glancing back at me over the next few minutes. Then, as with the first encounter, he let out a burp. I was tempted to laugh, but I didn't. Dodger turned in a semicircle before sliding down to the floor next to the right wheel of my chair. There he stayed til it was time to go.

"That's all right," I told him. "You ain't gotta talk about it."

All things considered, I was getting along pretty good by the end of the second month. Dr. Calvert was particularly surprised and delighted at my progress. To hear her tell it, a lot of people my age don't even make a recovery due to the complications associated with such a vicious injury. Infection and muscular atrophy, and so on and so forth. Even accelerated dementia. But, no, I reckon I could have been doing a sight worse. Between watching every rerun under the sun and failed attempts at setting Butch Jr. up with the good doctor or Caregiver Cheryl, I was getting by fine. I had become, at times, conversational with Missus Hunsucker and even civil with Missus Gibson. Which is to say we tolerated each other.

You could go as far as to say I was "adjusting" (they loved to use that word) to some aspects of my life in LH, dull and slow and depressing as it was. Other things I don't think I could ever get used to, though. Missus Ruby Lee's babydoll. Mr. Ernie's eating habits. Mr. Barbee's outbursts. He had the Sundowner's real bad. Could get mean and wild like you wouldn't believe. There was this one night I couldn't sleep, so I was up in bed, seeing what was on the tube. I kept having to turn the channel to avoid them animal cruelty commercials they run around the clock. The ones with the 1-800 numbers and sad music that makes you feel so godawful. Anyway, I was hunting me a program when I heard a big to-do in the hallway. I got to where I could hoist myself into my wheelchair so long as it was right next to my bed, so that's what I did. Managed to get over to the door and open it a crack.

Mr. Barbee was out there in his undershirt, pajama pants, and house slippers, pacing back and forth, raising Cain while the night crew tried to calm him down.

"Where the hell did I put my keys?" he said, patting his pockets.

"Mr. Barbee, you don't have keys, Sugar," one of the caregivers said. "Now, go on back to your room."

"Don't tell me my business, heifer. I gotta get down to the laundromat to fix that shittinass quarter machine for the thousandth time."

"It's all taken care of, Mr. Barbee. I promise."

"What would you know about it?"

I had it on good authority that Mr. Barbee's daughter was looking after the family business. Had been for the better part of three years, but the caregiver didn't want to tell him that. Even though he had likely been informed many, many times. When you're dealing with someone in that frame of mind, such information can only fan the flames.

"Go back to your room, now," the caregiver pleaded. "Please."

Missus Hunsucker, who had joined myself and a handful of other nosy residents—the ones who had the ability to get up and investigate what was going on—butted in: "It's late, dear. Do us a favor and go on back to bed."

"I don't wanna go back to bed, goddammit! I wanna go to my shop. Where's my keys? Where's my tools? Leave me alone. Y'all are wasting my time!"

Mr. Barbee slapped the wall with an open hand. Once, twice. He snorted like a damn bull and took a step in the caregiver's direction. Might have got to her, too, but a feller not quite as big as Edgar swooped in and bearhugged him. Man alive, how Mr. Barbee hollered. It made me hurt in my chest. Another gal came over, and they got him to the ground, and the caregiver he had been gunning for hit him with a shot of something, probably Valium, and I couldn't watch no more, so I closed my door and waited for the gasps and the screams to die down.

I couldn't think about nothing else that whole next day. Edgar must have sensed it when he come and got me for pet therapy.

"You all right, Missus Dale?" the former cheerleader asked.

"Why wouldn't I be?"

"I heard what happened last night, and I know it's hard to watch. Just thought I'd ask."

"I'd rather pretend like it didn't happen, Edgar. I really would."

"Fair enough."

The usual suspects were all present, human and canine alike, with the exception of Mr. Barbee, of course. And there was another absentee: Dodger. I looked all over for him, but he wasn't nowhere to be found.

"Where's that other dog?" I asked Cheryl.

"Other dog? You mean Dodger?"

"Sure."

"I don't rightly know. Why? You miss him?"

"Miss him? Oh, naw, child. I was just curious."

"Mhm."

A couple minutes passed before the little fool come prancing in with a case of the wigglebutts. Must have been outside, answering nature's call. He made a beeline for me, backed up against the right wheel of my chair, tilted his head to where he was looking right at me. His snout was wrinkling and curling above his teeth, but he wasn't baring them. No, it was almost like he was smiling. Whoever heard of such a thing? What a strange animal.

Would you believe me if I said a small part of me was happy to see him? Relieved?

I happened to glance over at Cheryl, and she give me this knowing grin that I didn't quite care for. Probably because, looking back, it meant she was onto me. Hell, I know she was. Dodger eventually settled, even took him a little nap next to me. At some point, something must have spooked him because he stood at attention. Maybe it was a nightmare.

"Don't worry," I told him. "Ain't nothing out to get you."

He didn't burp like I expected, but he did gulp. Then he rested his head on my leg next to my folded hands and sighed. I contemplated them hands. Calloused and harsh and sunspotted. Working hands.

"Could have used me a dog like you before," I said to Dodger. "Me and you might've run a fine farm." I spoke these words as a matter of pure fantasy, knowing damn well the dog I was talking to had been a couch pup his whole life. All the same, I thought about him on a piece of land. Protecting the garden from pesky rats and bunnyrabbits and squirrels. Having a good ole time. I was at once sad for what could never be but also grateful for the ability to daydream.

Dodger's eyes were getting heavy. He was dozing again, this time standing up. I could feel his breath on my hands. Them rough hands couldn't tend no vegetables at the moment—no herbs, no flowers—but they could pet the dog. If I wanted them to. And I reckon I did. But for the sake of both of us, I refrained.

You know, I was surprised it took as long as it did for someone to kick the bucket. Damn near eleven weeks. It ended up being Mr. Kiser. I didn't know much about him outside of the fact that he was fairly popular among the other residents. On account of his daughter kept him well-stocked in diet sodas that he had no problem sharing. It happened on a Tuesday morning—at least that's when they found him—and they tried to gloss over it by taking us to activities almost an hour earlier than usual. That day it was basketmaking. They had some hippie-dippie gal come in to teach us simple weaving techniques while they hauled poor Don (Mr. Kiser's first name) out to the funeral home. Like we wouldn't notice. The whole thing made me kindly melancholy, and I wasn't alone in that regard. Missus Hunsucker looked right down in the dumps, too. Being in such good shape, she'd typically be floating around, helping others, but she wasn't even showing interest in her own work. The tuft of beach rye sat before her, sad and unfinished.

"You okay?" I asked her.

"I'm fine," she said, as though someone had snapped their fingers in front of her face. "It's just hard, you know? Reminds me of my Roddy."

"That your husband?"

"Yes, dear."

"Did he pass?"

"It'll be five years next month."

"I hate that."

"I know it. Feels like it was yesterday. He was out in the backyard, fooling around with the firepit. Had hisself a heart attack and dropped right there. Fell in over the bricks face first. Just one of them things, you know. By the time I come home from shopping, he was gone. Burnt up above the waist like a s'more."

"Lord God," I said. What else could you say to such a thing as that?

"I know he had it a lot worse than Don, but that don't make it any better. Them grief people used to tell me it gets easier, but I cain't say I agree. Each loss is like a crack in the dam, no matter how big or small. You just gotta keep going, hope the wall holds."

I went quiet for a moment. Someone was saying, "Now, Mr. Ernie, don't eat your basket."

"You'll be all right," I finally managed, somewhat ashamed I couldn't come up with nothing better.

"Yes, dear," Missus Hunsucker said. "Yes, I will. But not today."

She got up and left. I sit there stewing in my emotions for a while. Longer than I probably should have. Feeling sorry for myself and Missus Hunsucker both. Mr. Kiser's family. I'm assuming he had one, but you never know. I didn't have time to dwell on it, though. I made up my mind right then and there that I was gonna bust my ass to get out of LH as soon as earthly possible. Do whatever I had to do.

The next week, when my cast come off, I could finally see the light at the end of the tunnel. Dr. Calvert brung in this orthopedist from Perch, and he used his little electric handsaw thingamajig to cut through the plaster. It's hard to put into words how good it felt when the air hit the skin that'd been covered up for three months. It was like taking a deep breath for the first time in a coon's age. Still, I was just as sore as I could be. My healed leg was achy and weak, and it wasn't no bigger around than a stalk of sugarcane. The road ahead was long, but I was ready to walk a million miles if it meant getting my life back.

"Well, Missus Dale," Dr. Calvert said. "I don't think you could have asked for the process to go any better than it has to this point. The bone healed beautifully."

"It don't look it," I replied.

She laughed. "Trust me, a lot of folks your age who have suffered a fractured femur would love to be in the same boat."

"So when can I start PT?"

"We'll give you another two weeks out of the cast before we go down that path."

"Two weeks?" I practically hollered.

"Just to be careful. We don't want to rush it and risk you having a setback. You're still well ahead of schedule."

I sighed. "You sure I cain't start any sooner than that?"

"I'm sure, Missus Dale. You'll just have to wait a little longer. Sorry."

And wait, I did. Many a long day and night. Going through the same old, same old. Trying to keep my mind busy. One evening I seen this program on the nature channel about herding dogs, and I got a kick out of that because it reminded me of Dodger. I told him all about it the next time I seen him, but he just rolled over, belly-up, and burped. Looked at me like he didn't know what I expected him to do with that information. It hit me: Sooner than later, I probably wasn't never gonna see him again. So, I left it at that and kept to myself for a bit. I was restless and crabby. Ready to get the show on the road. But Lord Jesus, if I'd have only known what I was in for, I wouldn't have pitched a fit about the waiting.

Physical therapy started simple enough, but you'd never know it the way it wore me out. They had this deal set up in the fitness room—a little track with rails on each side. I'd walk down it with the physical therapist behind me, his hands around my waist. It couldn't have been no more than ten yards long, but one trip down and back had me out of breath, feeling like my leg was gonna fall clean off at the hip. He give me a break, had me do it again. Then he laid me on the table back first, had me do leg lifts. Raise your leg, just so, off the table, put it back down, raise it up again. You get the picture. God Almighty, did that hurt. So much so that after a dozen of them, I had tears in my eyes.

"How are you feeling?" the physical therapist asked.

"All that schooling, and you cain't tell?" I chirped back.

He smiled more politely than I deserved. "It gets better."

"I sure hope so."

I lifted and lowered, lifted and lowered, all the while him saying, "That's it. That's it, Missus Dale." Finally, I hit a wall.

"I cain't do no more," I said.

"That's perfectly fine. Nothing to be ashamed of. We'll try again tomorrow."

He helped me down into my chair, and Edgar come and got me. Steered me back to my room. I didn't even make an appearance at supper that night. I just lay in bed and cried til I couldn't make no more tears. Had me a conversation with the Good Lord. Told Him I'd rather Him call me home than to feel so awful. I dreaded the next day, and I had good reason to. The second and third sessions were much the same as the first. By the fourth one, I told them I couldn't go because I was sick. Did they know I was full of it? Probably. I didn't care.

On the day of the fifth appointment, I talked myself up enough to go. Edgar took me, as usual, but when we got to the fitness room, it wasn't just the physical therapist. Cheryl was there, too.

"What you doing here?" I asked.

"We just thought we'd try a little something different today," she said.

The last word was hardly out of her mouth when Dodger made his entrance. He did his normal song and dance. The whining, the nubby wagging. He shoved his fluffy butt into my wheel, and it all just kind of happened before I even realized: I was petting the little booger. Heavens to Betsy! It's like I come out of a daze and found myself running my hand through the fur on his back, and his face was making that bizarre smile. Lips curling and smacking. When I looked over at Cheryl, she winked.

Now, I didn't rightly know how Dodger was supposed to fit into this equation, but it didn't take me long to figure it out. On my first lap down the rails, that old dog walked by my side the whole way. And that ain't even the half of it. When we were coming back, he was jumping up and down, nipping at my wrist! I swear! I kept fussing. "Cut that out, you silly thing," I said. "Cut that out." Irritated but wanting to laugh at the same time. He didn't listen to me. No, he reared up like a strange pony and playfully bit at me throughout the whole exercise. He never actually made contact, but it was as effective as if he had. When I went to the table for leg lifts, he plopped down on the ground right next to me. Was he being curious? Protective? It didn't occur to me then, but it's clear looking back. He was helping me.

Over the next couple weeks, I graduated from rail walking to double crutches. Then from double crutches to a single crutch, and free walking after that. I went from leg lifts to straight leg raises and standing hip extensions and stair work. Before it was all said and done, I was walking myself to appointments. It wasn't easy—not by a country mile—but I was determined to gut it out, and I did. Dodger was there through it all. Every day.

I was in good spirits when Butch Jr. come calling on a dreary Sunday afternoon, even though he hadn't visited since I was convalesced. Sure, we talked on the phone about once a week, but those chats were always full of awkward silence and beating around the bush. This time, I reckoned he might be there to talk about arrangements for getting me out of LH or at least to have a good conversation. There was something stuck in his craw from the minute he stepped foot in the room, though. He said hello and hugged my neck, but then he was real quiet, wouldn't look at me no more than he had to. I had Praise Hour on the TV, low volume.

"Well," I said from one of the sled chairs.

"Well?" he said from the other.

"Well, you ain't said nothing about how I look. I ain't even in a wheelchair no more, for crying out loud. In case you didn't notice."

"You already told me on the phone."

"I know it. I just thought you'd be more excited about it seeing me in person, is all."

"I'm proud of you, Mama. I really am."

"Uh huh."

The TV choir was singing "Power in the Blood," and I was humming along. I drummed the armrest with my fingers.

"How's my grangirl?" I asked.

"Good. She's at some Bible Study or another."

"I'm gonna have to get her out there to give me a hand in my garden when I get back home. Lord knows it's gonna need a lot of work. You never know, she might find her a new hobby yet."

Butch Sr. had this twisting thing he'd do to his mustache when he was fixing to hit me with bad news. He'd gotten snockered and plowed his truck into a gully, or else the Devil had tempted him into running around on me for the umpteenth time. His son was doing that now.

"Speaking of when I get back home," I continued, trying to ignore my intuition. "You had a chance to talk to Dr. Calvert about all that yet? I know I wasn't even expected to start physical therapy til around now, but everything's gone so smooth I figured there was a good chance I could be discharged early."

He stared at me with a boyish expression of shame. The same one I'd expect from one of his trademark childhood mischiefs. But the cat still had his tongue.

"Hell's bells, son," I said. "Talk to me. The way you're acting, you'd think I ain't even going back home at all."

"You ain't," he said. So quiet I almost didn't hear him.

"What?"

"You ain't going back home, Mama. That's what I come to tell you."

A Biblical fury caught fire in my throat, and by the time I had swallowed, it had raged across my whole body. Scalp to toes. For a minute there, I thought I was gonna pass out or catch the Holy Spirit one.

I said, "Son, let me tell you something: If this is some kind of bad joke, you better get to the punchline now."

"It ain't a joke, Mama."

"I don't understand."

"I've already made arrangements."

I couldn't believe my ears. "This is foolishness, boy. I won't stand for it."

"You ain't got a choice. I'm your power of attorney, remember? I ain't trying to be ugly. It's just better this way."

"Better for who?"

"Everybody. You'll always be looked after, and we won't have to worry about you. Peace of mind and all that, you know? It's win-win."

"You mean you won't have to put up with me."

"Don't be like that. I know it's gonna be hard at first, but you've already adjusted. Just look at how good they've took care of you. And look at how good they take care of everybody else. Whatshername and that Mr. … is it Mr. Barbee?"

"People like Mr. Barbee belong in here, son. I don't."

He stood up and walked over toward the window, turned back. I searched his eyes for any notion of guilt, but it seemed like the only thing he regretted was that he *had* to tell me, not *what* he was telling me. I'm not one to get lost for words—if you can't tell by now—but the betrayal froze me up so bad I was temporarily speechless. Running through my head were visions of me sipping coffee in my sunroom, tilling soil in my garden, watching the day melt away through the window above my kitchen sink. I took a deep breath.

"What about my house?"

He just give me a look.

"Lord, son. You cain't sell my house. You got no right."

"I don't know what to tell you, Mama."

"All my things is in there."

"I know. It ain't ready yet. But it will be."

The familiar prickle of tears took hold of my eyes. The thought of people coming in and walking on my floors with their grubby feet. Making plans. This goes here and that goes there. It tore me up.

"How can you do this to me?"

At this, he snapped. Just enough to get my attention. "I'm doing right by you. That's what I'm doing. This ain't even about this place or your house or this or that. It's about control. Always has been. You're too stubborn to lose your precious control. But you're gonna have to learn. You're almost eighty years old, Mama. You ain't gonna be able to take care of yourself forever."

I bit my tongue and looked away, determined to wait until after he left to break down.

"You're in good hands, and between your Medicare and the money you get for your house, you'll be squared away for the rest of your life.

They'll treat you right in here, and I'll still come to see you. I promise."

"Don't bother," I said.

"You don't mean that."

"I do. Just go, Butch. Leave me be."

He lingered there for a minute, hands on his hips. But then he stormed off. Ain't seen or heard from him since.

Since me and Dodger had gotten along so well during my PT, they started letting him come get me and walk me to pet therapy. See, that was where they messed up. They didn't realize it, hell, I didn't even realize it til a few weeks after Butch Jr.'s disastrous visit. The old feller shimmied into my room, ears flopping, and before I even had time to defend myself, he was in my face, giving me sugar. I'd been more depressed than at any other time in my life, so there were certainly worse things than getting affection from a dog, but man alive, could his breath gag a maggot.

"Stop that, you nasty buzzard," I said, and he smiled in embarrassment. He did his circling number and slid onto his back haunches. Waiting for me to get up off my ass so we could head out.

I meant to do just that, but when I gazed up at the door, something went off in my brain. I glanced at the dog, then back at the door. It was calling to me, but not to go to no activities room. No, it had something else in mind, and I nodded as though it had asked me a question. I'd be damned if I was gonna waste away in Lazarus Home for another minute.

"Come on, Dodger," I said. "Let's blow this joint."

There were people milling about in the hall—residents, visitors, and caregivers alike—but as long as we acted casual, I figured our cover wouldn't be blown. I took it slow, still getting used to my legs as I was. We moseyed atop the tile floor, Dodger sniffing all the while. I prayed for him to keep his cool, and he did. At the end of the corridor, you turn right to go to the activities room, left for the fitness room. Now, I knew two things. One: Nobody had PT on this particular day of the week. And two: There's a fire exit through the back of the fitness room. Going through it would set off the alarm, and someone would surely catch me before I made it very far. But my secret weapon was a hedgerow of honeysuckle about fifty feet from the back door. I could hide there and hope for the best. It was a risk I had to take.

I lingered at the end of the hallway until the coast was clear, then me and Dodger made a break for the fitness room. Finding it empty, we crossed to the fire exit. The color red never looked so purdy. I fixed my hands on the crashbar.

"If you want out, now's the time to say so," I told Dodger. "No turning back after this point."

He looked up at me, and I expected him to burp. But he didn't.

"All right, then," I said.

I pushed through, and sure enough, the alarm went to caterwauling. Hurrying over to the honeysuckle, it wasn't lost on me that this would have been a pretty funny sight to anyone who happened to be watching. This limping old lady scooting across a field with a stubby, nervous geriatric dog in tow. You'll have to excuse me for not laughing, though. Traversing LH's backyard felt like an eternity, but we reached the hedgerow before being found out, and I thanked the Good Lord for not making me a tall woman. I didn't even have to duck behind the foliage to conceal my body. Dodger was starting to pant a little, so I petted his head as we waited it out. I tried to remain calm for him, but I'm not gonna lie: My heart skipped a beat when I heard the door open a couple seconds later. It couldn't have been for more than one whole minute, but if you told me we hung there in limbo for one hour or more, I would've believed you. I just knew our escape was over before it could even begin. But then the door closed once more, and the alarm fell silent.

I breathed a sigh of relief. "Okay."

There was a wooded area another hundred some odd yards beyond the hedgerow, and if my memory served me correctly, a highway about a mile on the other side of that. I had been admitted at the first of spring, and now it was nearly fall, but summer wasn't going down without a fight.

It was plumb stifling out there. Upwards of eighty-five degrees, but even more with the humidity. I was already wore out and sweaty, but there was no time to rest. I snapped my fingers, and Dodger followed me into the trees. I didn't have any notion of where we were going. I just knew it was away from where we'd been, and that was good enough for me. I'd spent my fair share of time in the woods as a youngin, but they were a foreign land to me now. I navigated through the loblollies, doing my damnedest to keep my eyes open for any snakes hiding in the hammocks and pine boughs. Poor Dodger. He followed me no questions asked.

I wasn't never no account at math, but I tried to calculate how long it would be til the folks at LH realized we weren't in pet therapy. Probably they already knew. God Almighty, how they must have had a cow about that. Issued one of them silver alerts or whatever they do. I know it ain't Christian, but I kindly wished I was there to see it. I mean, imagine it: Me, Lou Dale Hill, an outlaw. On the run, like in one of them movies. Never thought I'd see the day.

We took our time, which was all right by my accomplice. He was so busy snuffling up all the new smells that he didn't have a chance to be worried. I even had to beckon him to catch up with me a time or two, and when he'd raise his head there would be debris on his nose. We'd been at it for maybe half an hour when I caught him rolling in something. He was on his back, whipping back and forth, tongue hanging out the side of his grinning mouth.

"Boy, you better cut that out," I said.

He popped up on all fours and give me this wide-eyed look. All I could do was shake my head. But I wasn't in no position to judge him. Who was I to tell him what to do with his newfound freedom?

More time passed. How much, I can't say because I didn't bother to put my watch on that morning. All I know is we'd been gone for a while, and I still had no indication that we were anywhere near a road. That was agitating, but I didn't want Dodger to pick up on it. You know, you never stop learning. Even at my ripe old age. The lesson I learned that day, aside from a refresher in coastal North Carolina geography, was that the power of adrenaline has its limits. And, child, did I learn it the hard way.

Once that adrenaline wore off, let me tell you. The pain running from my hip through my leg was so damn sharp you'd think it'd been rubbed against a whetstone. I caught a glimpse of a fallen tree up ahead, so I hobbled up to it and popped a squat. Getting my wind was more difficult than I thought it would be. My shirt was sticking to my back, and my mouth was dry as a pinecone. I didn't notice we were next to a crick til I heard Dodger lapping at it. A pitiful, shallow thing. He was really going to town at first, but then he stepped away and coughed a nasty wad of gunk onto the ground. Poor feller was thirsty, and that muddy water wasn't gonna cut it.

For the first time, I felt like a real fool. Maybe Butch Jr. was right. Maybe I did have a problem with control. But, dammit, shouldn't I have earned it? All I seen, all I been through in my life? Just seemed cruel, the way it was taken. Regardless, I had to admit that it was irresponsible getting Dodger involved in all this mess. Dogs may have been wild and self-sufficient thousands of years ago, but he wasn't cut out for this. He'd like to piss himself if he saw a squirrel, so expecting him to hunt one wasn't exactly fair. He licked his lips, lay down at my feet. Just a huffing and a puffing. I massaged my leg, but it didn't do no good. If anything, the pain was getting worse on account of the anxiety was setting in. I had been so busy trying to get away that the obvious question didn't dawn on me: What if I fell again? The answer was equally obvious. Up shit's creek, is where I'd be. Exposed to the elements and all creation. Nothing to defend me but a skittish, overgrown pup who's scared of the sound of his own farts.

I reached down and stroked his warm head. "I really did it this time, didn't I?"

He didn't respond.

"I'm sorry, darlin. I really am. If we get out of this pickle, I'll make it up to you."

Still no response, but he made this expression that I can only describe as a gesture of deep affection. It left me dizzy. Like I had the vertigo, only it wasn't unpleasant. Quite the opposite, actually. The dog's blue eye was Heaven and the brown one was Earth, and I was somewhere perfectly in between, sitting there on that log. I drank in the mossy smell of the land, listened to the birds pipe back and forth amidst the snapping treelimbs and the falling leaves. There was a breath of complete calm, the afternoon light flooding the forest with a color the consistency and sweetness of honey, and I was so comforted by it all that I damn near fell asleep.

Was this what it's like? Being called home?

I would have existed in that moment forever had Dodger's dappled ears not perked up. I thought his eyes might jump plumb out of his skull the way he stared off into the trees, back in the direction we'd come from. There were several echoes, and it didn't take long to recognize them as human voices. Dodger half woofed, half grumbled. The hair on his back was raised, and the closer the voices got, the more it looked like he had himself a mohawk on his spine. There were three men in total: two sporting the pecan brown of the Bayfort Police Department, and, of course, big ole Edgar in those lifeless green scrubs.

"Missus Dale," the caregiver said once he caught sight of us, his bald head sweating like an egg left out of the refrigerator too long. "What have you gone and done?"

As if it wasn't obvious.

My natural inclination was to be a smartass. "Well, I swear I was headed to pet therapy. Must've got turned around on account of how *senile* I am."

I think one of the cops was trying not to laugh.

Edgar put his hands on his hips. "You know good and well you got no business out here. You're just asking to get hurt. Or worse."

"Well."

"He's right, Missus Hill," the second cop—the one with the bad haircut and even worse tattoos—chimed in. "It's awful dangerous."

"Ain't no worse for my health than that place back there," I said, even though I knew it wasn't necessarily the truth.

Edgar shook his head.

"Come on, now," the second cop continued. "I bet a nice soft bed don't sound too bad. Some food. I'd wager you worked up quite the appetite coming all this way."

He obviously hadn't been to LH if he was using the word "nice" to describe any part of it. "That's all right," I said. "I'm fine right here. Might dig me out a hole to lay down in. If I get hungry, I'll have this here dog go fetch us something. He's a working breed, you know?"

Dodger's hair stayed upright and unruly on his back. His nub tail was still. Was there a burp stuck in his throat? Hard to say.

"I got a mother," the cop said. "Ain't quite your age, but she's getting there. Stubborn, too. I'd hate the thought of her being stranded and alone."

"Then you should understand better than anybody," I responded.

He thought on that one for a minute, came back with a platitude. "I know what you're going through."

"You don't know jack."

The cop scratched at his tattooed arms, annoyed. "All right, Missus Hill. I'm done playing around. Don't you think we got more important things to do than chase you all over God's Green Earth?"

"Not particularly."

Now it was Edgar trying not to laugh.

"Okay, then. How about this: We can do this the easy way, or we can do it the hard way." The cop nodded toward the caregiver.

"Oh, I see. Johnny Law gotta dope up the big, bad little old lady."

"Missus Hill, please," said Tattoo, taking a step toward me.

He'd no more than planted that boot when Dodger sprang up, situated himself firmly between me and the search party. Lord, you should've seen him. That dog lowered his head, pinned his ears back, and he *snarled*. Snarled! I'd liked to have fell out. He sure was making himself ugly, but he couldn't be intimidating to save his life. Bless his little heart. I was getting a kick out of it, though, until I studied the cop's face. It wasn't quite fear, but he was growing nervy. The last thing I wanted was for somebody to go getting excited and do something stupid.

"It's all right, Dodger," I said, petting the dog. Then I looked at Edgar. "I'll tell you what. I'll go back with you peaceful. Under one condition."

"What's that?"

"The dog comes to live with me. At Lazarus Home."

"Missus Dale."

"I can sit here all day, you know?."

"All right, all right," Edgar said. "I'm sure something can be arranged."

I grinned and stood up, grunting as I did. "You wouldn't happen to have any painkillers on you, would you, Edgar?"

He offered me his arm. "We'll get you squared away when we get back."

"Let's go home, Dodger," I said.

It didn't take as long as I thought it would, though the trip back to LH was a pain in the ass. Or, more specifically, a pain in everything around and below it. Edgar and the tattooed cop practically carried me out of the woods and over that last stretch as night fell, and with it a nip in the air. A fitting ending to my days on the run. Winter would be here before you knew it. It felt like I was doing a perp walk as I reentered the building, Dodger at my side. Oh, we had our share of spectators waiting for us, all right. Missus Hunsucker and Missus Gibson. Hell, even Mr. Ernie. The bunch of nosy nellies. I'd have plenty to tell them when the time was right, but just at that moment, I wanted to rest my bones. We were nearly to my room when I seen Missus Ruby Lee in the hallway. Rocking that doll, singing "You Are My Sunshine" to it in a real purdy voice. A voice like my grandmother had once upon a time. I stopped.

"This is my baby," Ruby Lee told me without looking up. "Yes, it is."

"I know it, honey," I said. "I know it."

Believe it or not, Lazarus Home held up their end of the bargain. I was half convinced they'd kick me to the curb after the stunt I pulled, but they let me stay, and they let my buddy move in with me. Edgar must've been mighty persuasive with the powers that be, though I'd bet my bottom dollar Caregiver Cheryl had a lot to do with it, too. Dodger come from the Bethesda Ranch with a container of food, a plastic zipper bag of medicine, and a wicker basket of toys: various chewies and stuffies and whatnot. He became the LH mascot in no time. Though he was partial to me, he also warmed up to other residents. Enough to not bark at nobody, at least. He'd accompany me almost everywhere except for meals—they were very firm on that—and at the end of the day, he'd retreat back to my room and watch TV with me. Had him a little poof on the floor, but he preferred to sleep by my feet.

He'd been staying at LH for a few weeks when a commotion woke me out of the deepest sleep I'd had in months. He was growling, and by the light of the TV screen, I could see him eyeing the door. Whatever was going on was happening in the hallway, and I had a good idea of what it was.

I flung the covers back. "It's all right," I said, patting the dog on the head. "You stay here. I'll be right back."

Sure enough, Mr. Barbee was out there in his PJs, this time wielding a corn broom—God knows where he got it—at the night crew. He took a swipe at some of the Thanksgiving artwork on the corkboard of the walls. "I'll kill every last one of you sorry sumbitches!" he cussed.

Somebody screamed.

"Mr. Barbee, Sugar, put the broom down before you hurt someone," one of the caregivers pleaded.

"I want some answers! You hear me? I want some answers right now!"

The face he was making, red and furrowed, was enough to get the Devil himself shaking in his britches. But I knew it was just a front. Behind that mask was fear. In its cruelest state. The fear of not knowing who or where you are. Of being robbed of your sanity. Your most basic human dignity, gone. Nothing in this world is more heart-wrenching to watch. I couldn't stand the thought of them wrestling and sedating him again. I shuffled over.

"Missus Dale, no," one of the caregivers was saying.

I gently reached out and touched Mr. Barbee on the arm. He turned to me. That meanness was there at first, and with it a healthy dose of confusion. But both of them emotions eroded into a river of sadness.

"You just go ahead and put that broom down, Mr. Barbee," I said. "Ain't nobody gonna pay you no mind. I promise you they won't."

He blinked, as if trying to clear his eyes, and I swear, if only for a fraction of a second, I saw him as the man he used to be. Leggy and fit. Proud but earnest. Important. His grip loosened.

"That's right," I said. "Just put it on down. Ain't closing time quite yet."

He let go of that broom, same as there's some things I'm gonna have to let go of. Because, in the end, I can't take them with me. Disaster averted, everybody went about their business. Back in my room, Dodger was waiting up for me. The silhouette of him filled me with a gratitude that only one in the twilight of her days can appreciate. One who understands her simple truth: I'm gonna die in here. We all do somewhere. But at least it won't be alone.

Had me a dream within a dream that same night:

Me and Dodger ended up going together. In our sleep, him curled up against me, real peaceful and heavy. When we came up on the other side of this life, we were in a great big field, the sweet ryegrass, green and knee-high, taking deep, lazy breaths under a sunless sky of not quite gold. A thick smell in the air of not quite spring. I was a younger gal then, in my baggy overalls, and he was older than he is now, for whatever reason, a handsome bright red bandana draped across his chest. In a strange way, it's like we met somewhere in the middle. I was chasing after him, no pain in my legs, no anything, laughing so hard I was coughing, and Lord, I had no idea he could bootscoot like that. Even as old as he was. He was on a tear, cutting figure eights and zigzags across the field before moving on, and I was hollering for him to slow down. Slow down. Out of nowhere a treeline of dark Carolina pines rose up ahead. Dodger stopped at the edge of it. His ears folded down but that nubby just kept a wagging. I stopped, too. He looked back at me, and there was something in them eyes that stole the breath right out of my lungs. Told me I didn't need such earthly mechanisms no more. Told me he knew things others couldn't know. That I, too, would soon know them. But not just yet. The dog went in. I would have, too, Lord, knows I wanted to, but I woke up before I could go after him.

Have you ever come out of a dream that felt so real you mourn its passing? Like you do a lost loved one?

I panicked til I realized Dodger was nestled up in a tight ball by my feet. The tears that came then could wash away an entire kingdom of grief. All my life, what I cared about most was myself. But let me tell you, honey, when it's my time to let go, when it's my time to follow that dog into the unknown, I'll be ready.

# of christmas past

It's Christmas Eve, and I'm playing Texas Hold'em with my dead uncles in a half-lit room while a Gene Autry album spins on the record player behind us. We sit in a circle, cutting eyes at one another, trading grunts and sniffs and coughs. I check my wristwatch, figure I've held out for long enough, and light a menthol. I'm trying to quit.

Uncle Roy looks at me with an envy so deep it must exist in a place that light cannot touch. "What I wouldn't give to have me one of them," he says.

"That's how you come to be in this situation in the first place," Uncle Marvin, the youngest, reminds him.

Uncle Roy huffs and looks at his cards. "Well."

"Your bet, Uncle Marvin," I say, exhaling.

He thinks about it for longer than he should. Then he says, "Bet ten." He flicks at his stack and sends two black chips into the pot.

Uncle Gil, the oldest of the three, is a mean sonofabitch. He looks it, too. Hunches over his hand and scowls at the cards like they just called his mother fat. His good eye dances, his glass eye sits still as night.

"Ten to call," I say, trying to move the action along.

"Check," Uncle Gil says.

"You cain't check after he bet," Uncle Roy replies. "That ain't how it works."

"The hell I cain't."

"Look, I didn't make the rules."

"Sounds like you think you did," Uncle Gil says. "You're just jealous because I'm beating you."

Uncle Roy, whose windswept hair and excess neck skin favor a disgruntled wild turkey when he's ill about something, glares at his older brother. "How could I be jealous of a man who cain't win unless he catches lucky cards?"

Uncle Gil calmly folds his hand facedown on the table. "The only thing anyone's fixing to catch around here is an asswhupping."

"Fellas," I say.

They shoot up from their chairs at the same time. Grab each other and go barreling through the wall and into the front yard. I can hear the dammits and the shits and the come here you little bastards. This isn't the first time this has happened. Not by a mile. Back in 1965, Uncle Gil was so drunk he pulled his pocketknife on Uncle Roy. Ended up slicing him across the forearm. Twenty some odd stitches.

"Don't pay them no mind," Uncle Marvin says, a cool nobility about him like the good guy out of a Country Western. He's always been the sweetest of the three. None of them made it to sixty, but he died the youngest, and it preserved him at an age not many years beyond mine.

I walk over to the fridge, pour myself some premade eggnog. "I don't see why y'all can't just go on to the by-and-by," I say. "Daddy did when he passed."

"You know why we cain't," Uncle Marvin says. "We vowed to *our* deddy on his deathbed. We swore we'd always watch over our sister."

I take a drink. "I told y'all. I can look out for Mama just fine."

"Where is your mama, anyway?" Uncle Marvin asks.

"Said she was out doing some last minute shopping. I tried to stop her."

"You know how she is."

Uncle Gil and Uncle Roy pass through the front door, both out of breath.

"Who won?" Uncle Marvin asks.

"You know how it goes," Uncle Gil says. "Boy gets too big for his britches, and I have to set him straight."

Uncle Roy appears more crestfallen than usual.

Lights flood the house as a car crawls into the driveway. Its choking motor quits, leaving only the barking of the Barringers' dogs down the street. After a few moments, Mama comes through the front door. She's a tiny lady—five feet tall if she's an inch—but her arms are bristling with bags from various places.

"What have you done, Mama?" I ask.

"I just picked up a few things," she says.

"You need some help?" Uncle Roy asks.

Uncle Gil snorts like a bull. "Why? You gonna be the one to do it? We can barely concentrate enough to hold a hand of cards."

"Don't y'all start," Mama says. If there's anything she hates more than conflict, it's conflict around Christmastime. She sits the bags down on the floor, removes a small artificial tree from one of them, and places it in the front windowsill. Its gold tinsel and multicolor lights sparkle in the dimness. "Ain't it purdy?" she asks.

"As a picture," Uncle Marvin says.

"You didn't have to go and do that, Mama."

The strands of teardrop bulbs fill her drowsy eyes with little jewels of red, blue, and orange. Yellow and purple. "I just wanna give you a good Christmas," she says. "Like you had when you was little. Before it happened."

I bury my cigarette into the ashtray.

"You're just like your daddy," Mama says, shaking her head.

There's a thumping at the door before I can respond. "You there, Aint Jo?" a hoarse voice calls from the other side of it. "It's me, Pepper."

"Don't let him in, Mama," I say.

She gives me that look.

"He's right, Josette," Uncle Marvin says. "Trouble on two legs is all he's ever been."

"Come on, y'all," Mama says. "He probably ain't had nothing to eat in a week."

Uncle Gil crosses his arms. "Let him starve."

"That's an awful thing to say about your son," Mama says.

Another knock. "Aint Jo?"

"Well, y'all can put up with it then," Uncle Gil says. "But count me out." He goes marching through the back of the house.

Mama heads for the door and opens it.

Cousin Pepper bolts in, hands in his pockets, limbs jerking. He's got no meat on his bones, and his clothes look more slept-in than usual. His pocked face always looks like someone's just told him something he can't believe. "Merry Christmas, Aint Jo," he says, hugging Mama's neck. "Uncle Roy, Uncle Marvin." He comes over to shake my hand. "Merry Christmas, Bobby."

"You come to spend Christmas with us, Pepper?" Mama asks.

"Naw, I just come to see what you was up to," Pepper says, wiping his nose. "I didn't think y'all even celebrated it anymore."

Mama glances at me. "Well, I decided to at the last minute this year. Just got it in my head."

"Ain't that something?" Pepper says. He pauses, but probably not for as long as he'd intended to when he workshopped this earlier. "Say, you wouldn't happen to have a couple extra dollars on you, would you?"

I sigh. "Here we go."

"What for?" Mama asks.

"Aw, I was just hoping to run up to the corner and get me a cheeseburger."

"How much trouble are you in this time, Pepper?" Mama asks.

It's a valid question. Pepper bugs Mama for heroin money at least once a week. Years ago, he pawned my old stereo to pay off a debt to a dealer. He's been in and out of jail and rehab for the past two decades, but he still can't seem to get clean. Mama says Uncle Gil tried to raise him right, but that he had demons of his own. I used to pity him, but these days I'm less forgiving.

"I ain't in no trouble," he says. "Just want me a cheeseburger, is all."

"You get turned away from the methadone clinic again?" I ask.

Pepper stares at me like he's seconds away from tears. That's how fast it happens. "Why do you hate me?" he asks.

"I don't."

"You do. You think you're better than everybody because you moved two towns over and only darken the doorway around Christmas and Easter. Think your shit smells sweet. You don't know what it's like."

"Stop it," Mama says. She reaches into her pocketbook, pulls out a five.

"Mama."

"It's my money, son." She hands it to Pepper.

He takes it and deposits it into his pocket. "God bless you, Aint Jo," he says, kissing her on the cheek. "Can I use your bathroom before I run up there?"

"Sure," she says.

He disappears into the back of the house.

"You ought not done that," Uncle Marvin says.

"Well, I did."

Moments later, Pepper rushes back into the living room. "I reckon I'll run up there," he says. "Thank you again, Aint Jo. Y'all have a Merry Christmas."

"Stay warm," Mama shouts as the door closes. She's the only one who says goodbye.

I light another cigarette, rub my eyes. "Mama. Where do you keep your medicine?"

She starts puttering with the bags she brought in. "In my bedroom. Why?"

When I was a kid, Christmas was a kind of uncomplicated magic that didn't require any spells or tricks or charms. It was just there, and even though I couldn't touch it, I could feel it in the same way that people at church talked about feeling the Lord. We listened to Country Christmas tunes until the cassette wore out. We went out and got a real tree from one of the lots past the old fairgrounds, and we wrapped presents in pretty paper, and we drove down Aycock Lane where the lights were so bright that I remember wondering how anybody there got any sleep. We prayed for snow. When it was all over, we'd spend weeks detoxing from the yuletide high and longing for a pastime that probably wasn't as enchanting as we remembered it in the first place. And in eleven more months, we'd do it all over again.

I was fifteen when all of that changed. It was the first weekend in December, and we were all over at the old house by the elementary school. Me and Mama were bringing in boxes of decorations from the shed, and Daddy was smoking a cigarette in his beat-up recliner. Uncle Roy, recently deceased, and Uncle Marvin, long gone, were lounging on the adjacent sofa. They weren't around every day back then, but they liked to pop in and out during the holidays. God knows where Uncle Gil was; he wouldn't be dead for another couple of years.

I sat the Nativity set on the dinner table and went into the living room. "Whatcha watching, Daddy?" I asked.

His eyes looked as heavy as a bucket full of water as he turned toward me. "I think it's 'A Christmas Carol' but with Muppets. Kindly weird, but not bad."

"We're fixing to go to the parade. You coming with?"

I knew the answer before he gave it. Daddy worked long, hard hours at the truck plant through the week, and whenever Saturday came, he wanted nothing more than to watch his programs and sink into that recliner until it became part of him. He stopped coming to the festivities with us when I was around eight or nine.

"Naw," he said. "Maybe next year."

"Hell, I'll come," Uncle Roy said.

"Ain't you got nothing better to do?" Uncle Marvin asked. "You got kids."

Uncle Roy frowned. "Well, Sheila and them *are* making gingerbread houses tonight. I reckon I'll go over there."

"Can I come?" Uncle Marvin asked.

Uncle Roy looked at him, spiteful. "Naw," he said. "You got kids."

But Uncle Marvin didn't.

Daddy laughed like he always did. Like it was the only thing he could do in certain situations. The older I get, the more I understand it.

Mama came into the room and grabbed her keys off the hook by the door. "You bout ready?" she asked.

"Yeah."

Daddy sparked another cigarette.

"Don't you fall asleep with one of those in your mouth," Mama said to him. "You'll wake up dead."

Mama had always been paranoid about things like that happening. Her hairdresser's sister's friend's cousin had a neighbor who'd left a candle going when she went to bed one night, and it burned her house to the ground.

"I won't, honey," Daddy replied.

She kissed him where his hairline had begun to recede. "We'll be back in a little."

We drove Mama's Chrysler the few miles to downtown and parked at the post office. Then we walked to the furniture store where we always found a pretty good seat. Along the sidewalks, parents bundled up in blankets as their kids pleaded for money for the passing vendor carts. Old folks gushed about their grandkids or lamented the disappointment of the high school football season. From beneath my windbreaker jacket, my heart yearned for light to cut through the growing darkness.

I got my wish when the high school marching band started things off. They donned Santa hats and lit-up tunics as they kicked left and right and played seasonal favorites. The local dance studio came next, its ballerinas becoming smaller by the row until there were only the tiniest girls left in the back, dressed in glittery costumes, carrying ribbon-topped boxes. A couple of churches with neon manger scenes followed. Then the girl who won Miss County.

I turned to Mama. I think I liked watching her watch the parade more than I liked looking at the procession itself. I imagine the people and the sounds and the colors reminded her of Christmases past with her mama and daddy and brothers. They didn't have much, but they had each other.

In her eyes, there was the faintest twinkle of something she knew deep down she'd never get back. But that didn't mean she'd stop trying.

A fire truck with a wreath on its grille and hundreds of lights wrapped around its ladder inched along behind the convertible carrying Miss County. It honked its horn as most people cheered, save some children covering their ears. But then there was this frantic chatter coming from inside. The truck's sirens rang out above the music and the laughter, and it turned off on a side road. Went screaming into the blue hour of the day.

I saw my mama's face as the fire truck drove off. It had gone from nostalgic to anxious in a matter of seconds. She was always like that at the drop of a hat, though, so I didn't think much of it as the parade continued for the next half hour or so. But as soon as Skinny Santa and his eight plastic reindeer passed by, Mama was itching to get home. It was all I could do to stay on her heels during the walk back to the car, and on the way to the house, she turned the volume on the radio all the way down.

We could smell it before we could see it—this acrid odor that was so strong you'd think it had always been there and would always be there. Our street was filled with a different kind of light display for that time of year: two or three fire trucks, including the one from the parade, several police cruisers, an ambulance. We had to park at the end of the block and run the rest of the way. Some of our neighbors were out in their front yards trying to wave us down, but we didn't stop. The house was unrecognizable by the time we reached it. The back half was mostly intact, but the front was black and smoldering, and with the heat it was giving off, you'd think we were standing at the mouth of Hell.

That's when Mama dropped her pocketbook, and I began to cry. She hollered my daddy's name, and a policeman cut her off before she could get to what was left of our front door. He kept telling her to take it easy. Take it easy. I dropped to my knees in the front yard, spiraling, and rocked back and forth until I felt something cold on my cheek. I half expected Uncle Marvin to be there, but when I looked up, a lone flurry floated past my face. Then another. Then a barrage. A full-blown shower of flakes in the hot darkness, some melting before they even hit the ground.

My daddy loved snow.

We go into Mama's bedroom. It's been almost twenty-five years since the fire, and we moved after it happened, but she's got all my daddy's belongings—what's left of them—the way he had them in the old house. His work hat hangs on the doorknob. His eyeglasses are in their case on the vanity, next to his cigar box. His shirts are up on one side of the closet. I've criticized her for it before, but I get it. Sometimes I think I started smoking just because it reminded me of him. Dumb as that sounds.

Mama sits down in front of her vanity. She grabs her pillminder; it's one of those containers that has seven compartments for scheduled doses of medicine, one for each day of the week. She opens the one for Monday and frowns. "He took my back pills," she says. "Some of my muscle relaxers, too."

"Dammit, I knew it."

She sits there, slouched and frail, looking grayer than usual. Defeated. Her brokenness makes me want to cry.

"You're inviting this type of behavior, Mama," I say.

"I know," she mumbles.

I pace back and forth across the little room. "You need to stop giving him money. That's your Social Security."

"I'm just too tender-hearted," she says. "I wish I could rip it out and beat it up. Go a couple of rounds with it. That might toughen me up."

I've offered Mama money when I could, but I don't make all that much with the city parks department. It wouldn't matter anyway. Mama has never been able to say no to anybody. It's the same mindset she had at Christmastime when I was younger. No matter what was on my list, she'd make it happen—even if it meant working overtime. She'd go without so that others didn't have to. That's just how she was and still is.

"Is he gone?" Uncle Gil asks, appearing from the hallway just outside the door.

"Yeah, he's gone," I say. "But not empty-handed."

"Well, what would you expect?" Uncle Roy calls from the other room. "That boy's slickern owl shit. I wonder where he gets it from."

"I'm fixing to wrassle this boy back to the grave," Uncle Gil says.

He barely finishes his sentence before Uncle Roy darts up the hall and takes hold of him. Then they go bounding through the wall again, this time into the backyard.

"I refuse to let this ruin our Christmas," Mama says, slowly standing to her feet.

She waddles back to her bags in the living room. For the next hour, she decorates as fast as her arthritic body will allow and says no every time I ask her if she needs help. Uncle Marvin sits on the loveseat and marvels at the smallest things. A couple of fake poinsettias and lengths of garland here. Some nutcracker dolls there. Mama goes outside and puts a big red bow on the mailbox. She grabs an extension cord and starts to wind strings of lights around the pillars of her front porch.

"Mama, no," I say. "It's cold out here, and you could hurt yourself."

She waves me off, so I curse under my breath, go into the front yard, and light a menthol as she fumbles with the lights behind me. I'm put off by how quiet it is out here. That's when I realize it's snowing a little. When it snows in the South, you make a mental picture of it and store it way back in your mind, where nobody can touch it because you never want to let it go. You're never sure how many more times you're going to see it. The flurries are coming down good when Mama goes back inside. She's been working so hard that she hasn't even noticed the snow's starting to cover the ground.

I step back in to find that my uncles have resumed their game of poker without me. Mama emerges from her bedroom with her special ornament. It's a glass bell with my daddy's picture inside. She hangs it on the tree in the windowsill and admires it. Its reflection shines in her now-glossy eyes.

I want to go put my arm around her, but there's a knock on the door, and this time, it's more aggressive than the last. "Aint Jo," the voice calls, cracking like ice in a glass of warm water.

Mama looks at the door, then at me.

I shake my head no.

"Aint Jo, please. It's an emergency."

"Mama, if you open that door, I'm leaving."

"He needs help," she says. She walks over to the door and cracks it open.

Pepper bursts through, gasping and wild, nearly knocking her over. "Oh, Aint Jo," he hollers. "Thank God. I'm in trouble."

"What kind of trouble?" she asks.

He whips up some crocodile tears. "I need some money."

"What happened to the money I give you earlier?"

"I need more."

"For more cheeseburgers?" I ask.

"Jimmy says he's gonna kill me if I don't pay him what I owe," Pepper says, sobbing so hard he can hardly get the words out.

"Is that why you took them pills?" I say.

"How much do you owe?" Mama asks.

Pepper wrings his hands. "Three hundred dollars."

I throw my arms up. "Absolutely not."

"Don't listen to that boy, Jo," Uncle Roy says. "He'd piss on your leg and tell you it's raining."

"I'll go get my checkbook," Mama says.

She starts off, but I snatch her arm, probably a little too hard. "Mama, no. This is ridiculous. Somebody's gonna kill him over three hundred dollars? Think about it."

"Have a heart," Pepper cries.

"Get out."

"Aint Jo."

I hold out my fist. "Pepper, get outta here before I kick your sorry ass up and down the street."

Lips trembling, Pepper spins around violently. He exits, slams the door behind him.

Mama rips her arm away from me and storms off into the guest bedroom.

"You did the right thing," Uncle Marvin says.

Uncle Gil hasn't looked up the whole time.

I take me a headache powder, give the situation some time to blow over. When I go into the guest bedroom, Mama is at the desktop computer, her face an inch away from the screen. Checking Facebook to see which member of her graduating class died today.

"You all right?" I ask.

She taps the mouse. "I'm okay."

"You know I just want what's best for you," I say, leaning against the wall. "You give, and give, and give, and someday, someone's gonna come around, and there ain't gonna be nothing left to take."

She looks away from the screen. "I don't know no better, darlin."

"Are you mad at me?"

She thinks about that for a minute. "No. I know you was looking out for me, and I appreciate it. But you know I cain't stand to see people want for nothing. Least of all family. Your cousin Pepper ain't never had a pot to piss in or a window to throw it out of."

She's right. Pepper *has* lived a rough life. Uncle Gil was in and out of the picture, and Pepper's mama died of cancer when he was just thirteen. He dropped out of school not long after that and never has been able to stay on the straight and narrow. But Mama hasn't had it easy, either. She's had no choice but to go full speed since she was little, and the unlived years of the dead have piled up on her pint-sized shoulders.

"Well, I don't wanna fight over it," I say. "I just think you deserve better. Can we still have a good Christmas?"

She smiles. "Yeah."

Later on, I'm relieved to see that Mama is no longer in the guest bedroom. But when I walk into the living room, I can't find her there, either. "Where'd she run off to?" I ask.

Uncle Marvin points at the front door.

I step out onto the porch to find a ladder propped against the rain gutters. I squint off into the driveway where Mama is unloading something from the trunk of her car. She opens it and begins to untangle hundreds of stringed lights.

"Mama, have you lost your mind? You don't have any business out here doing something crazy like this. It's almost ten o'clock at night, and you're seventy years old."

"Aw, it ain't hard," she hollers, the hood of her coat covering everything but her nose and mouth.

I start to say something else, but I'm interrupted by a commotion inside. "I'll be right back," I call to Mama.

As soon as I get into the house, Uncle Roy is in my face. "That bastard's here," he shrieks.

"What?"

"He broke in the back."

I run to Mama's bedroom. Pepper has ransacked most of her belongings, and now he's running his hand along the crease between the bed and the box springs. Uncle Marvin is throwing haymaker after haymaker at him, but his fists and arms are floating right through.

"Goddamn you," I scream, lunging at him.

He hardly has time to turn before I tackle him to the ground. We struggle there on the brown carpet for a good spell before I wind up on top. I punch him twice in the face, bloodying his nose as he digs his fingernails into my neck. I think I tell him I'm going to kill him. He wraps his bony fingers around my throat. I retch for air and hit him again. Then I beat at his hands, but he doesn't loosen his grip. He flips me over until he's on top. Punches me once, twice. I hold my hand up to protect my face, but he swings again, and it's a good one.

He gets up and sprints off.

"You don't have to do this, son," I hear Uncle Gil say as I roll over, and it's the first time I've ever heard him scared. "This ain't right."

I stagger into the living room, and the door's wide open.

"Hurry!" Uncle Roy shouts.

I scramble through the front door and jump off the porch and into the yard, where the snow has downgraded to a dusting. Above me, Mama has made her way up on the roof, and she's doddering across it, lights in hand. In front of me, Pepper has slid into the driver seat of Mama's car. He rakes at the ignition, and the engine struggles to life. I start that way when I notice a knot of the Christmas lights caught on the muffler.

"Let go of the lights, Mama!" I holler.

But I'm too late. Pepper throws the car into Drive and squeals off, picking up speed much too quick. As he does, the strand of lights yanks Mama off the roof. She plunges headfirst into the flowerbed, and I can hear the break. Pepper makes it halfway down the street before he hits a slick spot on the road and crashes into the tree in front of the Barringer house.

I hustle over to Mama and turn her over. I'm crying. Her eyes are shut, and she looks like she does when she dozes off on the couch during TV reruns. But I know better. There's some blood coming from her mouth, and she's limp, and she's not there. No, she's not there. I check for a pulse anyway. When I can't find one, I start the CPR. I stop because I don't want to break her ribs. I stop because I know she's gone.

I go over to the car. It's totaled. I sling the door open, and Pepper is sitting there, a gash in his forehead. His eyes are open, and he's blinking but not breathing. He turns toward me, face furrowed like he's trying to remember something. Something really important. "You know, I didn't want this life for myself," he says. Then he goes on. That quick. I can see him doing it. Like Uncle Marvin, and Uncle Roy, and Uncle Gil. But to another place. To where, I cannot see. Maybe someplace kinder than this.

When I glance back at the house, Mama is leaving, too. Her brothers are at her side, and they're grinning. It's hard to describe. Mama doesn't look any younger, but she seems lighter. Airier. Inseparable from the twinkles on the little tree in the window. She looks like she knows what's next, and she's grateful for it. Or perhaps she has no idea, and she's content all the same. She looks like she did on Christmas morning when I was seven years old.

Uncle Marvin waves at me. So does Uncle Roy and Uncle Gil.

Mama just smiles. And then she goes.

The cops are coming. The sirens are yowling across the night like wolves. In my mind, there are great angels of smoke. Crystalline tears falling through time. My heart burns somewhere in the space below. God. I don't know how I'm going to explain this. How could I?

But I think maybe I don't have to. Maybe the lights will tell my story for me. The parade of souls, lost and found, marching through town in a stream of infinite sound and color. Maybe the ghosts of yesterday, today, and tomorrow will meet again and share that story around a fire—this one beautiful and toasty and bright in a place where there is no pain. I have to hold out that hope.

acknowledgements

2024 was the worst fucking year of my life by a country mile. My mama died in March, and then my corgi followed in August, right around the thirteenth anniversary of my deddy's death. One of the only silver linings from that horrible time was the news that this book would be published. It is the culmination of seven-plus years of ass-busting hard work: The oldest story is from 2016, and the newest one was written in 2023. I poured my heart and soul into each and every one of them, by God.

Several thanks are in order. This book is dedicated to my dog and my mama, but it's also for my deddy and my brother and my wife and my pups, Raleigh and Stevie, and the people I grew up with, the people that raised me. It's for my Oma and Opa and my Maw Maw and Paw Paw and (some) of my other family. It's for all the editors who ever believed in my work and my writing professors and everyone who has been gracious enough to forget about my short-lived rap career (yikes). It's for the little mill town in the North Carolina Piedmont that's still trying to figure things out. And you, Reader. It's for you, too.

Thank you, April Gloaming, for the trust.

Hope is hard for a bastard like me, but you've gotta have it or the world will swallow you whole. Sure, it might chew you up and spit you out anyway, but at least you'll still be in pieces that can be put back together. I don't reckon we can ask for anything better than that. Especially in these crazy times. As Sam Dew sings on Kendrick Lamar's "United in Grief": I hope you find some peace of mind in this lifetime.

I hope we all do.

about the author

Matt Starr is from Kannapolis, North Carolina. He is the author of *Hell, or High Water* (Main Street Rag, 2018), as well as *Prepare to Meet Thy God* (2020) and *Things That Don't Belong in the Light* (2021) — both from Grinning Skull Press. His essays and stories have been featured in *Barren Magazine*, Empty House Press, *Farewell Transmission*, and *Shotgun Honey*, among other publications. He lives in a small town with his wife and children (Australian Shepherds).

comparable april gloaming titles

Love Letters from an Arsonist
David van den Berg

Possessing the Seasons
Charles Prowell

We Never Took a Bad Picture
Ashley N. Roth

Picking Over the Bones
Judith Ireland

*The Peril of Remembering
Nice Things*
Jeffrey Wade Gibbs

Frank's Bloody Books
Mack Green

APRIL GLOAMING

View our full catalogue at aprilgloaming.com

www.ingramcontent.com/pod-product-compliance
Lightning Source LLC
Chambersburg PA
CBHW011138190726
48289CB00012B/3075